Poppe Culture

Jaq Greenspon

Poppe Culture by Jaq Greenspon

Published by Xavier Patrick Books
©2020 Jaq Greenspon

All rights reserved. No portion of this book may be reproduced in any form without permission from the publisher, except as permitted by U.S. copyright law. For permissions contact: JaqGreenspon13@Gmail.com

Cover art by Lina Kišonytė - www.bookcoverillustrator.com

For the real life Guantanamo, who's been there since before the beginning.

Thanks also to everyone who has been a part of this since Skids starting writing for LA Bike. Special thanks to Scott Melamed, who had the faith to let Skids do what needed to be done. Heartfelt gratitude to Jeremy Bloom for late nights fixing my typos and making sure my tenses matched. And a big round of applause to the Monday Morning Mailing crew. You know who you are and what you did and for that, Skids is grateful.

Saturday

Saturday Morning

I should have known it was a mistake to answer the phone when I did. It was a Saturday morning and anyone who knows me knows not to call on Saturday morning. Even Guantanamo Bey, my faithful sidekick, wouldn't call me before noon on Saturday.

Besides, I knew it wasn't Guantanamo because he was asleep on the floor next to my bed. We'd had a pretty rough Friday night and I hadn't been planning on getting up to the sound of a damn telephone.

My first thought was it was my publisher. Most of you know that these days I write for a living (there ain't a hell of a lot an ex-member of the Diablo 143 can do which will make him money and keep him safely on the streets; I chose writing). I quickly figured it wasn't him. I had almost a week until deadline next Wednesday and he never calls unless he has to.

Poppe Culture

By the fifth ring, I was thinking it was my ex-wife. She's the only person I know who would let it ring that long. I thought about it while the phone went for rings six and seven. Nope, wasn't her. She only called when I was late on my alimony payment and that didn't happen until after I turned in my column and didn't get paid. I figured I had ten days until I'd get her call.

By the tenth ring I knew I had to get it because Guantanamo was waking up and if he answered it, who knows what might happen? I reached up behind me and grabbed the receiver off the wall hook. Yeah, I still had a phone on a wall hook. Thought about getting a mobile, but since you can't ride and talk, I just didn't see the point. I grabbed the receiver and mumbled into it. The first try I had the thing upside down. I told you I was tired. I got it right the second time.

"Skids here." I mumbled again.

"Skids, is that you?" His voice was frantic and high pitched, but I still recognized it. It was Bernie.

"Yeah, Bernie. It's Skids."

"Skids, it's me, Bernie."

Bernie was never that quick on the uptake, but he was a good guy. Even though he lived in LA, I first met him at Sturgis ten years ago and we'd been friendly off and on since then. Actually, since he moved to the West Side our friendship had been leaning more toward the "on" side. We'd been out riding a bunch of times and I usually had a drink with him at the Rock Store up on Mulholland four or five times a month. Like I said, he was a good guy.

"Skids, I need your help. I'm in trouble, man, and I

swear I didn't do it. You gotta believe me, man. There was no--"

I had to cut him off. "Bernie, slow down man, slow down."

"Sorry Skids. But you gotta help me."

"I gotta wake up. Can you call me back in an hour?" I didn't have Bernie's number and wasn't about to go and try to find a pen.

"Can I meet you somewhere?"

"Fine, you can buy me breakfast. Meet me at The Sidewalk Cafe in an hour and a half."

"I thought you said an hour?"

"That was for a phone call. For food, I gotta get dressed."

"But I'm not hungry."

"Ninety minutes and I'll have a table waiting." I hung up before he could argue with me. Bernie was a good guy but sometimes you just couldn't get him off the phone, especially when he wanted something. This time he sounded a bit more frenetic than usual, but he's needed my help before, so I really didn't give it much thought.

The first time I got a call like this from Bernie was when he tried to open a biker bar and had no idea why a bunch of young kids with black hair and pointy shoes were hanging out and asking for newspapers in French. I figured out how to make that one work (and made him a nice profit besides; that's why I let him buy me lunch) and since then, I'm on the top of his "people to call when I'm in trouble" list. Lucky me.

"Bey!" I yelled. "Get up! We got a lunch date."

Guantanamo Bey and I have been friends since before

Poppe Culture

I can remember. At least it feels that way. We'd been buds for nineteen, twenty years. Me and Bey started hanging out when we were twelve and with few exceptions haven't stopped yet. He was with me the first time I got popped for "excessive show of speed" on my Harley and I'm the one who got him shit-faced before putting him on the plane for his two-year army stint. It was supposed to be four years, but after the first two, Uncle Sam decided the world would be a safer place without Guantanamo Bey wearing the national colors and acting under orders. Definitely one of the wiser moves that Uncle ever made. According to Guantanamo, the best thing about the whole experience was he got to keep the clothes. You take the good where ya can, right?

"I don't wanna get up," Guantanamo mumbled. "I just got to sleep."

I got out of bed and stepped on him as I walked to the bathroom. He over-exaggerated a groan and rolled over, pulling the skull-and-crossbones flag he used as a blanket up over his head.

"You got to bed the same time I did," I yelled at him from the john. "And you passed out twice on the walk home. Besides, it's free food." I flushed.

###

Eighty-seven minutes later, Guantanamo and I were passing the short brick wall that separated those fortunate enough to afford food at The Sidewalk Cafe from those merely strolling the Venice Boardwalk. As we walked by, I looked to see if Bernie was already inside. I didn't think he would be, and I was right.

We rounded the corner and joined the group of people

waiting behind the red line. One great thing about The Sidewalk Cafe - there usually wasn't a long wait to get in. Then again, I was usually there during the week. Today, there was a wait. Besides, they wouldn't let us in without the complete party being there, so since we were waiting for Bernie, we waited behind the line.

Well... I waited. Bey went across the boardwalk to talk to the girl sculpting in the sand.

Okay, so she wasn't actually sculpting in the sand. She brought the sand to her and sculpted against the light post. The tourists loved it. Every day she'd create some babe and add that SoCal touch by putting a pair of Ray Bans on her. Used to be a guy doing it, then a couple of months ago this girl came in and took over. I think it was right around that time Guantanamo's interest in the fine art of sand sculpture began. Personally, I don't think he's going to get anywhere with her, but he still tries. Got to give the boy credit. When he picks a cause, he fights to the death. That kind of tenacity is a good thing to have in a friend. It's gotten me out of more than one jam in my life. Of course, it's also gotten me into most of them as well, but hey, you take the good with the bad, right?

I was watching Bey squat down to talk to the girl - Becky, I think her name was, or maybe that was Bey's last obsession - anyway I was so totally caught up with watching his mating rituals I didn't even see Bernie show up.

"Skids, man, am I glad to see you." He slapped me on the shoulder and pulled my hand forward to shake it. "How you been, man?"

"Bernie," I said. "It's good to see you, too. I'm doing

okay, you know?"

"Yeah. I read your last column. Man, you are funny."

As much as I wanted to think that the reason he had woken my ass up and consented to buy me breakfast was because he liked my last column, I could tell there was something else.

"Skids, there's something else."

Maybe I should go to work for one of those psychic hotlines.

"It's waited this long, it'll wait until we've ordered." I smiled at him. I hoped it was a reassuring, don't-worry-I'll-take-care-of-it, kind of smile. What it felt like was an I'm-hungry-and-don't-bother-me-until-I've-had-a-mug-of-Sam-Adams-and an-omelet kind of smile.

"Okay, yeah, sure."

I thought he could see through the smile.

"Bey!"

Guantanamo looked up. It took him a minute to find me even though I was only twenty feet away. Tourists were crowding the Boardwalk between us, holding everything from dogs to children on leashes.

"Let's go," I said when I finally caught his eye. "Our breakfast date is here." I turned away and told our hostess our entire party was present, and we'd like a table with a beer. She laughed.

Now, the great thing about The Sidewalk Cafe, aside from the fact it's on the Venice Boardwalk, is it's a literary Mecca. It has a background going back to 1905 and the very beginnings of Venice itself.

The building has housed all the big poets and artists

of every age. Rumor has it even Jack Kerouac crashed there during the fifties, but hey, that was a long time ago and no one really cares about him today. He is, however, still remembered at the Sidewalk. He's an omelet. Specifically, a chili omelet. With cheddar cheese and onions. Everything on the menu there is named after a famous literary figure. Makes sense, I guess, when you think that right next door is Small World Books, home of the world-famous Mystery Annex.

I've spent way too many hours there looking through old books and figuring out what items of my personal property I could sell to get a few more of them into my own collection. You know, for a guy with a reputation as a mean, nasty biker, I do have a soft, intellectual side. It doesn't come out too often, but in those quiet moments it makes life fun.

So, needless to say, I was well known in the area. Known enough, at least, to be led to a table by the wall. From this vantage point we could watch the crowds walk by and still enjoy our food in relative comfort. Granted, we were a little closer to the action, but for some reason the guys asking for spare change always seemed to avoid our table. I'm sure the fact we were three guys who looked like we had all served time and wouldn't be caught dead on a Honda had nothing to do with it.

Then again, maybe it did.

Guantanamo and I took the seats nearest the wall with Bernie sliding in next to Bey. I think he wanted to look at me when he asked for his favor. I handed him a menu. Me? I knew what I wanted. It was a Saturday and I had been mercifully drunk a mere six hours earlier. There wasn't much choice in my menu selection, but I figured I'd wait until the guys were ready.

"What can I get you gentlemen today?" Carol asked. Carol was a long-time waitress at the Sidewalk with long-time legs. Sure, it's a stupid line, but I figure it's something Chandler would have written.

It was always a treat to sit at her station. When she delivered food to the tables around yours, she bent over at the waist and, at least for me, proved the existence of God. But then, I'm easy.

"Carol," I smiled at her. "It's good to see you."

"Good to see you, too, Skids." She said. "It's been too long."

The look she gave me would have made me blush if I had been eating with Mom rather than Guantanamo. At least it would have made Mom blush.

"We'll take a pitcher for the table. My usual."

"I'll bet you will." She turned to get the beer, leaving Bernie astonished. Carol and I had had a, what do you want to call it? A fling? Okay, a fling. In fact, it was a series of flings, which meant she knew my usual and had it already written down on her little pad. She also knew what Guantanamo liked and would bring it just to make me happy. Besides, she thought he was cute, in a puppy dog kind of way…a huge, pit-bull kind of puppy dog, but a puppy nonetheless.

Carol was the kind of girl who didn't take me seriously and that was just the way I liked it. Whenever we got together, usually around my birthday or whenever her then-boyfriend was out of town and she was lonely, we had a great time, she cooked breakfast and then I didn't see her until the next time I walked down the street to the Cafe. It worked out rather nicely.

Bernie looked at me. "I knew I was doing the right thing in calling you, Skids."

"Of course, you were, Bern." I knew he was bursting to talk but I was still hungry.

"I know you're hungry Skids, but I gotta tell you this or I'm gonna burst."

Am I good, or what? "Unless this has to do with the body they found floating in the canals yesterday, it can wait."

Bernie was crushed. I could see it in his eyes. They were furtively (I looked that up) searching the menu, looking for a suitable entree. I had just punctured his balloon and he knew he would have to wait until after breakfast to talk. Maybe he would get something to eat after all. When he looked back up at me, I was sure he had discovered the Shibumi, a chicken sandwich named for that great Trevanian book. I knew he would like it.

"Skids, it's about the body they found floating in the canals yesterday."

What are the odds?

"Carol!" I wanted those beers quickly. She scooted her lovely legs through the crowd and didn't spill a drop. Setting the glasses down, she poured mine first. After she'd topped Guantanamo and Bernie's glasses, she refilled mine. Halfway through my third glass, when Carol brought a second pitcher, I had the coherence to remember why I never answer the phone on Saturday mornings.

Then I asked the all-important question: "What the fuck are you talking about?"

"It's about the body," he repeated.

"What about it?" I took another slug of the beer. I'm not a big guy, but I've built up a tolerance over the years, so it takes a lot to get me buzzed. I knew I had better be feeling the effects of the alcohol before Bernie told me anymore. I think Bernie knew it, too. He waited for me to get ready.

One more hit and I was almost there. Holding the mug with both hands, I looked straight at Guantanamo. He had been drinking slowly, finishing two beers to my five or six. He was smiling stupidly, staring past me toward the sand sculptress. I would put money on the fact he never heard a word of what Bernie said. So much for his providing moral support in getting me out of this.

Why do I do this to myself? I answer the phone and accept an invitation to breakfast. Now I'm obligated to listen and at least pretend to try and help out. Christ! Who knew having a moral code could be this much trouble? I drained the beer and set the mug down heavily on the table. My eyes stayed focused on that little puddle of beer at the bottom of the glass, the one you can never drink no matter how far back you tilt your neck. I watched it form, trying to figure out where it comes from. I took a deep breath and held it.

Finally, I spoke.

"Okay. Tell me."

"You already know about the body, right?"

I did. News like finding a well-dressed white guy floating face down in the canals spreads quickly. I heard about it from an ex-girlfriend who knew the girl who found the body. Said her dog started going nuts on their morning walk; running ahead, barking and carrying on until she caught up and saw the guy. She said she thought he might have been a passed out drunk until she saw the blood. As soon as I'd heard about it, I went down to check it out. He was found under the last bump of the Dell Street Bridge, the one over Carroll Canal. By the time I'd gotten there, the police had taped the place up pretty good and were busy dragging for bloody gloves.

The reason I went down was I needed to know if it was a brother. I may not ride with the gang anymore, but once you wear colors, they're yours for life. Besides, I knew my press credentials could get me in and I was hoping this real cute police photographer I knew would be there. She had taken my picture once and...but that's another story. Anyway, once I figured out I didn't know the guy (probably would never have known the guy, even if he were alive) I moved on and hit The Cow for my morning pick-me up.

So yeah, I knew about the body. What I didn't know, and really didn't want to know, was if Bernie had anything to do with it.

"Yeah, I know about the body. So?"

"The police think I had something to do with it."

How did I know this was coming?

I opened my mouth but couldn't say anything. I was a semi-respectable member of the community now. My days of hanging with murderers were long behind me. Hell, Bernie was even more respectable than I was. Sure, he looked evil, but he owned a business. A thriving business. I didn't know what to say. Thankfully, since my ever-faithful sidekick was present, I didn't have to say anything.

"Why in the hell would they think you did it?" Guantanamo asked. He had been paying attention.

Bernie looked at him. I think he was surprised. Most people who know both of us, know Guantanamo as the strong silent type. I knew him better.

Before Bernie could answer, our food arrived. Carol placed my omelet down last, her eyes never leaving mine. I knew she wanted me. Hell, I'm that type of guy. That, and I had heard she had just broken up with a guy she'd been seeing for five or six weeks. So we were due. And right then, I couldn't have done anything about it. I couldn't even grab the ketchup for my Faulkner (a ham and cheese). I was too busy doing nothing.

Guantanamo had no such problems. I mean what the hell did he care? He wasn't the one Bernie was asking for help. He took a huge bite of the Timothy Leary that Carol had set in front of him and re-asked the question around a mouthful of cheeseburger.

Bernie lifted his glass to his mouth. Thinking about it now, that was the first sip I had seen him take all morning. He tasted it very slowly, wetting his lips. Personally, I think he was savoring the moment. It's not often someone can say they left me, Skids Poppe, completely speechless. I don't care if you are up on possible murder charges, if you run in my crowd, you'd want that moment to last as long as possible.

Bernie carefully set his mug down and looked straight at me. As I watched, his eyes changed from proud and daring to scared and hunted. He'd been straight a long time and didn't want anything to fuck that up. I'd even heard he was serious about some girl and this would certainly complicate matters. I regained my composure as he started to talk.

"I knew the guy, Skids. He worked for me."

Like I said before, Bernie made an attempt a while back to open a biker bar. He'd run into a little bit of cash (no, the details of how he acquired it are not important at this, or any other, time) and figured the best thing to do would be invest it.

Well, there was this little run-down place over on Main Street in Santa Monica, which happened to go up for sale at just the right time so Bernie took it over. I mean, for Bernie, this was great. The place he felt most at home was a bar and since he owned the place he could have as many drinks on the house as he wanted. Of course, like all great drinkers who become businessmen, Bernie drank himself, along with me and not a few of the other brothers, into oblivion for the first month. Every other round was "on the house" until he sobered up enough to realize that "on the house" meant he was paying for it. The only thing that saved him was Main Street itself.

The Cup of Fools, which is what Bernie claims I named the bar, (The story goes: When he told me he was going to buy a bar, I told him he was a couple of fools; Evidently I'd been drinking enough to see double) would have been doomed if it wasn't for the wonderful restoration Santa Monica went through in the early 90s. See, once Bernie sobered up, he realized if he wanted to stay in business, he'd actually have to sell drinks. So, he did.

Well, we all supported him in his efforts, but somewhere along the line it became trendy to come to downtown Santa Monica and see the Harley riders drink. Not long after that, a couple of kids came in wearing all black clothes and talking about death and asking him to put some Nine Inch Nails in the jukebox.

At some point, Bernie asked me what to do and I suggested going with the flow. Before long, us bikers were outnumbered, and Bernie had himself a swinging hot spot. Most of us had retired by then anyway. I, myself, had become the brilliant columnist you all know and love. And because Bernie was making more money than he knew what to do with and I liked drinking with my friends, I ended up at a different bar and rarely ventured to The Cup, as the kids called it. I'm still known there, though, even though I haven't been in the place for over a year.

"He worked for you?" I asked. Sue me. It was still hard to get used to the idea of anyone being gainfully employed anywhere near Bernie.

"I know. Can you imagine how I feel? I have a whole fucking payroll I have to deal with."

It was a standard rule with us never to mention finances. I knew - hell we all knew - how much money Cup of Fools was bringing in for Bernie, but we never wanted to know. It was just something we never discussed in polite company. I mean, we're talking about a group of guys who used to lift Ding Dongs from the AM/PM just to get a sugar high, and now one of our own had a fucking payroll for chrissake. Sometimes it was a bit much for me to take and I really didn't like it being thrown in my face. Still...an employee of Bernie's was dead.

I knew the moment had come. I had been putting it off for as long as possible, but I had to finally bite the bullet and earn my omelet.

"Tell me the story."

God, I hated those words. Well, okay, I didn't exactly hate them since they were, in fact, how I made my - now - honest living, but they were four words I almost never asked a friend. The sad thing was that I knew exactly what I was getting myself into. From past experience, I knew where those four innocent little words could take you and they were certainly not a road I wanted to ride, especially not now when I didn't have my hog (metaphorically speaking. Look it up, it fits). I felt more like I was about to hit the canyons on an '84 Honda P.O.S. Ascot with a fuel problem. Not a great feeling. But when you gotta get someplace, any transport is better than none and I'd rather have two wheels than four any day.

As soon as I asked the question, Guantanamo refilled my glass. I made sure both hands were still around it and waited. With Bernie, I didn't have to wait long.

"You wanna hear the whole story, Skids?"

"No. I don't think I could take the whole story, not just yet at any rate." Then, before I could stop it, all the reporter training I told my publisher I had in order to get my job started coming out. "Who was he and what did he do for you?"

"His name is..." Bernie paused. "Was, I guess. His name was Alweighz. Jasper Alweighz."

"Always? Why would we think it had ever been different?" Guantanamo had this great knack for asking obvious questions.

Bernie looked at him as if he were insane. "Skids," he said, still looking at Bey, "how do you understand him?"

"Years of immersion. Even so, I'm only about 80% accurate."

Bernie looked at me like I was crazy. Then he continued his story. "His name is Alweighz. I guess his first name is–was–Jasper, but we never called him that. Everyone I knew called him Jā."

"Jay Always?" Guantanamo asked.

"Close enough," Bernie responded.

"Who was he?" I asked.

"He was a bartender, sort of."

"A bartender, sort of?" I had no idea what he was talking about. Not that I did before, but this made no sense. It could have had something to do with the fact that I don't have employees. If that was the case, I hoped I would never understand him.

"No one in LA is ever what they are." Bernie tried to explain. He was losing me quickly. "It's like this; He worked as a bartender but really considered himself something else. It's kind of like how you consider yourself a rebel outlaw but are, in fact, a well-respected member of the publishing world."

Okay, he got me with that one. I understood where he was coming from now, not that I wanted to admit it.

"So, what was this guy? Really?"

"A film director."

Now my interest was aroused. Those of you who have read my columns (and for those of you who haven't, shame on you) know I love movies. Any movie, any time, doesn't matter, I'm there. I may not like all of them, but as a whole, I think movies are the best thing ever to come out of Hollywood. And this guy was a film director. And he worked for my friend.

"What did he do? Anything I would know? I'll bet he's one of those guys who shoots in color and then turns it into black and white for art's sake. What were some of his films?"

"Well, it's not exactly like that, Skids. It's more like he wanted to be a film director and was working on that while he was tending bar for me."

"Where did the director part come in?"

"He was making his first film, about halfway done with it when he disappeared."

"Died," Guantanamo said plainly, then stuffed his mouth with ketchup-covered fries.

"He disappeared first." Bernie was getting annoyed with Guantanamo's direct approach. This was, in my opinion, why Guantanamo chose to be known as the strong, silent type and why he was my friend.

Of course, the fact this Jā character disappeared added a little granola to the yogurt of the story. Things were getting crunchy.

"When did he disappear?" I asked.

"A week ago. Last Saturday night he didn't show up for work. When he didn't show up the next three days, I figured something was wrong."

Not a bad guess, in my mind. Hell, if I didn't show up at the magazine for three days in a row...well, if I didn't show up, Publisher Steve would be damn glad not to see me, but he would figure something was wrong. I mean, I'm there almost every day when I'm not working on a story, so I could definitely see where Bernie was coming from, especially if he was paying this guy to be there.

"After the fifth day of no call, no show," Bernie continued, "I was pretty damn irritated. Here I lend this guy two hundred and fifty G and he doesn't--"

"You what?" I interrupted.

Guantanamo choked out some half eaten...something...and managed to cover his mouth with a napkin before completely disgusting everyone at the table. Needless to say, we were both taken by surprise.

Bernie kind of sunk into himself. I knew he thought he was going to just slip that one by and continue with his story. Uh uh. No way. See, now we're talking serious money. When we start talking serious money that requires a whole different approach to a conversation. I was not happy that this wasn't brought up to begin with.

"I should have brought that up to begin with, I know."

"From the beginning, Bernie. No more dancing around this. You are in way over your head and you're going to tell me what you want from me or I'm going home and getting back into bed."

Honestly, that wasn't a bad idea anyway, especially with Carol giving me the sexy eye (kind of like the evil eye but in a good way) every time I looked over at her. But I was here. I had to hear Bernie out and if there was a quarter million bucks at stake, I could at least find out how much of a cut he was going to offer me for my assistance.

Bernie took a deep breath. He did that whenever he needed to say something important. I waited.

He took another. I was getting bored.

A third breath and I signaled for the check.

"Okay, Skids," Finally. "It's like this. About three months ago, Jā comes to me with this great plan. He tells me he's got this great script by a kid he says is gonna be the next Robert Towne and all they need to make it $250,000. Now, that ain't a little bit, but, as it turns out, The Cup is doing pretty well and my accountant had just told me if I don't find an investment, I was gonna get hit hard on taxes."

Just the fact Bernie was sitting across from me telling me about his accountant with a straight face was worth getting out of bed this morning.

"You have an accountant?" I laughed. I know, it's not polite to laugh at a friend when he's down, but this was funny. The last time I'd heard Bernie mention an accountant was when he was recounting a boyhood story of a hallway beating he had participated in back in high school. The kid who was on the receiving end, according to Bernie when he told the story, had become an accountant. I believe Bernie's comment at the time was the only thing number crunchers were good for was being crunched. And now one of them is controlling enough of Bernie's interest to help him spend 250K. The irony was just too much for me.

I took several deep breaths and tried to control myself. Finally, I was calm enough.

"So this...accountant," I stifled another laugh, "he suggested giving the big bucks to a bartender?"

Bernie was starting to get irritated I wasn't taking him as seriously as he'd hoped, but it didn't last. We'd been friends way too long and besides, he knew if that was happening to someone else, he'd be laughing his ass off. "Yes...and no. Marty suggested an--"

"Marty?"

"My accountant. His name is Martin."

"Martin. Jewish?"

"Of course."

"How stereotypical of you."

"It's not like that, Skids."

Bernie was getting defensive. I wasn't sure why. I don't think he knew my family background was Jewish so that couldn't have been it, but there was something he was holding back.

"What's 'it' like, Bernie?"

He didn't want to say, I knew it, but if this was going to work, I had to know everything. Besides, anything you can hold over a friend will get you help later on.

"'Fess up, Bern. If this is gonna work, I gotta know everything."

Bernie knew I was right. He sighed. "He's..."

"It'll be easier if you just say it quick."

One more breath and Bernie spilled. "He's my cousin and my mom recommended him when she found out how much money the club was bringing in and knew I didn't have any money sense since as far as she knew I always lost my allowance through holes in my pocket instead of gambling it away which is what I really did and she thought cousin Marty might be able to help since he was always the good one in the family."

I was learning way more about Bernie than I really wanted to.

"Tell me about Cousin Marty."

"Marty says that if I don't have anything to offset the

profits I'm showing, then come April I could get hit hard."

"The Cup is doing that well?" Guantanamo asked.

"Better." Bernie seemed embarrassed by his good fortune. "I've been having to turn them away at the door. On nights when I have an out-of-town band - these small label acts touring the club circuit - on those nights I'm bringing in more than we used to make in a year. Legally. And nights with the house band are generally packed anyways, I just can't charge as much to get in."

He'd lost me when he started talking about small labels but who was I to argue. In any event, business seemed to be good. Before he could get too far sidetracked, I brought the conversation back to the topic at hand. "And Marty said...?"

"Marty said I should invest in something which wouldn't show any profit for a little while, if at all. He said I could write it off as a loss and wouldn't have to pay as much to the IRS."

"Not a bad plan." I wondered if I had ever paid anything to the IRS. I knew I filled out my forms every year, but it seemed to me I always got money back. In fact, I don't think I ever knew anyone who actually had to pay money to the government.

"Yeah. Anyway, a couple weeks ago, maybe six or so, Jā finally comes to me and hits me up with the plan. He's got everything all worked out on paper and says all he needs is the 250 and he could be like Chi Chi Rodriguez, you know the director of the next El Mariachi."

"Robert Rodriguez and that only cost 7 grand."

"Whatever."

"You read this great script of his?"

"Of course. I didn't understand it, but then Gina read it and loved it. Kept going on about how wonderful it was. We'd only been going out a little while then, so I figured what the hell, I'd impress her a bit. So, when Marty said this was a fine investment and that I should go for it, I did."

"Just handed him stacks of hundreds?"

"No...not exactly. With Marty's help I opened a separate bank account and deposited the money in there. According to Jā, I was the Executive Producer and as such I controlled the money. I was the one who was supposed to write all the checks and keep track and all that crap. I didn't want to do any of it. I mean I had my hands full with running The Cup and this was just more headache." He stopped long enough to take a long drink from his still nearly full glass.

"What did you do?" The pause was too much for me.

"I put his name on the signature card."

Now it was my turn to take a long swallow. "You handed this guy a checking account with two hundred fifty thousand dollars in it and walked away?"

"I didn't walk away, exactly. I made him sign papers and he had to work with Marty in making sure he got receipts for everything. It was all as above-board as I could make it. And besides, I wasn't looking to make any money back, at least not for a little while."

"Business is really that good?" I asked. I was amazed. I was also a little put out that I had chosen to make a living writing articles when I could have gone in with Bernie on the bar instead of blowing my share of the money on a rare edition of Alice's Adventures in Wonderland and an extended road trip to Disneyworld with Guantanamo. I could have been rich right now.

Bernie nodded his response to my question with the biggest grin I had ever seen outside of Chuck Jones' Grinch. "Makes you wish you'd gone in with me on the bar, doesn't it?"

I had to shoot him down, if only to make myself feel a little better about my own decision. "Then again, I could also be a murder suspect. I guess it all works out in the end, huh?"

Okay, I admit it. That was a low blow and I regretted it the moment I saw his face sink.

"I'm sorry, Bern. Really. Finish telling me. When did you set up this account?"

Bernie kept looking into his beer. "About a month ago. He first asked me for the money three months ago, back around that time you and me went for that ride up to Neptune's Net. Remember?"

Neptune's Net was a restaurant on the Pacific Coast Highway about an hours ride north of here, just below the Ventura County border. Last time I was there, the time Bernie was referring too, we got kicked out for trying to push all the tables together to create a dance stage.

"I remember."

"Anyway, Jā said he was doing all the pre-production and getting everyone together, he just needed the money before they started filming. Basically, if I didn't come through, he couldn't make his movie."

"A lot riding on you being able to come through. Did he pressure you at all?"

"With what? I was his boss. What was he going to do?

Quit? Yeah, that would show me."

Guantanamo laughed.

"No, he didn't threaten me, but he did make it sound exciting. He brought your name up a lot."

"My name?" This was a new development.

"Yeah, he kept mentioning your columns and how cool it would be to have it 'reviewed by your buddy, Skids.' I must admit the thought was attractive."

"He's read my stuff?"

"I keep several copies of that rag you write for around the bar. Makes me look hip when I mention Skids Poppe is a friend of mine. You don't realize how popular you are with the kids. They all think you're a modern-day cross between Hunter Thompson, William Burroughs, and Joe Bob Briggs, whoever that is. They think you're funnier than all of them."

I'd have been embarrassed if they weren't right.

"I'd be embarrassed if they weren't right."

"Tell him more," Guantanamo said.

"One night they even named a drink after you. Steely Jack, this guy we have to DJ when the band isn't playing, based it on something he said you wrote in a column about a year ago. Personally, I haven't had the guts to try it, although it is getting to be mighty popular."

Now I knew Bernie was buttering me up... and avoiding telling me the rest of the story. "Enough," I said, smiling. "Finish up."

"I'm serious about the drink. Okay, Jā finally convinced me, after I talked to Marty. I set up the account. He went out and rented all the equipment, got his crew lined up and got ready to shoot. My only stipulation was he still had to work. He's the best bartender I have."

"Had," Guantanamo interrupted. Bernie shot him a dirty look. Bey shrugged and went back to watching the girls rollerblading by on the bike path.

"Had," Bernie continued. "I needed him there. I told him it would be okay if he was late a night or two and he could even leave early, but during peak hours I really needed him there. He agreed, no problem. Said most of his stuff was daylight shots anyway, which would save him money on lights. He started shooting about two and a half weeks ago, said the entire thing would take 21 days."

"Three weeks."

"No. It was 21 days of shooting which meant closer to four weeks. They were scheduled to be shooting five or six days a week. He was a little more than halfway through and everything was going great. He would shoot all day and come in to work excited and full of energy, telling everyone how many shots he'd gotten done. Sure, the rush would leave, and he'd be dragging his feet long before last call, but he was a trooper and stuck to his side of the bargain." Bernie trailed off.

"And then..." I prompted.

"And then last Saturday he didn't show up. At first, I was upset, but I figured he'd been working hard trying to keep all cylinders firing, and probably just crashed. When he didn't show up Sunday, I began to get worried. Monday, I asked August if she knew what was going on."

I interrupted. "August?"

"She was Jā's girlfriend. They broke up right around the

time all this started. She sings for the house band. She didn't know anything. By Monday night, I knew something was wrong."

"You didn't think he was just too busy working on the film?"

"No. If he was having a problem, he would have told me. It was part of our agreement."

Silence. I could see Bernie was getting upset. I figured we should get moving. I picked up the check, looked at it and handed it to Bernie without saying a word. It would have been inappropriate to comment on how twenty-two bucks wasn't bad for breakfast. I wasn't going to pay it, though. I mean, friendship goes a long way and I know Bernie was having a hard time, emotionally, right now, but he was still making more money than I was and besides, he wanted my help, he had to buy me food. He knew it, too.

Bernie reached into his pocket and pulled out a crumpled wad of bills. He dropped several on the table without looking; I looked. It was about thirty bucks give or take.

We walked out of the restaurant and hit the Boardwalk, heading south, past where we had just been sitting. Carol yelled out something about getting together soon. I nodded and Bernie, Bey and I made our way towards Windward Avenue, the street where most tourists enter or exit the excitement that is Venice.

Time to finish the story.

"Let me finish the story," Bernie said. "On Tuesday I checked the bank account. There was still about $160,000 in it so I knew he hadn't split with the money. At least not then."

"What do you mean?"

"I mean I checked Tuesday morning. Wednesday morning there was $2,000 in the account. "

Bey whistled appreciatively. I wasn't sure if he was commenting on the group of girls we'd just passed or if he had been listening and was impressed with the sudden disappearance of $158,000. For me, it was the latter. For 158 grand, you could buy all the attractive women you wanted. I asked the obvious question, "What happened to the money?"

"Jā withdrew it in the form of a cashier's check Tuesday afternoon."

"Great."

"I didn't understand what was going on. I called Marty and he said Jā could do that since his name was on the signature card. He had to keep two thousand in the account to keep it open and he couldn't close it without me. Now I was pissed. It felt like Jā just wanted to take my money. I wasn't very happy."

And Bernie was not the kind of guy you wanted mad at you. He may be a respected member of the community now, but that didn't mean he didn't have a past...or friends who weren't as respected as he was and didn't have nearly as much to lose.

We were getting close to the end of the story.

"Thursday afternoon, there's a message on my machine. It's Jā. He says he needs to talk to me. Things have changed a little bit and he needs more money to finish the film. No apologies, no nothing. Just a message asking me to meet him at ten o'clock that night down at the end of the Venice

Pier."

"And did you?"

"What do you think? I had a band playing Thursday night. There was no way I could get out to meet him. At least not at that time. By the time I could get out, he wasn't there. I figured he'd already left."

"Was that the last time you heard from him?"

Bernie hesitated slightly. "Yeah. I spent the night at Gina's on Thursday and when I went home Friday afternoon to get a change of clothes, the police were there, looking for me."

"What did you do?"

"What did I do? I stayed away from my place and The Cup; I didn't even go back to Gina's. Spent the night at a motel in Santa Monica and called you when I got up this morning."

"What am I supposed to do?"

"Skids, you're the only one I can trust. You gotta get me out of this. I swear I didn't kill him."

I stopped walking and looked at him. He was my friend, true, but it had been a long time since I had been on the wrong side of a police line-up. His eyes were sad, desperate, and I knew he was in trouble, but how could I justify risking my own neck? I looked to Guantanamo to see if he could offer any clues as to what I should do. None. He was busy watching the guys at Muscle Beach and comparing his own biceps.

"C'mon, Skids, whaddya say?" Bernie knew it was now or never. If I backed out on him it would mean he was in this alone and it would irrevocably alter our friendship from this point forward. Hell, if I said no, they might even take away my drink down at The Cup.

I made up my mind. There really was no easy way to say it, so I just sucked in my breath and said those five words which, since I've been little, have gotten me into more trouble than I care to remember. And no, they weren't "Alright, I'll help you out."

I looked Bernie right in the eye. Took one last deep breath. "What's in it for me?"

Bernie clapped me on the shoulders and gratitude spread across his face. "Thank you, Skids. Thank you." He was causing a scene, a big one, and a group of body builders were beginning to look. I was afraid he was going to kiss me, which, under any circumstance wouldn't be good, but here might actually prove harmful.

I pulled out of his embrace and continued walking. Bernie kept up. Guantanamo said he'd meet me at home; he wanted to get back to his sand sculptress. That was fine with me. I mean, what help had he been so far? Besides, he knew me well enough to know I'd agreed to help out Bernie, no matter the offer, so he figured there was no need for him to stick around.

See, there is my biggest problem. I'm a sucker. If ever there was a situation that screamed, at the top of its lungs, "Stay away this will get you in trouble," this was it. And yet, here I was, about to negotiate my fee, and my sidekick knew me well enough to know I would do it no matter what. Some people would blame their parents for this kind of a good streak. Not me. Personally, I think God has it out for me.

Poppe Culture

We walked for a while not saying anything. Bernie was glowing like a radioactive rodent and I was still trying to figure out what I had gotten into. By the time we passed Washington Boulevard and started walking along the fancy houses which faced the water, I knew I better get Bernie to agree to some kind of payment. Friends, like I said, is one thing. But when you want someone to do you a favor, you're better off paying for it in advance, because if you take it on credit, there's no telling when and where that marker is going to come due. And me? What kind of a friend would I be if I put Ol' Bern into that kind of moral quandary?

"Seriously, Bern," I said. "What's in it for me?"

"What do you want, Skids? Name it."

"It doesn't work like that." He was supposed to make me an offer, which I could refuse. Then I counter-offer and end up settling on $200 a day plus expenses. I'd seen it work like that in an old Bogart film and if I was going to play detective and help out someone on a murder rap, I may as well crib from the best, right?

"How does it work? You want money, Skids? How much? I'm already into this for $250 G and if you don't come through, I'll be spending at least that much on a lawyer. Name a figure."

He was getting defensive.

"I didn't mean it like that, Bern." What was I saying? Of course I did.

"Look Skids, what would you do with money? Sure, I'll cover anything you put out while you're helping me, but do you really want to take money to help out a friend?"

I really wanted to say "yes." Instead, I said, "Don't I?"

"Skids, I can offer you something even better and something that, I think, will mean more in the long run."

Oh yeah, this was getting deep.

"The film is almost done. How 'bout I make you a producer?"

Now it was my turn to stop walking. I was floored. I thought about it. Me, Skids Poppe, Movie Producer. Mr. Poppe, Executive Producer. Skids Poppe Presents.... That last one sounded good. I looked over at Bernie. Christ was I a sucker.

"If the film doesn't get finished, I want $200 a day... plus expenses."

Saturday Afternoon

Guantanamo was already back at the apartment by the time we got there. It looked like it didn't go well with the sand sculptress.

"It didn't go well with the sand sculptress," he moaned.

"What happened?"

"Seems she's just not terribly interested in guys who've served time."

"What are you talking about?" I was confused. Bey was probably the only friend I had who hadn't spent any time behind bars. Hell, even nights he should have spent in the drunk tank were spent on someone's couch. He was always lucky that way.

"It was going along just great until I mentioned my two years blowing things up for peace and democracy."

"Ahhh," I said. It was all becoming clear. "Probably a pacifist."

"Probably right."

Bey seemed satisfied with my answer and grumbled his way into the bathroom. Bernie was still standing in the doorway.

"You guys both live here?"

"It's cozy, but we call it home."

I told Bernie to come inside and sit down.

"Where should I sit?"

I pointed to the couch and went into the kitchen to get a couple of beers. When I came back, Bernie was still standing.

"You can sit on the couch."

He seemed unsure what to say and stammered for a few seconds before anything coherent came out. "Where... exactly... is the couch?"

"Here." I moved a stack of old magazines and a pile of dirty clothes and, voila, a couch cushion appeared.

Now, I don't want to say our place isn't clean. I mean, we don't have rats or anything like that, but it hasn't been featured in Architectural Digest recently, if you know what I'm saying. Bernie took the offered cushion and dislodged a stack of books resting on the arm of the couch as he sat.

"Nice place you got here, Skids."

I knew he was being facetious, seeing as how he lived in a two-story place over in the Marina, right on the Silver Strand (I told you business was good for him), but I liked where I lived.

It was a one-bedroom place in a small building and it was right off the boardwalk. I'd been here for over a year and Guantanamo had been staying ever since he'd left the army, looking for a safe spot to let his hair grow out. It was a nice little setup. The bedroom had plenty of room in it for the both of us (as long as he slept on the floor) and I had a small area in the kitchen where I could set up my computer and files.

Yeah, I know, it just blows the image of me as a renegade writer to know I use a computer. Tough. I like my little laptop. I can throw it into a saddlebag and take it on the road with me so I can make money, legally, anyplace. And who would have thought the Internet could provide so much fun?

I handed Bernie a beer and grabbed a nearby stool. Actually, first, I put the magazines piled on said stool on top of the books Bernie had toppled and then moved it so I could sit in front of Bernie as we talked. He drank his beer more quickly than the one he'd had at the Sidewalk. Of course. This one I paid for, no reason to make it last. After he'd gotten the bottle parallel with the floor, he swallowed and looked up at me. "What do we do now, Skids?"

I knew this was coming. Ever since I agreed to help out, I'd been thinking about the answer. "First thing, Bern, is we hide you."

He set his mouth and tried to smile. It didn't work. He was worried about The Cup.

"What about The Cup?"

Told ya. "There is no way you can go back there right now. The police will be looking for you there as much as anyplace else. Maybe more. We'll hide you out while I try and figure out what happened. I'll even go and keep an eye on The Cup for you."

"Really?"

"I'm gonna have to go there and talk to people about this Jā character anyway, right? I can keep an eye on things while I'm there. Besides, I gotta check out this drink of mine."

"That makes sense. And if you have any questions, talk to Fyche. He's been running the place on weekends. That's Fyche with a Y-C-H-E."

"Fyche?" I needed to get a notebook to write all this shit down.

"Yeah. British guy, older. Rides a Triumph. I'm sure you've seen him around."

"Fyche. Got it." I shook my head to clear the dust. I went into the kitchen to find a notebook. I was sure I had an extra sitting around my desk.

"Where should I go?" Bernie asked.

"I'm thinking," I mumbled. I moved a stack of Hogs and Hooters, an old magazine I had done a couple of pieces for, and found a pocket-sized spiral-bound notebook with a picture of The Boomtown Rats on the cover. I'd rescued it years ago from the clearance bin at Platters and was waiting to use it for just the right occasion. This was it. I grabbed a pen from the coffee mug on my desk (I use it to store pens, not coffee) and went back into the living room.

"Well," I said, then exhaled. "You can't hide here. Aside from the fact there's no room, as soon as people realize I'm asking questions, they're going to think I know where you are." What was I getting myself into? "Probably, the best thing for you would be to get out of town immediately. Do you have any place you could go?"

"Not really."

"What about your mom's place?"

"She lives in a retirement community in Arizona. It'd be worse than going to a Young Republicans convention. Someone would call the cops."

"Why?"

"That's what they've done every other time I've visited. And Mom just can't take that kind of stress."

The more I learned, the more I realized I didn't want to meet Bernie's family.

"There's nowhere else you can go? Don't you have to scout for bands or something to play at the club?"

"They all send me CDs or links to their YouTube pages. Or their agents do. Everywhere I can think to go has someone with a felony record attached." Bernie trailed off.

It's amazing to me how people change. I mean, a few years ago, Bernie wouldn't have thought twice about beating the crap out of some punk who had ripped him off for 20 bucks in a Three Card Monte game on the boardwalk. I know, I'd seen him do it. And now, here he was, all 240 pounds of him, about to start weeping over a murder he claimed he didn't commit. Money certainly changes people. It's not like he dealt cocaine and then got his own sit-com. He was a bar owner. And he was innocent at that. At least he said he was and in order for me to help him, I had to believe that. I had to do something. I had to put him somewhere no one would think of looking and where, if need be, I could reach him.

"I have to make a phone call."

I got up and went into the bedroom. The message light

on the answering machine was blinking. Then again, it was always blinking since the damn thing didn't work right half the time. Maybe as a producer, I could get a new one. Or better yet, a secretary to answer the phone for me. That way I wouldn't have to commit to being at breakfast and then saving a buddy from a murder rap. You know, it's the simple thoughts in life that make you smile.

I grabbed the phone. Eventually I would have to check if there actually were any messages. I dialed the 702 number carefully. It had been a while since I called and it took a couple of tries before I got it right.

She answered on the third ring. "Hello."

"Brandy?" I asked. I sometimes got her voice confused with her roommate's.

"Yes?"

"It's Skids... Don't hang up!"

"What do you want?"

"Is that anyway to treat your brother, your big brother, who loves you? I don't want anything more than to say hello."

"You do want something. And it's big."

"It's not that big. I just have a friend going to Vegas and he needs a place to stay for a few days and-"

She interrupted me. "He's not staying here. The last time one of your friends stayed here I had to have a wall replaced. No way."

"He'll pay rent. A full month's worth."

"You want him to stay a month?" She was appalled.

"No, no. He just needs to stay a few days, but he'll pay for a month."

"Why doesn't he go to a hotel?"

"He likes the family atmosphere."

"What's his name?" She was weakening. "Do I know him?"

"His name is Bernie and I don't think you do."

"When would he be here?"

"Can you pick him up at the airport around four?"

There was a long silence on the other end of the phone. I knew I was going to have to pay for this one.

"You owe me. You owe me big."

"Tell Mom and Dad I said hi."

She hung up without saying good-bye.

Now all I had to do was figure out how to get him on a plane. In the old days this would have been easy, just buy a ticket in my name and away he goes, but not anymore.

I thought about it for a second. Maybe the old ways would still work…with just a little bit of modification.

"Bey," I called out. "Come here. I have an art project for you."

Guantanamo grumbled something about eating paste as he walked into the bedroom.

"What?"

"How long do you think it would take to turn Bernie into me?"

Bey looked at me like I was insane, but then, that's how he always looked at me. Then a grin spread slowly across his face.

"Can I use your good digital camera?"

I should have seen that coming. I winced, pursed my lips and said "yes" before I could change my mind.

My sidekick's eyes lit up bigger than his smile.

"45 minutes. Hour max."

"Good. Should be just about right. Bernie," I yelled. "Pack a bag. You're going to Vegas."

75 minutes later and we were stopped at the Ralph's on the way to the airport. At this point, packing Bernie's bag consisted of getting a toothbrush and some deodorant (and for Bernie, the deodorant was the important thing) and hoping he could pick up clothes once he got to Vegas. I paid for the toiletries and we headed for LAX, me riding on the back of Bernie's Fat Boy. Okay, I know riding on the back is not the most masculine place to be, but we couldn't leave Bernie's bike parked at the beach for God knows how long, could we? This way I could take the bike after Bern got on a plane and I could park it someplace out of the way where it wouldn't get scratched, dented, or stolen. Besides, his bike was newer than my Sportster and I really wanted to ride it back.

I told Bernie to park at a meter near Terminal One. We got off the bike, I hung a handicapped placard on the handlebar, and we headed off to get Bernie out of town.

"Why'd we park there?" Bernie asked.

"Two reasons. One, it's free with a handicapped sign."

"You're not handicapped."

"And you're not a murderer, but here we are, right?" The logic confused him. "And two, most important, they take pictures of your license plate when you leave from the big structures. That's all we need, the police seeing your bike at the airport." I was starting to think like a detective and I liked it. Actually, I was thinking like a criminal, but I had more practice at that so I figured you should start with what you know, right? In any case the point was the same.

Inside the terminal, I sent Bernie to stand in line at the Southwest counter while I checked flights. I really am a product of television, man. The only reason I picked Southwest was because their TV ads said they had flights leaving every hour for Vegas and they weren't lying. Right there in multi-colored phosphorescence was flight 931 to Las Vegas, arriving at 4:03. Perfect.

I rejoined Bernie in line. We were three people away from his freedom.

"Got it," I told him. "There's a flight landing at just about four and Brandy will pick you up at the airport."

"Who's Brandy?"

"My sister."

"Sister?"

"Look, you got an accountant named Marty, I got a sister named Brandy. Is that a problem?" So I was a bit touchy on the subject, so what?

"Bit touchy, huh?"

I glared at him. True, Bernie was twice my size, but I was a pretty fair scrapper in my own right and besides, I was helping him out. He looked away.

"No problem, Skids," He said. He took a step forward in line as person number one got their ticket and checked their baggage. Two more in front of us. "It's just you've never mentioned her, is all."

"Well now I have. Happy?"

He looked at me and decided not to press it. Things

hadn't been great between my sister and I since the whole skydiving incident and I just didn't feel like talking about it.

We moved up one more space in line.

"How will I know her?"

"She looks like me... with less facial hair."

"No, seriously, Skids."

I wasn't kidding.

"You're not kidding?"

I shook my head and smiled. "Nope. She's a little shorter than me, about 5'6" or so. And she's got really long hair."

"How long?"

"Remember how long mine was before I cut it for that girl?" Don't ask.

"Yeah."

"Longer. And it's purple."

"Purple?"

"It was last time I saw her, about two years ago. I have no reason to believe she's changed it."

We were next in line.

"Does she know what I look like?" Bernie asked.

"Nope. I bet she has a sign saying something like 'Asshole Friend of Skids, I'm your ride."

Bernie laughed. I was serious about the sign, too. He'll learn soon enough about the Poppe Family. We are all cut from the same cloth.

"Next, please."

It was our turn. Bernie and I walked up to the counter.

"How can I help you today?"

"Hi," I read her name tag, "... Wendy. I'd like an open-ended round-trip ticket to Las Vegas, please. Flight

931."

"For both of you?" She was very pleasant.

Bernie opened his mouth. I kicked him, hard.

"Just me, thanks."

"Your name?"

"Skids Poppe."

She stopped typing and looked up at me like she recognized me from somewhere. I stared back at her.

"You're Skids Poppe?"

"Yes...." At least I thought I was.

"My boyfriend reads your stuff." She shook her head in disbelief then went back to typing up my ticket.

I nudged Bernie, grinning like the cat with the canary. I was famous. "Would you like me to sign something for your boyfriend?"

"Naw. He thinks your columns are full of shit. Although from what he says, I would have thought you were taller." She smiled at me, handing over the ticket. "Cash or charge?"

I handed over the money and stood as tall as possible as we walked away.

I stood with Bernie a little ways back from the security checkpoint and handed him the ticket. Then I held up the "art" project Bey had completed in record time. It showed Bernie's face but every other bit of information on it claimed to be me. I scrutinized it closer then handed it off.

"Thanks, Skids," Bernie said, placing the laminated card into his wallet.

"Don't thank me. Remember, with great power comes

great responsibility." For the next hour and a half, he was going to be me. Why did that make me so nervous?

He looked at me confused, not knowing what I was talking about. "Never mind," I waved him off. "I'll call you in a few days, as soon as I find out something."

"Yeah. Okay." He paused. "I owe you one." He put his hand out. I shook it.

"Anytime, Bern. Anytime. And no, you owe me two. Two hundred actually. Give me a check dated sometime last week for two hundred bucks." Bernie looked hurt. "You didn't think I was actually paying for this flight, did you?"

"I guess not."

"Good."

"Why am I dating it last week?" He asked as he started writing.

"Because if I deposit it with today's date, the cops are going to know I saw you and then I won't be able to ask questions and clear your name. Better make it two fifty." Bernie looked at me. "Gas for the scooter, man." He nodded and ripped the check from his book. "And your keys."

"Right."

"Now get on the plane. I'll know something soon."

"Thanks again, Skids."

He started to walk away as I thought of one last piece of advice.

"Bernie!" I yelled.

He turned around. "What?"

"Don't piss off my sister."

"Why?"

"Just don't." He nodded without understanding. Hopefully he'd listen to me. Lord help him if he didn't.

I stayed to make sure he made it through security. I held my breath as he pulled out his wallet and showed it along with my boarding pass. The old guy standing guard didn't look at it for more than a second before waving him through.

I exhaled and went back the way we'd come.

As I left the terminal, I looked to see if Wendy was still at the counter. She was but she didn't see me. Good. It wouldn't look good to have me leaving the airport just as my flight was taxiing down the runway. We must keep up appearances.

The bike was where we'd left it. I climbed on and put Bernie's keys in the ignition. I must tell you; his bike is nice. Like I said, it's newer than mine and his paint job is sweet. It's the type of bike we could only dream about when we were riding full time. I mean, the last guy in our little gang who rode a bike this nice is now serving time for killing the previous owner...but what a chase he led the cops on.

I turned the key and the v-twin engine hummed to life. Once it was warmed up, which only took a few minutes, the hum became a purr, then a full-throated growl as I twisted the throttle wide open. The entire bike vibrated between my legs. There is only one feeling in the world better than a Harley-Davidson showing off its muscle. And this you can do all by yourself.

I rolled the throttle back down, kicked the bike into neutral and backed out of the parking space. As soon as the front tire cleared the Mazda I was parked next to, I pulled the clutch and gently nudged the bike into first, feeling the slight jump as the gears took hold. There was a lot of power here, just waiting to be unleashed. I knew how jockeys felt just before the gate opened and the race started. And I really wished my bike made me feel like this. Maybe when this was over, after I cleared Bernie's name, I could get him to buy me one of these things. Hell, he could just give me this one and we could declare it stolen. Wouldn't be the first time I'd driven hot property.

I released the clutch and navigated around parked cars until I found the right exit to put me back on Sepulveda heading north. Once I hit Lincoln, I looked over and saw a Southwest plane rolling towards take-off. I raced it, thinking it might be Bernie's flight. I got the bike up over a 100 before I decided I would never win and besides, I had a red light coming up. I skidded and came to a stop inches away from the ass-end of a '73 Buick. I've never hit a car yet, although there have been several which deserved hitting. I could never justify damaging my bike enough to actually do it.

"What to do next?" I wondered, as I drove down the hill into Marina del Rey. It was still too early to hit The Cup and I doubted if I would be able to get back to sleep. I saw Bartels' up ahead on the left and immediately nixed going in. They not only knew me, but they knew Bernie's bike and I didn't want to explain. Maybe a movie would be good? I turned right on Maxella to see what was playing at the multiplex and as soon as I did, I knew I wasn't going to the movies. I pulled the bike into the parking lot of the big two-story copy place and parked as close as I could legally get to the door. I had things to take care of before I started my new investigative career.

I walked through the blue doors knowing exactly what I had in mind. All I needed was someone to help me put it all together. I made my way to the counter and asked the first guy I could find for help.

"Ye be wantin' help then do ya?"

At least that's what I thought he said. I could barely understand him through his thick Scottish accent.

"Yeah... I think so."

He was a big man, not as big as Bernie, but big, with red hair and a beard which would have felt at home in a Mel Gibson movie. "Well, then, my nem is Bram and w'at ken I dew to mek yer day t'at much moor pleasurable?"

I swear that is what he sounded like. Although I will not swear that is what he said. In fact, I'm just going to tell you what I think he said because, let's face it, that's all that's really important anyway.

"Well, Bram," I said, trying my best not to mock his accent. He didn't look like the kind of guy who would take my mocking with the sense of humor in which it was meant. "I just started a new business and need some things."

"Then you've certainly come to the right place, haven't ya?"

Bram turned out to be a full-service copy guy. When I told him what I wanted, he led me first to the computer department to get everything type-set. He pulled all the text over, sized it up just right then started printing. We argued a couple of times over color and stock, but eventually we got it all worked out. When I left there, I had a box of supplies for me and a perfect gift for a few friends. I was feeling quite proud of myself. I wondered why I'd never done this before.

I slipped the box into the bike's saddlebags, wedging it in nice and tight to avoid any damage, and buckled the bag shut. I still had plenty of time and nothing to do. My little printing excursion had only taken a little over an hour (although it felt like less) and even though I had a stop I wanted to make before I went home and changed, I knew it wouldn't take all that long, either.

I sat sideways against the bike and thought about what was around. Were there any errands I needed to run as long as I was out? Guantanamo had said something a couple days before about wanting me to pick up something from the store, but I couldn't remember what. I looked around.

"Oh my God," I thought. "There's a branch of my bank." I'd never noticed it before since all my checks were direct deposited by Publisher Steve. He thought it best if I wasn't allowed to handle the checks personally. Now, though, I had a check in my pocket. I walked over and convinced a teller I was who I said I was. Eventually, she upped the balance of my account by two hundred fifty bucks.

Walking out I thought about all the things I should spend that money on. Things like groceries or dish soap. I definitely should not spend it frivolously.

What the hell, I thought and headed over to Ellpee's, the mostly used but primarily underground and off-beat record store across the parking lot.

Now, as most of you know, my musical tastes are somewhat eclectic. Being raised by parents who left the country when The Beatle's Revolver album came out because, as Pop

Poppe Culture

Poppe put it, "Things were just getting a bit too weird." can have that effect on a growing boy. Since then, I've listened to just about everything, being introduced to new music by each successive girlfriend who didn't like what the last one made me listen to. And with the exception of the Country-Western singer I dated briefly, I still listen to most of that music.

Sure, I've picked up a few favorites along the way and these I collect with reckless abandon, regardless of what anyone else thinks. Those of you who read my column (Wendy's boyfriend aside) have been fairly appreciative of my wide range of interests. I only say this so it won't shock you to find out I was in Ellpee's looking for the new album from Driftwood Messiah. They're a relatively new band from the area. I used to see 'em play on the Santa Monica Pier for free and now they had a record deal. Their first two CDs rocked pretty hard and I knew the third had just come out so I figured since I had the time and a couple of extra bucks, I may as well grab it.

While I was there, I also picked up a few replacement discs for ones I lost in the divorce. It is so annoying to know you have a record and then when you go to play it realize the ex-wife now has it. I grabbed a copy of Bowie's Diamond Dogs, Costello's Armed Forces and, since they had it in stock and I wouldn't have to go through the trouble of special ordering, Marillion's Misplaced Childhood. How I ever let her walk out the door with that one, I will never know. Guantanamo swears I told her to leave it but what are you going to do? I hope she listens to it often and curses my name.

When I got home, I discovered Guantanamo fast asleep in front of some documentary on "Firepower in The Military" on the History Channel. Without waking him, not that I didn't try, I grabbed a stack of my new supplies and headed over to Windward to visit some friends.

Windward Avenue is the heart of the Venice Boardwalk. It's not in the exact center, but everything else radiates out from it. Originally, Windward was Venice's main street and the original pieces of architecture which still remain lends a sense of history and culture to a city less than a hundred years old.

On the beach side, Windward dead-ends amid rows of swap-meet style vendors at the Venice Pavilion, a building once used for outdoor concerts and now a haven for skateboard punks. It's also where you can find more cops than a donut stand. With the Pavilion at your back, the stores become a little more permanent. Two blocks up you hit the Windward Circle and a great sushi bar. I wasn't going that far.

I stopped before I hit Pacific at Runaway Squid Tattoo. The Squid has only been in this location for a couple of years, but all the guys working there had become long-time drinking buddies. And this had nothing to do with the fact the closest bar to my house was next door to the shop. Nothing. Nope, these guys were my friends because they were the best in the field. I won't let anyone else touch me when it comes to ink.

I walked in and was greeted like a long-lost relative.

"Skids, you bastard, you owe me money."

I smiled and walked straight through to the back of the store. Mutt, the one who claimed I owed him money, was hanging out with Slick who was busy putting a butterfly on some girl's ass. Lucky guy, whoever that butterfly would be landing on next. Slick grunted hello as Mutt came around the counter.

"Skids, my man. I'm serious. You owe me money. Drinks Thursday night were not complimentary." He smiled at me. Mutt has been doing my color for the past two years. It's good to have a positive relationship with your tattoo artist.

"I owe everyone money, get in line." I smiled back and held my hand to shake his. When our hands connected, I slipped him one of the pieces of paper I had made at Kinko's.

"What's this?" Mutt looked at the card I'd given him. "'Skids Poppe, Private Detective.' Oh this is good." He laughed and handed the card back.

"Keep it," I said. "I had a bunch made."

"For what?"

"New job."

"You mean to tell me you actually work? I thought you were like Angelyne. Don't tell me just being the world-famous Skids Poppe doesn't bring in fortune and fame?" He was giving me a hard time and I knew it. Today was not the day to ask for a free tatt.

"Fame, sure. I got that in spades. The fortune thing, though..." I paused.

"The ex is still wringing your balls for alimony?" I nodded. "Christ," Mutt continued, disgusted, "Why doesn't the bitch just get married already and leave you the hell alone?"

Mutt was a friend. He didn't own a bike of his own,

but every now and again we'd score an extra and he'd come cruising with me and Guantanamo and a few of the other boys. He also had an extreme dislike of ex-wives, having three of them himself.

"Early next year, she said." Mutt looked at me with an accusing eye. He'd heard this before. "No really. I asked him, not her." That seemed to placate him. At least he lowered his eyebrow. Always creeps me out when he does that, looks like he's doing a bad Leonard Nimoy impression.

"What's with the business cards?"

"Cool, huh? I had 'em made at that copy place in the Marina. You can have them made up for anything. My copy guy, Bram," I said it in the appropriate accent, "he explained the whole thing to me. Said he could put up to eight different cards on a sheet then just cut it so they all look right. I got me a couple of different ones." I handed him several cards.

"'Skids Poppe, Movie Producer,' this one's nice. 'Skids Poppe, Famous Writer,' good, your head isn't big enough as it is. 'Mutt Jefferson, Male Prostitute.' What the hell is this?"

"I had some made for you." I was so proud of myself. I handed Mutt a whole stack of the cards with his name on them. He was touched

"Thanks, Skids, I'm touched. I don't know what to say."

"How about 'we're even and please let me give you a free tattoo'?"

"How about get the fuck out of my store?"

"Almost the same." We both laughed.

Mutt stopped first. "I know you Skids, you don't just

go out and spend time with people who wear ties unless you have to. What gives?"

I told him. Not everything, I'm not stupid. I just told him I was looking into a local murder for the magazine and thought it would be easier to ask questions if people thought I was a real detective. He thought I was insane, but that was par for the course. Before we could talk more, he got a client and had to run.

"Skids," he yelled out as I was leaving. "You wanna go for a beer or something later on?"

"I'm going to The Cup tonight, if you wanna stop by."

"Too packed for me. But have you had a Skids on the Rocks?"

"No. I just heard about it today. Is it good?"

"It certainly ain't nothing like you."

"What's that mean?"

"It means the drink can kick my ass."

I walked along the beach, my thick, steel-toed black boots making deep indentations in the wet sand as the water came up, licked them tentatively, then receded meekly away. By the time the sun set, very few people were left on the beach itself. It would take another hour or so before the boardwalk cleared itself of the day's visitors, leaving only residents and the brave couples walking along as the end of a romantic evening after eating at a nearby restaurant. Although how anyone can think the Venice Boardwalk after dark is romantic is beyond me. Romantic is the end of the jetty in Marina del Rey, the Ferris wheel on the pier, that kind of thing. Guantanamo is the kind of guy who finds

Venice after dark romantic, but then, he's spent time in combat, so you decide.

As I walked, I thought about what I was going to do about Bernie. I promised to help him, true, but what was that worth? Not my word - that's worth its weight in gold (or two hundred a day plus expenses, whichever is more) - but my detective skills. Why was I the one always getting called upon to solve my friends' problems? Just because I'd been able to help out in the past didn't mean I could always give the right answer.

Then again, I did have business cards in my pocket that said I was a private detective. If Bernie was right, and LA was indeed a place where you were what you said you were, then I should have no problem. In reality, I've been a lot of things in my life and I've been at least a dozen more when I was trying to pick up drunk girls at various bars around the country and no one has ever questioned me. Even Publisher Steve hired me because I told him I could write. I was just as surprised as he was when we discovered I actually could.

So I could do this. Bernie was my friend and the least I could do was pretend to be a detective for him. And if it turned out okay, there were worse things in life than being a movie producer. I've been writing and talking about movies for so long, it would be nice to actually be a part of one and all I had to do for it was find out who killed one guy. How hard could that be? Philip Marlowe did it all the time. Hell, Guantanamo once told me about a book where a pair of cats solved the crime. If a couple of pussies could do it, so could Skids Poppe.

I was feeling pretty damn sure of myself when I left the

sand and headed back to my apartment. Guantanamo was sprawled on the couch, watching some behind-the-scenes program about how they do special effects in movies. At least he wasn't asleep.

"Where you been?" he asked during a commercial.

"Walking down by the beach."

"Figuring out how to get to South America?"

He said it like it's what he would have been thinking about if he was in my position. And even though I wasn't, I knew exactly what he was talking about.

"Sorry, Sundance. We're not going to South America. We're going to The Cup for drinks."

"Sorry, Butch. You're going alone. I have a date with the sand sculptress."

"Sure. Desert me in my hour of need. And all for a woman."

"And when you have a woman of your own, Skids, who isn't inflatable, then maybe you'll understand."

"Hey! Wait a --" I was interrupted by his hand being held straight up in my face. The program was back on and my favorite sidekick was deeply engrossed, again.

I tossed him a stack of business cards which read "Guantanamo Bey, Sidekick." They landed on his lap.

"I got you a present," I laughed. "And tomorrow you will tell me the story." I think he said he would, but I was already in my bedroom, deciding which outfit would best suit my new job of asking questions at The Cup. I opted for jeans and a clean t-shirt. I threw them on the bed and hopped in the shower. I wanted to be clean for my first night of work.

Saturday Evening

The front of The Cup of Fools looked just like I remembered. The sign Bernie'd been so proud of was hanging up over the door: The jester still sitting on the bottom with his foot hanging down over the edge, and the foot still kicking away at an imaginary monkey. Bernie's dream of getting an actual monkey for him to kick had even been realized, metaphorically, by the large group of people with multi-colored waistcoats and funny hats standing in line outside the door.

I rode past, heading north on Main Street until I could find a decent place to park. I was riding my own bike, having parked Bernie's behind my place for the night. It would be safe there, at least until morning, and then I would figure out where to leave it for a while. Now my bike was nothing like Bernie's, but that didn't mean I didn't take care of it, which is why I needed a good place to park. About a block and a half away, I found one.

Granted, I hate paying for parking. Sue me. I have found the best way to avoid this particular little trap is to park on someone else's quarter. And if you're not lucky enough to find a completely empty space with a full meter some idiot has just left, well then, you have to borrow a little of an occupied space. I have found, in my travels, this isn't as hard as it may sound. In Bernie's bike it would have been a little more difficult (not the reason I didn't take it) since he's got a wider rear tire, not to mention those huge, studded saddlebags. But, I hear you asking, what about getting your bike dinged or knocked over by the car whose space you're sharing? This is why space selection is so very important.

I slipped my 883 backwards in between a BMW Z3 painted a brilliant fire engine red and a white Mercedes 450SEL. I told you Santa Monica was becoming more up-scale.

I positioned my bike evenly between the two, knowing neither driver would hit my bike for fear of denting, scratching, folding, spindling, or mutilating their shiny boxes. The minds of the car-driving public are so easy to predict. Also why I chose not to park between a piece-of-shit yellow Honda CVCC wagon with a cracked windshield and a beat-up Dodge Omni. Whoever drove those cars didn't give a damn about who they hit.

I locked the front forks and got off, hanging my helmet on the handlebars. I hated that helmet and the fact I had to wear it. I kept hoping it would get stolen but somehow, it never did. Lucky, lucky me.

I walked back the block and a half and joined the group of kids standing in line. On my own personal timeline, I was standing in the shadow of 30, if you count birth as sunrise, so I wasn't much older than most of the crowd I was with, but somehow knowing that fact didn't stop me from feeling old. Maybe it was just I had never had to wait in a line to get into a bar in my life, even before I was legal. Well, I could always console myself with the knowledge Guantanamo was older than me. Why wasn't he here, anyway?

"Oh well," I thought. "Time to get to work."

I got in line and waited for a few minutes. This was really boring. I could hear music coming from inside and knew I would be doing much better in there than out here.

Some new kids showed up, went right past the line and to the doorman, who, after a brief conversation and a consultation with his clipboard, let them inside.

"What's all that about?" I asked, to no one in particular.

"They must be on the guest list," answered a little pimply-faced kid standing next to me in line. He was dressed in what I could only assume were trend-following clothes. All I could think when I looked at him was he looked like a skinny white boy trying to be cool.

"Guest list?"

"If you know someone, they put you on the guest list and you don't have to wait in line." The skinny white boy explained as if I were insane to have even asked. He seemed like the kind of guy who always wished he were on the guest list but never was, and probably never would be.

"I know what a guest list is," I snarled back in the same attitude. But I was wondering if my name was on it. Bernie had said once, a long time ago, about the time we all stopped coming here, that my name would always be left at the door in case I ever wanted to stop by. I decided to test it. I grabbed the kid by the arm, pulling him along with me to the front of the line.

"Hey," he protested. "What do you think you're doing?"

"You wanna get in? Shut up and come with me."

He didn't seem sure, but at least he followed.

We stopped in front of the big doorman.

"What." It wasn't a question. This guy couldn't formulate a question.

"I'm on the guest list."

"Yeah. And I'm Trent Reznor. Get back in line, buddy."

My new friend took this as a sign to walk away but I stood firm. My hand shot out and I grabbed the kid before he could get too far. My eyes never left the doorman's. "Look under 'P' for Poppe." I spelled it for him so he'd get it right.

"Skids Poppe?" I was wrong, he could formulate a question.

"You are correct, sir." No matter how many times I say that, I never sound like Ed McMahon.

Then he recognized me and the doorman became my best friend, ushering me and the skinny white kid, whose name I never did find out, into the club. It pays to be friends with the owner.

The inside of the Cup of Fools had changed a bit since I had been there last, but not enough that I wouldn't be able to find my way to the bathroom. Just inside the door was where the bar started. It ran a good twenty-five feet before it turned and started its second leg. High tables with high stools were scattered haphazardly around the place and a dance floor was packed with clones of the same kids I had just been in line with. What is it about kids that says they all have to dress the same way? I have never understood fashion, myself. To me, jeans and a clean shirt always seemed to fit any occasion.

The crowd was part of what had changed. Sure, the bar was bigger, and it looked like Bernie had gotten rid of the pool table which used to be in a back corner, but the reason I left The Cup was because it was getting too crowded. And even back then, it had never even been this packed. The other main change was the source of the music the kids were all dancing to.

Across the dance floor, at the far end of the room, was a stage. The way it was built, chairs could be set up like a school assembly in front of it to fill the whole place and no one would have a bad seat. I figured if you moved the tables aside, you could get two hundred people in to see a band. Two fifty if they were all close friends. And at twenty-five bucks a head, plus drinks, Bernie would clear…Shit. I wasn't charging him nearly enough. No wonder he was driving a new Hog.

Currently, though, the band playing seemed to be part of the crowd. That is to say they just fit in. No one was paying particular attention to them, but everyone was dancing and enjoying themselves. I shuffled to a stop and created a hole among the people at the bar so I could get close to the wood. I signaled for a bartender.

"What can I get for you?" He yelled over the music.

"Hi," I yelled back. "I'm Skids Poppe."

He looked at me, his eyebrows furrowed as if trying to figure something out. Once he had his answer, he nodded appreciatively and walked away.

I tried to get his attention again, but my yells were ignored as he busied himself making a drink. Maybe I was going nuts and he never heard me. That was it, he was talking to someone else. I looked around. Everyone around me already had drinks.

When I turned back to try and reintroduce myself, my bartender was setting a large glass down in front of me. I didn't recall ordering a drink, but okay, I was ready to go with the flow.

Then he poured the drink. Not from a regular shaker, mind you, but from what looked like the crankcase of a '59 panhead. In my mind, I was thinking it couldn't be real, it would be too heavy, but the bartender was a big guy and he was having a bit of difficulty lifting it so maybe it was. Certainly, what came out of it looked real. I mean the liquid he was pouring into my cup looked like it could have come from the crankcase of a '59 panhead. It was thick and syrupy and looked like it needed changing about 5000 miles ago.

I leaned in to smell it. It smelled sweet and very alcoholic. The bartender smiled at me and put a small appliance around the rim of my glass. By this point, everyone around me at the bar was paying attention. Obviously, this wasn't a regular occurrence and I was wondering what I did to deserve such an honor. By the time the bartender finished fiddling with my glass, it looked like something out of one of the Mad Max films. It now had a twisted metal handle and a small area along the lip to drink from. No subtlety here. The piece de resistance came when the bartender pulled an unopened spark plug box from someplace under the bar. He fitted the plug into the contraption on the glass and set the whole thing down in front of me.

Suddenly, the music stopped. The woman who was singing announced the band would be taking a little break and they would be back in 20 minutes. I used the momentary lull to my advantage.

I looked the bartender in the eye. "What the hell is this?"

"This," he said, grabbing the handle, "is a 'Skids Poppe.'" He pushed the mug closer while triggering an unseen battery, which set off the spark plug, which in turn lit the entire thing on fire. I felt like I had just been handed the remains of an accident and was being asked to drink the blood of the vanquished. Something about the scene seemed vaguely familiar but I couldn't place it.

I eyed the flames carefully. "I didn't order this."

"Yes you did. You came up and said 'Skids Poppe.'"

I nodded and pointed to myself. "That's me. I'm Skids Poppe."

Finally, a light of understanding came on in the bartender's eye. He nodded sagely. "Well, then," he said. "This is your drink."

I couldn't argue with logic like that.

"I'm honored, really."

Now all I had to figure out was how to drink it.

"Hey, who ordered the Skids?" The question was asked by a female voice. I looked up to see a beautiful girl with blonde hair standing next to me and looking down at my drink.

"He did," my bartender said, nodding in my direction.

"Good call," the girl said. "That's a great drink."

I saw my salvation. "You want it? I ordered it by accident."

The girl looked at me then at the bartender, who nodded back at her. "Sure," she said.

She grabbed the mug and lifted it to her mouth. She closed her eyes and took a deep breath, her breasts lifting slightly as her lungs filled with air. A second later she opened her eyes and blew. The flames vanished and she upended the glass, connecting it with her lips as she tilted her head back. I could see her swallowing quickly as the glass drained.

She set the empty glass down on the bar. The crowd around me erupted in applause. The girl smiled, proud of herself.

"Thanks for the drink," she said. "It really hit the spot. See ya around." She turned and walked away. I watched her as far as the entrance to the ladies' room.

Some girl. I had met a lot of people in my life who could drink but I had the feeling she could beat most of them in a flat-out contest. I was impressed. I was also thirsty. I raised my hand to get the bartender's attention again.

"What microbrews you got on tap?"

"Most everything."

"Fat Weasel, then."

The bartender nodded and a few seconds later brought me a frosty mug with a nice head on it. I took a deep slug and felt a lot better.

"That'll be $17.50," the bartender said.

"$17.50? For a beer?" Bernie was doing even better than I thought.

"Two and a half for the beer and fifteen bucks for the Skids."

"But I didn't order the Skids."

"True enough, but you gave it away, therefore, you pay for it."

Again, his logic seemed sound. I pulled out a twenty and set it on the bar. When the bartender came back with change, I stopped him.

"Can I ask you a question?"

"August," he said.

"August what?"

"August Everywhere."

"What are you talking about?" I was perplexed. Usually I'm far drunker when I'm this confused, although the name rang a bell. Then again, maybe it was a contact high from the fumes of the Skids drink.

The bartender could see I was confused. "Can I get you another beer?" Bernie trained his people very well. I nodded. He brought it.

"About that question," I said.

"The name of the girl you just bought a fifteen-dollar drink for?"

"That's a good question, but not the one I was going to ask."

The bartender looked bored. "Go ahead."

"What can you tell me about Jā Alweighz?"

That got his attention.

"You a cop?"

"Please. I told you, I'm Skids Poppe."

"Then I don't have to answer any questions, do I? Excuse

me, I have other customers." He walked away, forgetting the money for my drinks. This detective work was harder than I thought it would be.

I sat there drinking my beer. What was my next move? Obviously, I had to talk to someone and that someone was not going to be our friendly neighborhood bartender. Somehow, I had the feeling I would be lucky to get another drink out of him.

I reached into my leather jacket and pulled out my notebook. Who were the people Bernie told me to talk to? Some guy named Fyche was first on the list. I looked around. No one who looked like a "Fyche" was anywhere to be seen.

I went to the next name on the list, the last name on the list. It was a short list. August, it said. She was Jā's ex-girlfriend and I had just bought her a drink. That's why her name sounded familiar. Maybe I would do okay at this detective thing after all.

Now what? I knew I had to talk to her, but how to approach it? Maybe the fact I bought her a drink would be my in. Obviously, I couldn't do what I did with the bartender. Contrary to popular belief (and my ex-wife), I can learn from my mistakes.

The band had returned so I picked up my beer and walked toward the stage. As I threaded my way through the crowded dance floor, I actually started listening to the song they were playing. They weren't bad. I settled myself at a conveniently abandoned table off to one side, right near the stage, to wait out the set.

From where I sat, I had a great view of the band. And

they were worth looking at. Ms. Everywhere looked like she was just now feeling the effects of the drink she downed ten minutes ago. She was shaking her body behind the mic stand, doing things which would have gotten her kicked off American Idol. The only thing anchoring her to any fixed point was her slim hand, wrapped around the microphone. She was using it to pull herself in close when the song required her voice and then she was doing things to that mic that David Bowie used to do to a guitar thirty-five years ago. It looked better when she did it. I couldn't understand a bit of what she was singing, though I was thinking I would definitely have to come back and see this band again. Soon.

I looked at the little plastic stand-up thing in the middle of the table which had a specialty drink menu on one side (a "Skids Poppe" was listed at "market value") and a promo for The Cup announcing future band appearances on the other. It listed the house band as Bridesmaid's Protocol. I put the plastic down as the musical interlude started and pulled my attention back to the stage.

August had let go of her land-line and was free floating across the stage, leading my eyes to the other members of the all-girl group, each beautiful in her own right. But I couldn't stop looking at the lead singer. It just seemed weird to me. She was very casual for a girl whose former lover was found floating in a canal yesterday morning. I know I would be creeped out if someone told me Carol had died. Hell, even if my ex-wife was dead, I'd feel a little something, and I didn't even like her all that much anymore. Just the thought of a dead person being someone I used to sleep with gave me the heebie-jeebies. Then again, with my ex-wife, I don't know if I would be able to tell the difference.

But this wasn't right. She knew something. No one could be that blasé about an ex getting killed without knowing something. I definitely had to talk to her.

I pulled the paper out of the plastic holder, the sheet with the drink specials on it, and wrote a note to August, asking her to meet me for another drink after her next set. I flagged the waitress over, ordered another beer, and tipped her five bucks to give August the note. She smiled, if not exactly at me then somewhere near my direction, and said sure.

Then I wrote my five-dollar tip in my notebook. Bernie was paying for it, after all. This was considered expenses, right? At the very top of the page I wrote "Expenses" in large capital letters. While I was thinking about it, I wrote the word beer down and made three slashes next to it. At the very least, I was going to get my beer covered.

The next song started, a cover of The Beatles' "Norwegian Wood." The Beatles never rocked it like this.

Bridesmaid's Protocol did a great job, despite changing the lyrics to make more sense coming from the all-girl band. My feet were tapping away, and I was really getting into the music when the waitress brought me my beer. When I tried to pay her, she informed me it had been taken care of by a girl on the other side of the dance floor. I looked across and could tell immediately which girl it was. She was sitting alone and staring at me. I lifted my glass to her and smiled. She smiled back and walked over.

We danced for several songs, but I didn't really enjoy it. Normally, I would be flying. I mean, having a girl buy me a drink and ask me to dance gets written down in my journal, generally, as a red-letter day. But not today. Today, I was dancing but my eyes kept looking back to the band. August Everywhere had captured my attention. I wanted to know what she knew. And I wanted to know if what she knew could get my friend Bernie off the hook.

Of course, I didn't want to find out too soon. Sure, eventually I wanted Bernie cleared and back here at The Cup where he belonged, but if I could get a few bucks and a couple of beers out of him beforehand, who was I to argue? And this is what was going through my mind while I was dancing with Julie, who worked as a secretary someplace.

By the time August introduced the rest of the band and said her "good nights" for the evening, Bernie had bought both Julie and me another couple of beers and I had discovered that Julie thought working as a secretary was really boring and was just trying to sample the dangerous side of life. She figured her safest entry was to start with a well-known biker journalist and work her way up to rock star and junkie. Granted, everything after the part about her job being boring was all my own opinion and I could have been wrong. But I don't think so.

I said good-bye to Julie, giving her Mutt's number when she asked for mine, and headed towards the stage. August met me halfway there. She had my note in her hand.

"Thanks again for the drink."

"No problem."

"You wanted to talk to me?" She turned and walked back towards the stage, I followed her.

"Yeah," I said to her back.

"What about?"

My first impulse was to just blurt out "Jasper Alweighz" but I felt I had learned my lesson on that one. What did I want to talk to her about? I looked around for a reason. My eyes rested on her ass, squeezed beautifully into a pair of jeans with strategic rips several inches above her knee.

"I figured since I already bought you a drink, we could get to know each other better." It sounded natural. Sure, it wasn't the first time I'd used the line, but I was happy with it in this context. I looked up at the back of her head.

She turned and looked me straight in the eye. She was thinking it over. After a few seconds she cocked her head to one side, smiled, and said sure.

"If nothing else, I want to know why you'd order a Skids if you had no intention of drinking it."

Suddenly it hit me. She didn't know who I was. I had signed the note as the "guy who bought you the drink, Skids." I guess she didn't realize why the comma was there. I laughed to myself and followed her up onto the stage.

"Here." A stage monitor was thrust into my hands. It was heavy. August had an identical one in her hands. "I can't leave until the truck is packed up. You wanna go out, you gotta help load out."

I took the speaker and followed her out the back door. A black Chevy Blazer was parked nearby, the rear gate down and the back seat folded forward. A skinny guy with glasses was loading the gear in as the various band members set it down on the asphalt. I put my speaker next to August's and went back inside to grab some more. I was used to this. There were plenty of times I'd helped "load out" a store with a couple of buddies. Lugging sound equipment was nothing.

The rest of the band just assumed I knew someone and didn't question me when I started coiling cables. Every five bundles, I'd grab the stacks and take them out to the truck. Every time I went out to the truck, it was sitting lower and lower, sagging under the weight of all the gear.

A second truck, a pick-up, pulled alongside the Blazer and drum cases were thrown in the bed. I went back inside and found the stage completely cleared. These girls knew what they were doing. Bernie had said they were the house band, so I figured they had to pull their gear apart whenever another act was coming in. They were waiting for me outside, so I jumped back to my table and grabbed the other sheet of paper from the plastic holder. It had a listing of who was coming in. I folded the paper and stuck it in my pocket.

By the time I got back outside, everyone was saying goodnight. A lot of "good gig" and "See you Tuesday night" were going around. Two girls - the drummer and bassist - climbed into the pick-up, waving as they drove off.

The guitarist opened the door on the passenger side of the Blazer and stood on the running board, shouting at August over the roof of the truck. "You coming?"

"I got a ride home," August looked over at me. "Right?"

I nodded. "Of course."

"Cool," Spring said. She got into the truck and slammed the door. The skinny guy got into the driver's side.

"Night, August," He said.

"Night, Specs. Great sound tonight."

The guy smiled shyly, almost embarrassed. He didn't

say a word as he started the truck and drove off.

All of a sudden August and I were left alone in the parking lot. "Where's your car?" She asked.

"I don't have a car."

She wheeled on the ball of her foot, spinning to glare at me in the dim light of the club's loading dock. "How in the hell are you going to give me a ride home?"

"I can give you a ride all right, as long as you like motorcycles."

"Motorcycle?"

"Yeah."

"Harley?"

"Yeah."

"You're Skids Poppe, the guy the drink is named for?"

"Yeah."

There was a long pause before she responded with a well thought out come back.

"Yeah."

It's amazing how much one word can mean depending on inflection. I was pretty sure if someone didn't say something soon, we would be staring at each other all night long saying "yeah" over and over again. She was dumb struck so I knew it would have to be me.

Now, I've never been one to hesitate once I realized the moment of action had come and it was up to me. I looked her right in the eye and said "Yeah!" It sounded good at the time.

She just looked at me with what I can only hope was admiration in her eyes. I was a celebrity. I mean her favorite drink was named after me, that had to count for something, right?

"Where's it parked?" she asked.

I bowed slightly and made a sweeping gesture with my arm. "Right this way. Your chariot awaits."

I took her for coffee at Van Go's Ear on Main Street. It was the closest place I could think of which would be open at that time of night, especially since they'd torn down Tiny Naylor's.

I must say, she was an excellent passenger. Those of my loyal readers who ride know how important this is. For those of you who have never ridden a bike in any capacity, let me explain.

Riding a motorcycle is unlike riding a horse no matter how many stupid "iron horse" comparisons are made. A horse has a mind of its own as well as four legs for stability. It won't fall over if you don't balance it properly at a stoplight. Bikes have a tendency to do that, especially if you're tired and completely forget to take your feet off the pegs at a red light. Trust me on this one. Learn from my mistake.

Anyway, it's hard enough to get the balance right riding one person on a bike. Remember your little Huffy with the banana seat from third grade? It's like that only faster. You have to lean into the curves, counter-steer (which means turning the handlebars right if you want to go left, it has something to do with gyroscopes and Guantanamo can explain it if you get him drunk enough, he never remembers physics theory when he's sober) and never let the bike get below a certain speed or it'll fall over, like I've said.

Adding a second person complicates matters entirely

too much. If you have a passenger who, for some reason, wants to see where they're going, and they decide to wiggle around to see past your head, it's gonna cause the bike to scatter all over the road (and from the back, it looks like you're drunk; again, don't ask me how I know, just trust that I do).

August was an excellent passenger. She held on tight, pressed her breasts into my back and kept her head firmly on my shoulder. She knew the procedure. Whenever I leaned into a curve, she leaned with me. This was the kind of girl I could ride with on a regular basis. In fact, I even went the long way around just to see how she would handle the Main Street traffic circle. She took it like a pro. Guantanamo says you can tell a lot about a girl by the way she takes to the back of a bike. I would have to consult with him about this one.

We pulled into the lot at Van Go's Ear and I parked right up front. I climbed off the bike and waited until she had taken off the helmet before I helped her dismount.

"That was some ride," she said.

I shrugged and hung the helmet on the handlebar. I only had the one since I wasn't expecting company. I was a perfect gentleman and I rode topless. Chivalrous, huh?

She continued, "Didn't you go the long way around? The Cup is just up the street from here."

"I thought about going to Tiny Naylor's first."

"Tiny's was torn down years ago."

"That's why we didn't go there."

I opened the door and followed her in.

The menu, written in big letters, was hanging on the

wall. After looking it over, August decided on a hot chocolate and a turkey sandwich. I wanted a coke, straight up; something to counteract the beer already in my system. I ordered for both of us at the register. They put a little numbered cone, the kind auto mechanics use to differentiate between the cars they're fixing, on the countertop. We grabbed it and headed upstairs.

At 2 a.m., you usually won't find a huge group of people hanging out in a coffeehouse unless it's near a college. And then there's Venice. Upstairs, the tables were mostly filled. August and I were able to grab a couple of seats near the door leading to the balcony.

We sat and took in the local artwork hanging on the walls for a few minutes before either of us said anything. I sipped my coke.

"Thanks for the drink," she said.

The ice was broken. I don't know why, but I had the feeling I was on a date. "No problem," I smiled at her, trying to make a good impression. Date or not, I had a reason for being here. "I just have one question?"

"What?"

Now was my chance to ask her about Jā.

"When you order a Skids, do you get to keep the glass? I mean for fifteen bucks, you'd think you'd at least get to keep the glass."

Like I could really be expected to jump right in after what happened when I asked the bartender about him.

"You get the glass, it has a nice etching of the clown from the sign, but you have to give back the igniter. They reuse those."

"You're really good. Singing I mean. I liked the band."

"Thanks. We're really close to getting signed."

"So, you'll be putting out a record soon?"

"CD actually."

I was being corrected over the use of the word "record"? Suddenly I felt very old. "You recorded a CD?"

"Yeah," She was getting excited. This was good. If she was talking about herself, maybe I could get her to talk about Dead Guy Jā. I would be able to get all the information I needed and still not piss her off, which was something I definitely did not want to do.

"That must be expensive?"

"Not really. Well, yeah, it usually is, but we all have friends who owe us favors and our producer really has faith in us, and he has his own studio. He lets us record there for free. He says our first record is going to be one of the biggest breakthrough albums ever. I believe him when he says our demo will open a lot of doors. I have to. Sometimes it's the only thing keeping me going."

It sounded to me like he was hoping to open a lot of zippers. I watched them play and not one of them would get kicked out of my bed for eating crackers. "And what does he get out of it?"

"He gets to produce us, which is something he wants to do. It's not like he needs the money or anything. Me and his wife are friends, that's how I met him. She's an actress. We took a singing class together."

"And you don't pay him anything?" I was skeptical. If she were having a fling with this record producer guy, and I know that sort of stuff goes on all the time, it would go a long way to explaining her indifference at her boyfriend's murder.

"Well..." she started. She seemed embarrassed. "Sometimes, when his wife is in a play and not going to be home during the day because of rehearsals..." She trailed off.

"Look, it's really none of my business."

"It's just I can get in trouble... but you won't tell anyone, will you?"

I was being taken into her confidence, this was good, but I wasn't sure I wanted to hear what she was about to say. I shook my head and put a finger to my lips.

"Okay, but you really can't say anything. I mean it's not like you know his wife or anything, but you really can't."

"I promise." I was almost laughing at the absurdity of the situation.

"Okay... Sometimes I baby-sit for his two kids and he slips me a couple of bucks, but she doesn't know. I'm supposed to do it for nothing since he's giving us all this free recording time, but the extra cash helps out at the end of the month, you know?"

Then I did laugh. Not a lot, but enough to let her know I was thinking she was going to say something else.

"I thought you were going to say something else."

"What did you think I was going to say?"

"Something a little more worthy of blackmail than under-the-table baby-sitting money."

"You didn't think I was sleeping with him, did you?"

I had to nod

"Please. He's a great guy, and not bad looking, but he's old enough to be my dad. He graduated high school before

I was born."

Don't ask me why, but I was relieved.

"When did he graduate high school?"

"You trying to find out how old I am?"

Nothing got past her. I nodded again.

"Just ask. I'll tell you. You'll find I like it straightforward."

I wasn't sure how to take that last comment, so I just let it slip away. Instead I went back to the original. "Okay," I said. "How old are you?"

"Don't you know it's not polite to ask a girl her age? And here I thought you were a gentleman." Her eyes glowed.

I was stuck. I couldn't tell where I had gone wrong, but this girl was walking all over me. Before I could say anything, a waiter brought the sandwich and set it down in the middle of the table, not knowing who it was for.

"Can I get you anything else?" he asked.

"I need some mustard and ketchup and he needs a refill of his Coke." August was enjoying herself.

The waiter left to get the condiments.

She looked at me. "You did want more to drink, right?"

"Sure."

"I'm 26. Just fucking with ya." She grinned wide and took a huge bite out of her sandwich. "Mmmm... I love sprouts and avocado. I think that's why I originally moved to California, for the sprouts and avocados. Every plate here has an avocado hidden somewhere on it. The tomato is a little crunchy, though." She took the top piece of bread off and plucked off an under ripe tomato slice. "They're never good like that. Tomatoes should be a little soft, so the skin doesn't get caught in your teeth. That's what apples are for and I don't eat apples."

The waiter brought the red and yellow bottles and my Coke while she was still picking at the tomato. He set them down without a word.

August grabbed the mustard and spurted a little from the squeeze top onto her turkey. She spelled the word "hi", upside down so I could read it without straining, then used the top piece of bread to spread it around. She took another bite.

"Much better, although I prefer Dijon. This yellow crap is for the birds, but it's better than nothing. When I'm famous and on tour, I'm going to have it written into my contract I only get sandwiches with Dijon and if there's any yellow mustard backstage we don't have to play. Like Van Halen and the brown M & M's."

She looked at me like I was supposed to know what she was talking about. I hid my confusion well.

I countered with a question of my own. "You're not from out here originally?"

"Is anyone?"

"I heard there was someone out in the valley, once."

She laughed at my joke. I could get to like this girl. Once I made sure she didn't kill Jā and frame Bernie for it. That would be too "Maltese Falcon" for me.

"I was born in Portland. My folks and sister still live there. I've been out here for five years, though, so I almost qualify for native status."

"You live in this area?"

"Isn't that awfully forward of you, Mr. Poppe?"

I had her this time. I was getting the hang of her patter. "Not unless you want to take a cab home. As I recall, I got drafted into being your ride, and picking up your meal besides."

"Good point. And good sandwich," she smiled at me again. "I live over on the canals. I rent a back house. It's not like a real house, more like a garage with a bathroom and a fridge, but they call it a house and I pay $650 a month. And I get a yard."

"That's important if you have a dog."

"No dogs. Don't like 'em. It's important if you have friends who want to have parties on the canals."

"Don't like dogs?"

"Animals in general bug me. I mean if you have to have one, I guess a dog would be the best way to go."

"Which Canal?"

"Linnie. It's the second one in from Venice Boulevard."

I knew where it was. "How close to the bridge are you? Dell Street?"

"Does it matter? You have to go all the way around to Washington to drive there no matter where it is. I'll direct you, don't worry."

"Just asking."

She was finished with her sandwich and making a soup of ketchup and mustard for her fries. She used the fries themselves to mix it all together.

"That looks gross," I said.

"But it's yummy. Here, try one." She covered a fry with the concoction and held it up to my mouth. I took it. It was one of the worst tastes I'd ever had on my tongue.

"It's better with Dijon."

"I'm sure it is." I used her napkin to wipe my lips and finished my second Coke in one swallow, trying to wipe the taste out. I succeeded only in spreading it evenly around my mouth. "So, what really brought you out to LA?"

"Music. Doesn't everyone come out here to be in show business? You're a writer, don't you want to write a great novel and have it turned into a movie or a TV series? Can't you just picture 'The Skids Poppe Show' based on your columns?"

"You read my columns?"

"Yeah. I think you're really funny." She paused for just a fraction of a second too long. "At least on paper."

"That hurts."

"Still fucking with ya."

"I know." I didn't, but I wasn't about to let her know it.

"I've been playing guitar and singing and writing songs since I could talk so I figured I'd come out here and try it out."

"I thought Seattle was the big music scene?" One of the other writers at the magazine did a piece on Seattle music. I tried to get them to send me up there, too, on expense account, but Publisher Steve couldn't justify it.

"It is, and I went up there for school. I met a lot of people there and one of them convinced me I should come down here after the band he was in started doing something."

Suddenly I was very attentive. Not that I hadn't been paying attention before, but now I may finally get a clue as to what was going on. "Who was that?"

"You probably wouldn't know him. He's in a band called Driftwood Messiah. They're not very big, yet, but they will be. They just put out a new album."

"Laryngitis Nightingale. I picked it up this afternoon. I've been listening to those guys for a while."

"You've heard of them?"

"If they play Venice and are any good, I've heard of them."

She stopped eating her fries and looked at me. Already, in the short time I'd known her, I could see the difference in her eyes. This time she wasn't fucking with me.

"Had you heard of us before tonight?"

All of a sudden, the dreams of her future rested in what I said. Okay, maybe I was being a bit over-dramatic, and egotistical besides, but that's what it felt like. I knew I had to make it okay.

"Why do you think I was at the club?"

"And you liked us?"

"I already told you, I think you're great. How did you come by such a great gig in the first place? I mean, house band at such a popular club would seem to be a pretty tough spot to fill for an unsigned band."

"An ex-boyfriend of mine works there and introduced me to the owner."

"What does he do?"

"Tends bar." She was getting defensive. I had to play dumb.

"So how come he didn't drive you home?"

"A couple of reasons. One, he's an ex-boyfriend; two, you asked, and three, he wasn't even at work tonight."

Either she was being really coy, or she didn't know Jasper Alweighz was dead.

I had to say something. If I didn't, my entire first evening as a detective was shot all to hell. "Why wasn't he at work tonight? I mean I would think Saturday would be a prime work night?"

"You interested in my boyfriend or in me?" She wiped her plate clean with the last of her fries. When she was done, she pushed the whole thing over to the side, away from her. She looked back up at me. "Well?"

What could I say? If you were there, looking into those eyes, you would be interested. I was interested after following her up a flight of stairs. I told her so. "It's definitely you I'm interested in. I just don't want to have to deal with your jealous ex-boyfriend every time I come to pick you up from work, you know? How would that look? They might even take my drink away from me."

"Trust me, if you ever pick me up from work, he won't be there to make a big deal out of it."

"Works the early shift, does he?"

"It's not that...." She stopped herself. "Let's go for a walk," she said.

She did know he was dead. Well, at least I could figure out that much of it. And now she wanted to go for a walk. Maybe she wanted to tell me something and just needed the time and space to do it. I was ready to give it to her.

"A walk?"

She nodded and stood up.

"Sure thing," I continued.

She turned and walked down the outside back stairs.

Following her down a flight wasn't as good as going up, but it still left me feeling good to know she was going to be wrapping her hands around my body in just a few minutes.

We stopped at my bike. I looked around. Main Street in Venice was not the best place in the world to go for a walk in the middle of the night. Sure, there have been times when I've been wandering the beach or streets in the 'hood well past my bedtime and I've never been harassed. But, then, I don't look like August. I knew I could protect her if it came to that; I just didn't want it to come to that. We were having a perfectly good time so far and I didn't want to blow it by beating up someone to defend the honor of a girl who wasn't even mine. Yet.

"You don't want to walk around here, do you?" I asked.

"Of course not. It's too dangerous around here. By my place. I want to change clothes anyway and grab a pack of smokes." She grabbed the helmet off the handlebar and put it on, turning to me to tighten it like I had before.

Saturday Night

I parked my bike in front of August's place, being careful not to block any of the three garage doors behind the main house. I didn't want to get too close to the white Ferrari parked there, either. My un-muffled engine could set off the alarm, if they had the thing armed.

August was off the bike and running to her house by the time I had killed the ignition. I waited, leaning against the bike.

"What are you waiting for?" She whispered at me from her doorway. "Come on in."

I did.

She was right. Her place wasn't much more than a single large room. A couple of doors led to a bathroom and a closet. A breakfast bar separated what passed for a kitchen from the rest of the apartment. August was in the closet when I walked in.

"Shut the door, will ya? What, were you born in a bar?"

"A bar? Don't you mean 'barn?'" If nothing else, I knew my cliché phrases.

"I'm sorry, Skids, but you just don't look like the kind of guy who has ever been anywhere near a barn. I just figured 'bar' was more appropriate." She came out of the closet and stepped behind one of those three-fold Chinese rice-paper screen things. "Now don't look."

Like I could help it if I did. But I tried not to. As soon as the top she had been wearing was tossed over the partition, I looked around the rest of the room.

"I went to a farm once," I said. "I was in 2nd grade. I got in trouble for trying to ride a hog."

Her room was not messy, but it wasn't clean, either. There were piles of stuff everywhere, but neat, orderly piles. I walked over to the kitchen. The dishes had been in the sink for a while. Sitting open on the counter was a book of Elvis Costello sheet music. An electric guitar was sitting in a stand behind the door. I hadn't seen it when I walked in. I wasn't a very good judge of guitars, but this looked like a nice one. A second guitar, an acoustic, was laid across the top of the single bookshelf in the room. I thumbed through some of the titles.

Guantanamo may have his theories about women, but I have found you can tell an awful lot about people in general by what books are on their shelves and what records – sorry, CDs – are in their collection. August had some good books: classics like Little Women, Wuthering Heights and The Hunchback of Notre Dame, all of them bookstore editions. She also had a shelf of paperbacks and a beat-up hard cover of George MacDonald's The Princess and The Goblin, an old fairy-tale from the mid 1800s. She was a romantic. The rest of the shelves held books on music theory, reference books on the music industry and sheet music for everything from Cole Porter to Alanis Morissette and Liz Phair.

"Find anything interesting?" She had finished changing and snuck up behind me.

I answered without looking back. "I was wondering if you had the music for 'The Night Chicago Died?' I really love that song."

"If I did, it would be under 'P' for 'Paper Lace.' I know they didn't write it, but they are the ones who made it famous."

She was good. I kept looking. "So, do you have it?"

"Let's go."

Unlike Main Street, the canals at night are beautiful. I've seen more than one girl seduced while sitting on a bridge, legs dangling over the side. I followed August through the yard of the main house and out next to the water. She had changed into loose jeans and a baggy sweatshirt, put her hair up into a ponytail covered by a Tasmanian Devil ball cap and she still looked great.

She turned left and led me towards Dell Street. We were one canal away from where Jā's body was found yesterday morning. She didn't mention it.

The Venice Canals were originally built in 1905 to create "Venice of America," a playground for the rich and famous. All those original canals were filled in long ago, though, paved over to make roadways for the "new" automobiles. The canals we were walking along were an extension system built shortly after the originals. For years, back when I first moved into the neighborhood, these canals stank. Without circulation, the water stagnated and became like the swampland Venice used to be.

In the early '90s, right around the time Main Street in Santa Monica was getting its own resurgence, someone decided the Venice canals needed to be fixed, and did. They were all drained, shored up with pretty stone sidings, a circulation system was added, and they were refilled. Since then, property values had soared.

I walked next to August without saying a word until we got to Grand Canal, the main waterway which had originally joined this new section with the old. Now, though, it just marked the west end of three tiny, but very expensive islands and connected, underneath Washington Boulevard, to the Marina del Rey Silver Strand and from there to the marina channel itself. We walked side by side as she turned south.

Again, I was in that wonderfully awkward position where I had to say something or no one would.

"He died," August said out of the blue.

Okay, maybe I was wrong. Maybe she would be the first to talk. I was still acting dumb. "Who died?"

"My ex-boyfriend, Jasper Alweighz. He was found dead in that canal over there," she jerked her thumb over her shoulder. "That's what you wanted to know, right?"

"What do you mean?" I thought I was playing dumb really well.

"Stop playing dumb, you're not very good at it. I told you, I like things straightforward." She stopped walking. I noticed we were in the middle of a bridge. Somehow the thought of seduction was increasingly far from my mind.

She continued, "So what's up?"

Now was my turn to be straightforward. Or at least as straightforward as I knew how to be. I reached into my pocket, pulled out a business card and handed it to her. She read it in the light of an overhead streetlamp.

"Skids Poppe, Movie Producer? Let me guess, you heard my boyfriend was making a movie and wanted to move in on his action?"

Shit. I took the card out of her hand and gave her another one, reading it first myself to make sure it was the right one.

"Skids Poppe, Private Investigator? That's almost better than the movie producer one. I still don't get it. Are you investigating me?" She held the card up close. "There's no license number on here. What the hell are you doing?"

License number? "Bernie - you know, your boss, the guy who owns The Cup? He asked me to check things out for him. They think he killed your boyfriend."

"Who thinks? And he's my ex-boyfriend. Or was. Get that straight."

"Why is it so important he's your ex?"

"Are you accusing me of something?"

"Keep your voice down, people are probably in bed, trying to sleep or otherwise. And no, I'm not accusing you. Why? Have you done something wrong?"

"No, I haven't."

"Then why are you getting so defensive?"

She walked away. I followed her.

By the time I caught up with her I could see shiny tear

tracks on her cheeks.

She saw me, but she didn't stop. She was moving faster than when we had been casually strolling, as if she were trying to get someplace in a hurry.

"So this is all about Jā, huh?"

"I just want to know what happened," I said. I had no idea why she was crying.

"It's always about Jā. You didn't want to go out with me, did you? You probably never even heard of my band before you walked into The Cup tonight. Just once it would have been nice if someone actually wanted to see me for me, because they liked the way I sang or played guitar or wrote music or looked or anything but not because I am now or have ever been fucking Jā Alweighz."

"Listen. I like the way you play music and the way you sing and the way you look. I like all of that. Really."

August snorted, as if I was just trying to butter her up. I kept talking.

"True, I probably would never have met you if Jā hadn't been killed..." I paused for a breath. Big mistake. She started walking faster. I took a big breath of air so I could get everything else out in one go.

"But now that I have, I would really like to get to know you better. Now how about slowing down a little so I can stop running after you? I'm supposed to do that after we've been together for a while, not on our first date."

She slowed. I think she even chuckled a little under the tears. "Is this our first date?"

"Well, I'd like there to be another one, therefore, this, hopefully, is the first."

She smiled at me. I held my hand out to take hers as we crossed Washington, rejoining Grand Canal on the other side. Now we were holding hands. I don't think I'd held hands with anyone since Beth Ann Jacobs in third grade. I also wondered if I was breaking another rule of being a private detective? I'd already fucked up on the license thing, but I didn't know the rules on getting involved with a suspect.

No, wait, it was okay. Sam Spade did it. So did Philip Marlowe. As long as you didn't get too involved before you found out who did it, because if the girl was guilty, you had to be willing to send her up the river. I remembered Bogey's speech at the end of "Falcon." Okay, I was still within proper guidelines. Now I just wondered how far I could take it on the first night.

"Why didn't you say anything right away?" She asked.

"I just met you. What am I gonna do? Say 'Hi, I know your boyfriend--'"

"Ex," she interrupted.

"'Ex-boyfriend.' Happy?" She was. "'I know your ex-boyfriend was just stabbed to death, but would you mind not only answering a few questions for me but also let me buy you dinner and take you for a romantic moonlight walk?' Would that approach have worked?"

"It just might've. And by the way, he was shot."

"What?"

"He wasn't stabbed, he was shot."

"Really?"

"Yup." She squeezed my hand a little bit tighter.

"How do you know?"

"The police came over this morning to ask me questions."

"Were they more straightforward than I was?"

"Yup. Came right out and asked me all about things like alibis and had we had any fights recently and did I know anyone who would want to kill him."

"Did you go out with any of them?"

"No. I just don't like guys in uniform. Although the detective was kinda cute. But he didn't know anything about music. Actually tried to impress me by saying he knew Hootie personally."

"Sucker play. He was hitting on you. How do you know I'm not just saying stuff so you'll answer my questions, too?"

"You listen to Driftwood Messiah and if you just wanted answers, you would have let me walk away."

I looked at her. She continued, "I majored in psychology in school. My folks insisted I have something to fall back on."

"So can I ask you questions now? I mean I should ask them at some point."

"Not yet."

"Why not?"

"We're not there yet?"

"Where?"

"C'mon." She let go of my hand and ran ahead of me. I've spent too many years riding motorized vehicles and drinking beer to run very far, very fast, without wheezing and gasping for air. So I didn't. I let her run ahead of me, knowing she wouldn't let me fall too far behind.

"There" turned out to be the end of the stone jetty marking off the northern boundary of the Marina del Rey channel. We had to climb through some chains to get to the rocks and we had to climb over the rocks to get out past the light, down by the water.

"This is one of my favorite places in LA," August said. She was sitting on a spot which would probably be covered by water at high tide. Me? I wasn't so daring. I stood on a rock several feet above her. "Isn't it beautiful? I come out here when I'm working on lyrics."

I agreed it was. But now was time to start asking questions.

"Are you working on any lyrics now?" I asked.

"I'm always working on lyrics. It's a bad habit. Whenever I see something or hear something that's cool, I file it away to use as a lyric sometime." She turned and looked up at me, smiling in the moonlight.

Enough of this. I really had to know some answers before things got way out of hand. "You writing a song about Jā?"

There was silence. August looked out towards the ocean. She reached into her pocket and pulled out a crumpled pack of cigarettes, removing one and putting it between her lips. She made no move to light it.

"That's straightforward alright," she said.

I grunted in agreement. The water splashed around her feet, not getting them wet, but close enough I would have moved them had it been up to me.

A series of waves hit while my question hung in the air. I knew she would answer it. I just didn't know when, and I didn't want to push.

I fished my lighter out of my pocket and leaned down next to her. Balancing on a rock, leaning close into her, I reached out to light her cigarette. She took hold of my arm and pushed it away.

"I don't smoke," she said. "I used to, but it hurt my throat. Now I just like playing with a cigarette when I'm nervous. I kind of had a feeling I would be nervous tonight." I snapped the lid of my custom Zippo closed and stood back up.

"Writing a song for Jā?" August started talking again, this time much softer. I could barely hear her over the sound of the waves on the rocks. She seemed to be talking to herself and it really didn't matter I was there. I had to kneel down next to her again to make out what she was saying.

"No, I'm not writing a song for Jā. I already did that. I thought he was the only one I would be writing songs about forever." She laughed softly, as if she needed a way to get all the air out of her lungs and that was the quickest way to do it. "Well, him and Robert Downey Jr., but that was my own thing." I chuckled along with her.

"When did you write your first song for him?" I asked.

"When did we start going out? Is that what you're asking?"

"Yeah, I guess it is."

"Then ask it. Straightforward is best, it may shock me a little, but ultimately it really is the best. When did we start going out? About a year and a half ago."

"How'd you two hook up?"

"That sounds like we're a couple of trailers."

"Cut me some slack, will ya? I'm new to this whole detective thing."

She laughed openly this time, the smile reaching her eyes. She lay back on the rocks, using her hands as a pillow.

"I met Jasper Alweighz where all good girls meet all good boys. I met him where I met you, at The Cup. He had just started working there a couple of months before and that night I was with a few friends and they all had boyfriends or were in the process of getting them and I wasn't. So, I spent a lot of time at the bar. Every few minutes, Jā would come around and chat. He bought me a few drinks and when my friends came by to say they were ready to go to another club, he asked if I would call him."

"If you would call him? I thought the good boys were supposed to call the good girls."

"That's exactly what I said. He told me no. He said if I was interested, then I should call him. If I wasn't interested, he didn't want my number. It would just torture him knowing he had screwed up somewhere and that he couldn't use it to call me."

"How long did you make him wait?"

"All good girls know three days is the appropriate time before you call the good boy. Aren't the stars beautiful?"

I looked up, the bones in my neck creaking with the effort.

"You'll kill your neck, you do it like that. You have to lay down."

I wasn't so sure about that.

"So you waited three days?" I asked, trying to get the conversation back on track.

"Lay down," she said, patting the rock next to her. "You're wearing a leather jacket, you're not going to hurt your nice clean t-shirt."

She'd noticed the shirt. The least I could do was look at the stars for a few minutes. I lay down, my head next to hers. She started humming, mumbling something to herself.

"What are you singing?" I asked.

"You asked if I was writing a song for Jā and I told you I already had. That was it. Want to hear it?"

I answered with absolute honesty. "Not one part of me wants to hear that song right now."

"Jā would never do this. I could never get him to come out here and just look at the stars."

Great, so far, I was up on points over Mr. Alweighz. "What happened after three days?"

"We went out. He took me for dinner and then to a screening of a film at the Director's Guild. He talked about how he had this great film he was going to make and how it would win all these awards. He loved movies." Her voice trailed off.

"I love movies. A lot of people do."

"Not like this. Jā could watch a film and tell you what other films Cop No. 3 had been in and where the director had gone to school. It was what he lived for. Everything he did was about getting his movie made." She shifted slightly, swinging a little to the right. Her head now nestled on my stomach. I didn't mind.

"I hope you don't mind," she said, "but the rock is so hard."

"So what happened?" I felt like a complete schmuck

for asking questions about her dead ex-boyfriend when she was lying across me, her hair begging to have my fingers run through it. But then, that could very well have been her plan.

She sighed and answered. "Things were great for a while. He treated me like a movie star. We would go to movie premieres of films his friends worked on, we went to dinner at Spago and Le Dome; I met all sorts of celebrities. Well, I didn't really meet them, but I saw a bunch of them."

Her voice became giddy with excitement. "I had dinner once with Gil Gerard. Jā thought he'd be perfect for his film, so we all went out for dinner to discuss it. When I was little, I thought Buck Rogers was the cutest thing. In the end, though, Gil decided he didn't want to do the film."

"When was this?"

"About 6 months ago. Jā had a gotten the rights to this great script called Body Mechanics. It's a thriller but with a ton of plot twists."

"You've read it?"

"Yeah. It was really good."

"Do you still have a copy of the script?"

"No. I gave it back to Jā when I gave him the rest of his shit."

"When was that?"

"A couple of days ago. Monday or Tuesday"

"This past Monday or Tuesday?" I sat up, and August slid into my lap. I looked down at her.

"Yeah. And it was Tuesday. Because Monday is when Spring told me."

I had asked for it and it was coming. Too much information was being thrown my way. I rattled off my questions as quickly as I could think of them.

"Who is Spring? What did she tell you? You saw Jā after he supposedly disappeared? Did you tell any of this to the police?"

August let me finish. Then she waited a little longer to make sure I was done.

"Jā called me on Tuesday morning to say he needed my help. He didn't offer any explanation as to where he'd been or anything. Just called me in the morning, woke me up, and said he needed help. Someone was after him."

"Did he say who? Or why? Did you help him?"

"I didn't care. After what he did, I couldn't give a shit what kind of trouble he was in. He got into it himself; he could get out of it himself as far as I was concerned."

"What did he do?"

"He was fucking Spring Tyme, the guitarist in my band."

That was a bad thing. "How did you find out?"

August spoke like it happened years ago. She seemed so disconnected from it I knew it hadn't hit her yet. It certainly explained her reaction, though.

"Spring told me. On Monday. She called me Monday night to let me know."

"Why?" It seemed like a logical question to me.

"She was my friend. We've been friends since I moved out here."

"But why now? What prompted her to tell you on Monday night, two days after your boyfriend - I'm assuming he didn't become an 'ex' until after Spring's phone call

- disappeared and didn't show up for work?"

August sat up. Her arms stretched out behind her, holding her up. Her fingers rested under me, so the physical connection wasn't broken.

"Why? I don't know. She said she felt guilty about it."

"How long had it been going on?"

"Not long she said. A couple of weeks. Jā and I had been drifting apart since he started working on the film. He got the money he needed from someplace and started production a few weeks ago."

"You don't know who he got the money from?"

"No."

"So, what happened?"

"When he started working on the film, doing pre-production and getting his crew together, he stopped having time for me. It's not like I didn't understand. I mean, I knew it would take time away from us, but once he started getting into it, he didn't even call me. For days at a time. I'd see him at work - between sets at the bar - but whenever I said anything to him, he'd brush me off, saying he had too much on his mind."

"Maybe he was busy?" Don't ask me why I was defending him.

"Why are you defending him? Of course he was busy, but I'll bet when you're busy, you still make time for your girl, right? I've read your columns. I think you would find the time to at least say 'hi.' Or have sex." She looked over at me, eyebrows raised questioningly.

"You stopped having sex?" She had a point. If I was dating someone who looked like her, I would always find time for sex. Call me shallow.

"He didn't have time for anything having to do with me. The only thing we talked about was that I was going to write a song for his movie. And I think the only reason I was still doing that was I'm talented and he was getting it for free."

I could hear the anger and bitterness creeping into her voice. Now was the time to go back and get the rest of the answers.

"What happened when he called you?"

She stood up. Now all contact was broken. She stepped away, climbing down closer to the water.

"He said he needed my help."

"That's what you said before." I wanted to know what was going on. Part of me wanted to know to help Bernie. The other part of me? Well that part wanted to know for personal reasons. Sue me.

She turned on me. "Do you want to hear the story or not?"

I nodded. She turned back around. I don't think she wanted to look at me when she told me the rest.

"I told him what Spring had said. Jā said she was lying, that she had tried to start something with him, but he had turned her down. He said she was just jealous of what we had."

"Did you believe him?" I knew it was a dumb question as it was leaving my lips.

"Six months ago, I would have. Around the time of our Gil Gerard dinner. But not recently. Not after the way he had been treating me."

"Did he say what you could do to help him?"

"He didn't want to say over the phone. He asked to meet me. I agreed so I could give him back his stuff. I didn't tell him that. I just told him I'd meet him, and he could tell me the rest then."

"Did you meet him?"

"Yeah. I didn't even give him a chance to say anything. I just handed him the box of all the stuff he had left at my place and told him I didn't care."

"Where did this all happen?"

"You know the Washington Street Pier? He asked me to meet him out on the end."

"But that's all locked up."

"You mean to tell me you've never gone out to the pavilion on the end there? You, Mr. Renegade Biker Guy who writes about all the bad things he's done, have never climbed the fence and gone out to the end of that pier? I find that hard to believe."

She had me. "Okay, I've been there. But never during the day. I go out there at night sometimes to write, when Guantanamo is snoring too loud. It takes some guts to go out there during the day."

"Not really. Jā was going to use it as a location for his film and got permission. All he had to do was call and tell them he needed to get some stills so he could figure out his shots and they said fine. When I got there, the gate was open and he was waiting down at the end. I walked right up to him, dropped the box at his feet and walked away."

"He let you walk away, just like that?"

"Not really." She seemed uncomfortable.

"If this makes you uncomfortable..." I said, letting the words trail off.

"He grabbed me, said he really needed me. When I told him to let me go, he said I didn't understand. He said someone would kill him if I didn't help. When I tried to pull away, he slapped me and told me to calm down."

"He hit you?"

She nodded.

"Good thing he's dead." I've been in a lot of fights in my day, enough to make any NHL veteran proud of me (and a few have told me so themselves), but I have never hit a woman. Even if she hit me first. Again, it's that morality my parents instilled in me when I was still living at home. Burglary I could rationalize, sneaking into a movie even, but hitting a woman just don't cut it. In fact, more than one of my fights has been due to my objecting to that very thing.

August smiled up at me. I had a feeling I was looking more like a white knight than I really had any reason to. "What did you do?" I asked.

"What could I do? I slapped him back." She paused. "And then I ran. Almost all the way back home."

"He didn't follow you?"

"I don't know. I didn't look back." She climbed back up a couple of rocks until she was standing close to me. "Did I do the right thing?"

How should I know if she did the right thing? I could tell it didn't matter if I answered or not, so I didn't. "Was that the last time you saw him?" She nodded.

For a few seconds we both just stood there, wrapped in our own thoughts. The stars she had been admiring a few minutes before now seemed like so many lighters in a large concert hall. I felt like I was on display. I had done well so far, well enough for the gods to want an encore, but I didn't know where to go. Some things just didn't make any sense. I spoke some of them out loud.

"Why did he meet you at the end of the pier when you lived right around the corner?"

She answered me. "He didn't live around the corner. He lived down in Redondo Beach. He used to stay over a lot, when things were good, because it was easier for him than going home, especially if he had to be up in this part of town the next day, but he didn't live here."

"Did he have a key to your place?"

"Yeah, but I had the locks changed."

"After the pier?"

"Yup. Why did you think he lived here? Because of where they found him?"

I nodded. It was a dumb assumption on my part, but I was feeling my way along slowly. I was entitled to make some mistakes. "Did you tell any of this to the police?" She shook her head. "Why not?"

"They didn't ask. I answered the questions they asked and nothing more. I mean, I don't want you to get the wrong impression, like I'm a chronic lawbreaker or something, but I've had dealings with the police before and I find it best not to say any more than you have to. You might say something and the next thing you know your sister is being arrested... or something like that."

I let it pass. "So what did you tell the police?"

"They wanted to know where I was on Thursday night"

"And where were you?"

"I was playing."

Seemed like a reasonable response to me. If someone had asked me what I was doing Thursday night I would have said drinking. Even if I wasn't, I do it often enough it would make sense. "What else did they want to know?"

August suddenly got defensive. "You don't think I did it, do you?"

"Of course not," I said sweetly. "But I have to find out who did."

"Why don't you let the police handle it?"

"Ironically enough, I don't trust them as far as I can throw them. Sure, every now and again they come up with the right answer, but not often enough. And this time, the answer they've come up with is one of my friends. Personally, I don't think he did it either and he asked me to prove it so he can come back to work. You've already told me things you said they don't know. Maybe I can put together the whole puzzle from pieces you and everyone else gives me and then we can all go home and you and I can go out again on a real date with dinner and a movie and a ride up the coast on the back of my hog. How's that for an answer?"

"Not bad," she was smiling again. "Okay, you want to know details, I'll tell you."

I pulled my little notebook out of my back pocket, realizing, a little late, that I should have been taking notes all along. I uncapped the pen. "Ready."

She started, "So they wanted to know if we'd had any major fights recently--"

"And you told them...?"

"I told them yes but didn't tell them about Spring. I said we'd been fighting ever since he'd gotten the half million for the movie. I told them about him not spending time with me."

I wrote quickly.

"They asked when I'd seen him last and I told them a week ago Friday, the day before he disappeared. I didn't want to tell them about the pier."

"I understand, " I said. "And what about--" I stopped short, looking back over my notes. "How much did he get for the film?"

"Five hundred thousand dollars. He said he really needed seven hundred fifty, but he could cut enough corners that he could make it work."

I was in shock. Somewhere along the lines Jā Alweighz had acquired another quarter million. I was definitely going to need to find out where that money had come from. I circled it in my notebook.

"Five hundred thousand dollars? That's a whole lot of money. Did you ever see it?"

"In cash?" August laughed. "No. I did see a deposit slip once, though. Why? Is that important?"

"I don't know. But I know I've never seen that much money in one place outside a Vegas tourist trap and it just impresses the hell out of me. Do you happen to know which bank he was depositing to?"

She screwed her eyes shut and crinkled her nose as she thought. She looked like a constipated rabbit, not that I'd ever say that out loud. Finally, she relaxed her face and answered. "I think it was First National."

I wrote it down. I'd have to check with Bernie about which bank he used. Things were getting interesting.

"It's getting early," August said.

I looked up from my notes. "Huh?"

She pointed behind me. The sky was brightening in the east, turning a shade of blue you'd never find in a Harley shop. This was the only way to see the sunrise, in my opinion, as the end of a great night. Seeing it any other way means you are up way too early.

"Don't you mean it's getting late?"

"Nope. It's getting early. I have the firm belief that we shouldn't change dates until after the sun comes up, that's the mark. As long as it's still dark out, it's late yesterday, but when the sun starts to rise, suddenly it becomes early tomorrow." She grabbed my hand and pulled me along the rocks to the asphalt walkway leading back towards shore.

"What about today?" I asked.

"What about it? It's Sunday and I think you should walk me home because it's not respectable for a nice young girl to be walking around this early by herself."

On the way back we went a different route so she could stop at a bagel shop and pick up breakfast. I didn't have anything. Eating right before I go to bed always gives me nightmares and I could feel the weight of the day on my eyelids. It's like when I'm writing a big piece right before a deadline; I can go all night as long as I keep on working, but the moment I stop and think about what I'm doing or if someone points out the last time I slept, I'm out like a light.

August and I made it back to her place just as the sun was peeking over whatever mountains are there to the east.

I never bothered to learn their names, since, usually, by the time I'm awake you can't see them for the smog. August unlocked the door and ran inside to throw away her empty bagel bag and orange juice container. I waited at the doorstep.

She came back and stood just inside the house, holding the door like a security blanket. After one night, I knew I wasn't going to have to speak first.

"Thanks for a really wonderful evening, Skids," she said. She had a coy little smile on her face, but I wasn't sure if it was caused by lack of sleep or not.

"You're very welcome, Ms. Everywhere." I was trying to be as professional as I could be. "Sorry about all the questions."

"You know you can call me August." Her face was reproachful, just for a second, then she smiled again. "And you can ask me questions anytime. I mean, how else are two people supposed to get to know each other if they don't ask questions, right? Only next time I get to ask you some questions. That way we're even. Fair enough?"

"Next time?"

"I believe you said you thought of this as a first date and if, indeed, you did, then that means you wanted more and so I'm accepting. Here's my number." She handed me a business card. I mumbled my thanks and put it in my pocket without looking at it. She continued: "I already have your number, if the one on the card you gave me is the right one?"

"It is." I couldn't help but laugh at her enthusiasm. We'd been out for almost five hours and I know she'd been playing for the seven hours before that. Now here she was, perky as Julie, your cruise director, after a powder stop in Columbia. What was I getting myself into?

"And now, Mr. Poppe, I'm going to go to sleep. And I suggest you do the same. You look very tired. We'll talk soon, right?"

I nodded. "I believe we will, August. And you know you can call me Skids..."

She smiled a big Cheshire cat grin at me, one reaching deep into her eyes. "Good." She bit her lower lip and tilted her head down, looking at me through her eyelashes. "Good night, Skids."

"Good night, August."

She was still looking at me as she shut the door, softly so as not to wake the neighbors. I stood there for a few minutes, basking in the glow of her smile, imagining her going behind the Chinese screen and getting ready for bed.

A few minutes later I cranked the throttle on my Harley wide open, hopefully waking the neighbors she had wanted to let sleep. I was in a good mood and I wanted the world to know. I had successfully completed, almost, my first day of being a detective, had a date with a beautiful singer/songwriter and, hopefully, was well on my way to figuring out who killed Jā Alweighz. Or at least figuring out who didn't.

Guantanamo was fast asleep on the couch when I got home. I guess he figured since it had been cleaned off for Bernie to sit, he may as well make use of it as a bed as long as he could. I didn't worry about making too much noise as I walked around the apartment. Within certain circles, Guantanamo Bey was known as "The man who slept through the mortar attack," so my kicking off my boots and turning on the TV wasn't going to bother him.

I put the TV on the Cartoon Network just so I could have some background noise while I brushed my teeth and checked for phone messages. As far as brushing my teeth goes, I just want to say Mrs. Poppe didn't raise no dentally deficient children. I don't care what your opinion of bad bikers is, there is nothing worse than getting up-close and personal with a guy, trying to go over the evening's plans, and he's got teeth worse than the French under Napoleon. Gross.

After my final rinse and spit I checked the phone machine. The red light was blinking, as always. I hit the play button.

To my surprise, there actually were a couple of new messages. The first was from Publisher Steve, reminding me I still had a column due and not to come into the office on Monday or Tuesday. I stopped the tape for a second and looked at the calendar. My column wasn't due until the 17th and that was... yesterday. Shit. And I hadn't even thought about what I was going to write. Oh well, I'd figure it out. I always had before.

I hit the side of the answering machine until it started playing again. Publisher Steve was back talking, although it was slower than before. He was going to be out of town with his wife and kid and he didn't want me scaring the art department girls.

I fast-forwarded when he started talking about how hard it was to replace the last girl and he really should fire me, and he would if I didn't have such an ardent following. Publisher Steve loves me. I've made more money for his magazine than any three other writers combined.

Have I seen any of it? No. But then he takes care of me most of the time. And as long as I can reasonably justify something, he'll let me put it on my expense account. But at six in the morning, I couldn't take his complaining.

The second message was from Guantanamo reminding me to return the movies we'd gotten from Redbox. I looked. Yup, there they were sitting on top of the DVD player. What the hell, they were already late, and they were on the magazine's credit card. That's what Publisher Steve gets for calling me on a Saturday. The last message was from my sister. She had picked Bernie up okay, decided he wasn't all that bad after he'd offered to take her for dinner, but I should call her when I got the message. I'd call her later, maybe tomorrow.

That done, I turned the computer on, set it to check my e-mail and popped a beer while I was waiting.

Today's mail was nothing special. Two offers to make millions on the Internet, an offer to make either my breasts or penis grow, depending on which was appropriate, one chain letter from an old riding buddy who was now serving time up in a state prison in Utah, and a letter from "Doc Darcy," an actor friend in Hollywood, telling me about his latest audition. He was an on-line buddy. We'd met in a "What do you know about Hollywood?" trivia group. Between the two of us, we were cleaning up. Since then, we'd kept in touch by instant message and liking each other's posts. He told me about his auditions, and I told him about whatever I was doing. I would certainly have to let him know about this new gig. He'd get a big kick out of it.

I logged off and headed to bed. When I took my pants off, I emptied my back pockets of all the papers I had collected during the course of the evening and threw them on the bed to look at once I was under the covers.

August's card did have her phone number and listed her occupation as "Tunesmith." I liked it. I put it inside the book I was reading, knowing I wouldn't lose it there. The other paper was the list of bands playing at The Cup. Tonight - Sunday - some band called Magnificent Octopus was playing, confirming my theory as to why Bridesmaid's Protocol had packed up. I looked over the rest of the schedule. Damn, last Thursday I'd missed Airheads of State, a real fun band. They were all a bunch of people who did other things and got together occasionally to play music of a satirically political bent. I'd seen them a few times and interviewed them once for the magazine. They were definitely worth seeing. Oh well. I rolled over and closed my eyes, hoping to be asleep within seconds.

I wasn't. Something was nagging at me. It wasn't August. So far, I could see nothing wrong with her. Maybe it was the idea of the "Skids Poppe" drink? No. I liked that. It was something else. After a while, getting no closer to an answer, exhaustion took over and forced me into unconsciousness.

Sunday

Sunday Afternoon

At least the phone didn't wake me. I woke up just fine on my own at what most people would consider a lazy hour, even for a Sunday. I did the math in my head and figured I'd gotten about five hours of sleep. It wasn't enough but it would have to do. By this point in my life, I knew there was no use arguing with my body. If it said it was time to get up, I wouldn't be going back to bed until it had clocked a full day. I used to be able to take naps, back when I considered illegal activity my moral obligation, but ever since I got respectable (and a loyal following besides) there were no more daytime soirees to dreamland. I often wondered what I'd do if I ever moved to Spain. Thankfully, it wasn't on the agenda.

Of course, even though I wasn't going to get any more sleep, that didn't mean I actually had to get out of bed, so I didn't. I lay there, my head propped up on a pillow, and thought about my night. All I'd really learned was Jā was playing some sort of scam and when I found out where he'd gotten the other part of his money, I'd have someone else to pin his murder on. If I could do that, Bernie was in the clear, I'd get my producer's credit and maybe August and I could go on a real date.

Ahhh...August. Time to get up.

Guantanamo was still sleeping soundly, bless his little heart. I checked the pot on the stove. It still had water, so I turned the burner on high and walked around to my desk. I flipped on my laptop and waited for the screens to come to life. One of the few concessions I've made in the way of creature comforts is a large external monitor for my PowerBook. No, I can't take it with me on the road, but it sure is easy on the eyes, especially when I'm surfing the net. This morning, though, I was just playing a game of solitaire while I waited for my water to boil.

By the time I had put a red jack on a black queen the tea pot was getting ready to scream. I grabbed it off the stove and set about fixing my cup. The way I figure it, once the water has boiled, I still have time to get everything together, pour the water in and it'll still be too hot to drink right away. I just cut my wait time by a few minutes.

I poured some honey into a mug, tossed in a splash of lemon juice and a tea bag and I was all set. Sure, you'd think a tough guy like me would be drinking coffee on a Sunday morning, but I find tea a quicker pick-me-up. Particularly my own special blend of pirate tea: a nice dollop of rum (Captain Morgan's, I'm a pirate from way back) in a mug of Earl Grey. When my tea was adjusted just right, I took my mug and stepped outside. It was a beautiful day, the kind of day you only find in Southern California. I figured I should appreciate it. I went back inside, grabbed my notebook and took it up the two flights of stairs to the roof of my building.

The rooftop deck was a major reason I decided on renting this particular apartment. Well, that and the fact they actually approved me. I think Publisher Steve had something to do with that, since before I'd moved in here two years ago, I'd been sleeping on his couch. For some reason, I don't think he thought I was a good influence on his kid. Oh well, what are ya gonna do?

But the deck, the deck was magnificent. There were a couple of old restaurant booths up there, complete with Formica tabletops, and an old weight set. I never used the weights, but one of the booths was definitively reserved as mine. It was my usual table, so to speak. Whenever the sun was shining and I was ready to work before dusk, this was a great place to do it. I didn't have the distractions of the TV or the phone or Guantanamo. I could bring the computer up here and crank out a column.

It was also a nice place to entertain guests, especially female guests. Carol had been up here more than once. From the roof, during the day, you had a clear view of the ocean and the Venice Boardwalk to the west. At night, when the place was lighted up with tiki torches, the lights of the city stretched out to the east as far as the eye could see. On an all too rare clear day, you could even make out the Hollywood sign. All in all, a great place to call home.

Today, though, I had work to do. I sat facing the water and opened my notebook. Yesterday had been mildly productive but I really needed to get down to business if this was going to work. Sipping my pirate tea, I went over my notes. I'd added several people to my "worth talking to" list yesterday and so far, I'd only talked to August Everywhere. Granted, she was well worth talking to, but I had a whole list of other people who had information. Today was going to be busy.

"Skids!"

It was Guantanamo. He was yelling from inside the apartment. Odds are it was a phone call for me.

I called down to him. "I'm on the roof."

"Phone call for you."

"Bring the phone up here, would ya?"

I could hear him below, struggling to get out past the screen door.

"It won't reach," he yelled.

Guantanamo is my best friend. I have seen him through as many different aspects of life as is possible to see another human being you're not married to and I can say, unequivocally, that he is not a morning person.

I yelled back "Bring the cordless!"

"Oh, right."

You really had to wonder how he made it through basic training.

A moment later he appeared, holding the cordless phone out to me. I took it, putting my hand over the mouthpiece.

"Who is it?" I mouthed at him.

"How the hell should I know?" He said, loudly.

"Are you up?"

He looked around, saw where the sun was in the sky, and shrugged. In the language handed down from one Bey generation to the next, that meant, "I guess so."

"Go get something to drink and come up here."

He nodded. I knew I had a good twenty minutes before he came back. Enough time to get a start on my day's work and then I could find out what happened between him and the sand sculptress.

"Hello?" I said into the phone.

"Is this Skids Poppe?" It was a female voice. With my past, this was not always a good sign.

"It could be," I answered hesitantly. "Who's this?"

"My name is Spring Tyme. I'm in the band with August?" She was asking if I'd heard of her. I had. Her name was staring up at me from my notebook. Boy, was this easy. When the people you wanted to talk to just called you right up, I couldn't understand why people thought this was hard.

I decided the polite approach was the best way to handle her. "What can I do for you, Ms. Tyme?"

"I talked to August this morning and she said you were asking questions about Jā."

"That's right. I'm looking into his death for a friend of mine. In fact, you were on my list of people to call today."

"I thought I might be. Figured I could save you the dime."

"Great." I could have this whole thing wrapped up by the end of the week and still have plenty of time to do my column in time for press day. "Can I ask you a few questions?"

"No."

"Okay, so where were you--I'm sorry. Did you say 'no'?"

"Yes."

"Yes you said no?"

"Yes."

"So, I can't ask you questions?"

"Yes."

I was lost. I had to stop this before it turned into a bad Abbot and Costello routine.

"I'm confused," I said.

"Let's meet for lunch," she said.

Now there was something I could understand. "You can't talk there?" She didn't say anything. "I see. You have a roommate and you don't want them to know what's going on so we have to meet someplace out of the way so you can talk freely?"

"Something like that."

"Right. I'm with ya. What time is it?"

"About one. Can you meet me at two? At H & R on Washington?"

"I'll be there. How will I know you?"

"Don't worry. I'll know you. I'll have a table outside waiting."

"See you then." She hung up before I could say goodbye.

H & R was a little trattoria known for its breakfasts and weekend brunches. They catered to the beach crowd by supplying bicycle parking and had a little grassy patch for dogs to play in while their owners ate. I'd eaten there once, at night, when I had to interview someone for an article for a magazine which has since been swallowed up by some corporation. As I recall, that particular magazine only paid like 35 cents a word and since they went corporate, they never hired me again. I'll tell you; this freelance writing thing is tough.

The nice thing about H & R, though, is it's right down the street. I still had plenty of time to do some leg work before meeting her.

Guantanamo joined me on the roof. He had a beer in one hand and was wearing my bathrobe over a pair of faded army fatigues. He looked like Hawkeye Pierce's evil twin. He plopped himself into the booth opposite me. His stare suggested he really hadn't wanted to get up yet.

"Who was it?" He asked.

"A girl."

"I could figure that much out when I answered it. Any girl in particular? Was it the girl you were out with all night? Do I know this girl?"

"It had to do with this Bernie thing and what makes you think I was with a girl last night?"

He drained his beer. He took another one out of one of the side pockets of his pants and twisted the cap off without taking his eyes off me. Then he raised his eyebrows.

"All right, I was with a girl last night." We knew each other too well. "I met her at The Cup. She's the dead guy's ex-girlfriend."

"Did she do it?"

"I don't think so."

"But you haven't ruled her out completely?"

"Not yet."

I was getting uncomfortable. Guantanamo had this wonderful way of making me question every decision I ever made. Not that he thought they were wrong, he just wanted me to make sure they were right. Every now and again, it helped. I tried to defend August. "I should have her cleared by tonight, though."

"Okay, but just remember, you can't fall for her until after she's been cleared. You don't have a Joel Cairo to pin it on yet." Like I said, we knew each other far too well.

"What about you?" I asked. "What about sand girl?"

"I went back out after you left to take Bernie to the airport. I convinced her she really wanted to go out with me."

"How'd you do that?"

"I told her I had some dirt on her and if she gave me half a chance, she'd really dig me." He took a quick swallow of his beer.

I couldn't believe he was able to say it with a straight face. The least I could do was play along. "The pun approach worked for you?"

"It got me the date. She said I was cute and she liked a guy with perseverance. And it didn't hurt that I helped carry several buckets of sand for her."

"So, what happened last night?"

"What time you get home?"

"Sometime after dawn, why? Who are you, my mother?"

"Just asking to see how much I missed you by. I crawled in around four." He finished off the second beer. I really wanted to look under the table to see if there was another waiting, but I refrained. I once saw Guantanamo bring out enough beers to serve a morning minyan so there was no telling how many he had on him now.

"Four? Not bad. The date went well?"

"Not too bad, but I don't think I'll see her again."

"Why not?" Guantanamo had this way of being disappointed by girls he was enamored of in a physical way. Especially if the sex wasn't good.

He pulled another beer out (I knew he had another beer) and turned to look at the beach. "Everything was going great. I'd convinced her my time in the army was a benefit for humanity and everything. We went for drinks and then ended up back at her place."

"Sounds good so far," I said.

"It was. So was she. Sure, there was a little grit from all the sand, but generally she was pretty good."

"So, what happened?"

"Afterwards, we were lying there, talking, and somehow it comes out that I ride a motorcycle. Next thing I know, she's going off on some journalist she had read who claimed motorcyclists were more socially aware than regular drivers due to the fact they filled out their little pink organ donor cards. Then she wanted to know what I thought."

I felt for him. I knew the article. In fact, I'd written it. "What'd you say?"

"What could I say? I told her whoever wrote that article was a sad pathetic loser and that I never rode my motorcycle in the city, just in the country and on deserted highways, except for today because my car was in the shop. She said good and gave me a great blow job."

I was proud of him. "Of course you can't go out with her again because you'd have to tell her I'm your roommate and that just won't serve any productive use. What are you gonna say?"

He smiled at me. A great big cheesy smile, the kind you only find in Southern California. But his was sincere. "That's the best part. I don't have to say anything. She decided early in the evening she was going to go back to her boyfriend, but still wanted to know what I'd be like in bed. Seems her boyfriend is a pansy-ass poet who wears black all the time and snaps his fingers instead of clapping. I was just the bad-boy one-night stand."

"Good for you."

"Thank you. Now how was your night?"

I told him all about August and what I'd learned.

"Sounds like you have your work cut out for you," he said. "When are you going to talk to the film crew?"

I hadn't even thought about talking to the film crew. "Tomorrow," I covered. "Even you should know they don't shoot on Sundays."

He looked at me like I was insane.

"Unless it's a low budget film," he said. "Then they shoot all weekend, because they get Sunday free from the rental places."

"Really?" He had me. I had no choice but to tell him the truth. "Well, I already had it scheduled for tomorrow."

He nodded like that was the most logical answer I could be expected to come up with. "And what's on your agenda for today?"

"Lunch with another prospective killer."

"Sounds like fun. I'm going down to the Promenade to catch a double feature of whatever I can sneak into."

I'd seen a lot of films in my day. I mean, part of my job is to watch movies and tell people what I think of 'em, but I'm nothing next to my sidekick. Ever since he made it back to civilian life, he spent any free time he had watching movies. It didn't matter if they were on tape or in the theatre (although he did prefer the dark box as opposed to the idiot box), he watched them all. And when he was in a movie jag kind of mood, I'd even known him to catch three or four films in a day. I think Guantanamo took the multiplex as a personal challenge.

"If you see anything good," I told him, "let me know. I'm looking for a good date film."

"Dead guy's girl?"

"She has a name, you know."

"They all have names. I'll wait 'til she's innocent before I learn hers."

He finished his beer and set the empty on the table with the other two. "I think the first show is at two," he said as he got up to leave. "I always feel better sneaking into a matinee. Somehow, I don't feel like I'm stealing as much. Be home around eight or nine if you need me. Later."

He vanished down the stairs.

"August," I said quietly, a minute after he was gone. "Her name is August.

Okay, I had a half hour to do some work and still have time to shower and meet Spring at H & R. The first thing I had to do was call Brandy and Bernie. This time I got the number right on the first try.

"Brandy?" I asked when someone finally answered.

"No."

"Janet?"

"Yes."

Janet was Brandy's roommate. They had been living together for about three years. The first time I'd met her, I decided instantly she was the kind of person who enjoys making your life miserable because it gives her a reason to exist. I know, not exactly charitable of me, but then again, there are some people you just get feelings for. But for some reason, Brandy was still living with her. I guess she sees something in Janet I don't, but that's what makes the world go around, right? The biggest thing about Janet was her lack of conversational skills, at least with Brandy Poppe's favorite brother (Okay, so I'm her only brother; details).

"It's Skids. Brandy around?"

"Out back."

"Could you get her?"

There was no noise on the other end.

"Please?" I asked again.

Then I heard something in the distance. The reason there had been no response was she had set the phone down and gone to get her before I'd said anything. I love talking to her. Before I could think any more sarcastic thoughts, someone picked up the phone.

"Skids?"

"Brandy. How are ya? How's Bernie?"

"I'm fine. Bernie is here. He drinks a lot."

"I'll pay for anything he drinks." And of course, I'll put it on Bernie's expense report. And I'll tack on an extra 20%. I had to make money somehow.

"Like you have money. You still owe me for the last road trip you and Guantanamo took."

"This is different. I'll pay for all of it, just don't let him go anywhere. Or get into any trouble."

"Have you ever tried to keep this guy out of trouble?"

"Yeah."

"What'd you do?"

"I sent him to you. Listen, is he there?"

"Yeah. I'll get him." There was a pause. "Skids, what kind of trouble is this guy in?"

"Honestly?"

"You're my brother, if you can't be honest with me... well, then you're a typical guy... but yeah, tell me the truth."

"He's wanted by the police for murder."

There was another long silence. "Oh... is that all. I thought it was something serious like an angry girlfriend. I'll get him. Oh yeah. You still owe me... big."

I had to be honest with her, didn't I?

"Skids, it's me, Bernie."

"I know, Bern. How's it going?"

"Great. Your sister is great. Her roommate is a babe."

Like I said, it takes all types.

"Bernie, I just have a quick question for ya."

"Shoot."

"Bad choice of words for a murder suspect. Anyway, how much did you deposit into the joint account, did you do the depositing, and what bank did you use?"

"Marty and I made the deposit, transfer actually, from one of my accounts at Southwest Savings into the trust account. And I already told you, it was two hundred and fifty grand."

"I just wanted to make sure." I opened my notebook

to a clean page and made a note of the bank name and the particulars. "Do you know the account number, off hand?"

"Marty would have it. I have it but it's back at my house. You could ask Gina to let you in, she has a key. It's in a file in the bottom drawer of my desk called Body Mechanics. That's the name of the film."

"I know." I had it written on the other page. "Give me Marty's number. And you may as well give me Gina's while you're at it." He did. "I'll call her and let her know what's going on. You haven't called her, have you?"

"No. Your sister wouldn't let me make any calls."

Good girl. "Okay, you take care and I'll get back to you in a couple of days."

"Hey, Skids?" His voice was serious.

"Yeah?"

"Am I getting my money's worth?"

"I'm finding out a bunch of stuff, Bern. I'll call you in a couple of days. Just hang tight and I'll get you out of this."

I heard him saying thank you as I hung up the phone. Was he getting his money's worth? Did he expect any less?

I looked at my notebook. In all the years I had owned notebooks, going back to when I was in school, I never, ever used an entire one. Every time I've moved, I've thrown out spiral-bound blank pages. I'll bet over the years I, personally, have been responsible for at least a small garden portion of the redwood's destruction.

My point, though, is this notebook was getting filled up pretty quick. I had a list of potential bad guys three pages long and every time I talked to one of them, they just added three names to the list rather than subtracting their own. I looked back over my previous notes.

The thing that struck me, which I hadn't thought of before, was Jā being shot. For some reason I'd thought he was stabbed. Maybe it was my own background. I know whenever we got into serious, heavy-duty fights and someone ended up dead, it was because of steel, not lead. It was so much easier to hide (and then use) a knife. But since Jā was shot, I should probably find out something about what shot him. That meant a visit with Cricket, my police photographer friend. I made a note of it, right next to 'contact the film crew' on the list of things to do tomorrow. Now, though, I had to get going if I was going to be on time to meet Spring.

I drove down to the H & R. Yes, I know I could have walked, but this is Los Angeles. No one walks if they don't have to, not in this air.

When I got there, a line of people was standing outside, half of them Rollerbladers who still hadn't mastered the "full stop." I really hate Rollerbladers. These people wear so much protection I think they've forgotten why it is they picked a semi-dangerous sport to begin with. I have a sneaking suspicion the helmet law lobbyists are all Rollerbladers.

I parked my bike in front of the place, just inside the non-painted curb. Two inches to the left and I'd be in danger of a ticket. Dropping my helmet (damn those Rollerbladers) on my handlebars, I began looking for Spring Tyme. I had seen her last night at The Cup but that didn't mean I'd recognize her in glaring sunlight. In fact, I wasn't even sure which band member she had been.

"Skids Poppe?"

I turned around. It was one of the waiters.

"Yes?" I answered.

"Mr. Poppe, your table is waiting this way. If you'll please follow me." I followed him.

He led me through a maze of crowded tables to the back patio. Well, 'back' wasn't entirely accurate. It was actually off to the side, closer to the beach. It was also closer to the grassy area reserved for dogs, which is why I thought of it as "out back." I recognized Spring the moment I saw her sitting at a table on the edge of the grass, petting a beautiful black-and-white Siberian Husky. And wearing a pair of Rollerblades. Don't ask me why, but I didn't like her.

She flagged me over. As I got closer, more of last night came back to me. She was Bridesmaid's Protocol's guitarist, the one who drove off in the truck with the sound guy. She was wearing a pair of sweat pants, which had been cut off just above the knees (to make room for her hard plastic knee pads); a t-shirt (dripping sweat under the arms and bearing the slogan of another band) was tied loosely in a knot under her breasts.

Looking at the way she was dressed today, I figured what she had been wearing last night was more of a costume than anything else. Her hair was pulled off her face and piled on her head like some sort of Gordian knot. Needless to say, I felt rather stupid for having gone to the trouble of showering and putting on a clean pair of jeans. At least I was wearing yesterday's t-shirt, and that made me feel a little better.

The waiter pulled out my chair for me and the dog she

was petting growled at me as I sat.

"Shhh... Quiet, Jack," she admonished the dog. She held out her hand to me as I got settled, moving my legs to the side of the table away from the dog's mouth. "Hi, Mr. Poppe. I'm Spring Tyme."

I shook her hand. "Nice dog you got there," I said. The dog growled again.

"He's the best. I hope you don't mind that I mixed our meeting with taking him for a walk."

"Not at all." I eyed the menu sitting in front of me and casually opened it up. One look at the prices and I suddenly wondered what protocol was. Okay, I didn't really wonder, I knew what protocol was. I had to buy. My next question was if I had enough cash on me. Better eat light, just in case.

When I looked up, I saw she was staring at me. "Do you already know what you want to eat?" I asked.

"Yes." But she didn't stop staring at me.

Right I thought. I went back to studying the menu and decided on a couple of eggs, some crispy bacon, toast and a beer. I turned the menu over to see what they had on tap.

"I hear you had a late night last night," she said.

I knew if I looked up before I had made my beer selection, she would still be staring at me. What had August told her?

"What did August tell you?" I continued to look at the beer list. Finally, I decided on a Rogue Dead Guy. It wasn't on tap, but I was developing a cultivated taste for micro brews. Besides, the irony killed me.

"What makes you think August told me anything?"

When I looked up, she was still staring at me. "Where

else would you hear about my late night?"

"Maybe your roommate told me when I called you?"

"He didn't. What are you staring at?"

She stopped staring. Instead, she sipped her water, then poured some into her hand to let her dog drink.

"August told me the two of you were out until very early and you were asking questions about Jā. She also told me she told you Jā and I had had a relationship in the past and that you would probably want to talk to me. Does that cover it?"

That was pretty much everything. Great, so now we were both up to date.

"It doesn't explain why you were staring at me." She looked at me again, keeping one hand under the table where the dog was still licking the last drops of liquid from it. "August said you were something to look at. You are."

The way she said it, I knew it wasn't the compliment I was sure it had been from August.

"Can I ask you some questions now?"

She smiled sweetly. "Let's order first."

She used the dog hand to flag over a waiter and ordered a seafood omelet and two large glasses of orange juice. The omelet was one of the pricier things on the menu and orange juice, no matter where you order it, is too expensive for what it is. I hate people who order orange juice in restaurants. You end up paying six bucks for a shot glass and that's what they call a "large." I did some quick figuring in my head, revised it when she suddenly 'remembered' a plain beef patty for Jack the dog, and when the waiter turned to take my order, I made do with just the beer and a bagel.

Poppe Culture

Even at that, I was concerned about my cash flow.

As soon as the waiter left, I resumed my line of questioning. I don't know why, maybe it was the sunlight, maybe I was getting used to it, maybe it was just that I had been screwed out of breakfast, but for some reason I felt very comfortable getting right to the point with Miss Tyme.

"You don't deny having a sexual relationship with Jā Alweighz?" I pulled out my notebook so could keep track of her answers.

"I don't deny it. We were screwing around. Had been for a couple of months."

"Hell of a way to treat a friend, huh?"

"I told her about it."

"Eventually." I finished the sentence for her. "Why Monday? What had changed?"

For the first time, she looked at me like I was a real person. "Mr. Poppe, I'm answering your questions because August asked me too. She told me you were doing this for Bernie and it's only because of those two people I'm talking to you at all. Both of them are good people who have helped me out. A lot. "

I nodded in what I could only hope was a sagely, knowing way. It felt like a get-on-with-it way. "Thank you."

"Personally," she continued, "I don't like you. I've read your columns and I don't think you're all that clever, but you do seem to have a take on things and if I can help Bernie, I will. But please, whatever I tell you, you can't tell August."

She was serious. I didn't like her, either, but obviously we had one thing in common; we both liked August and evidently neither of us wanted to hurt her. "Fair enough. I think you're protected under motorcycle-rider confidentiality laws anyway." I smiled at her.

She smiled back. A real smile. Maybe I was getting through to her. Then she flashed the same smile on the dog. Naw, probably not.

I asked again, "Why Monday?"

"Jā called me Sunday afternoon. He said he was going to tell August about us if I didn't give him fifty thousand dollars."

Wow. Fifty grand was a lot of money. I looked at the girl sitting across from me. She had ordered the most expensive thing on the menu without batting an eyelash. But did that mean she had that kind of money lying around? Her clothes didn't say much about her income. So okay, just looking at her there was no way to know. I decided on the rude approach.

"Could you afford that?"

She continued to look at her dog. Maybe it was the dog that had the money. I had read of some woman who was worth millions when she died and left all her money to her cats since she didn't like any of her relatives. So maybe the dog was worth some bucks and this girl was just caretaking. Okay, it was crazy, but live in LA long enough and you begin to believe anything is possible.

"Could I afford fifty thousand dollars?" She repeated my question, but not to me. She asked the dog. And she asked him in the kind of baby voice which just makes me sick.

If you're going to have a pet, at least have the decency to treat it with a little respect. Jack, the dog, looked up at me with sad eyes. I'm with ya buddy, I thought. I was connecting more with the dog at this point. Then again, if she was asking him maybe my first theory wasn't so far off.

She reached down to him, grabbing the scruff of his neck and shaking hard. Jack seemed to really like it. His tail started wagging and his tongue lolled out. His eyes said to me: "Yeah, sure, she talks like I'm an imbecile, but who's complaining? I get this!" He had a point.

Finally, Spring answered my question. "Ironically enough, at this point in time, I can afford it."

"What do you mean?"

She left her hand on the dog's back but answered me. "I mean a very wealthy relative just died and, when all was said and done, I inherited just over fifty-three thousand." She stopped. Getting any information from her was going to be like pulling teeth.

"When did this come through?"

"Last week."

"Did Jā know about this money?" Stupid question.

"Stupid question. Of course he knew about it. Everyone at The Cup knew about it."

"You make it a habit telling people you're suddenly rich?"

"You think that's rich?"

It was more take home money than I had legally made most years of my adult life, but still. "No, it's not rich, but it's a nice chunk of change. Evidently it was enough to warrant blackmail."

She shivered slightly in the cool ocean breeze. Jack had stretched out completely on the ground, so she had a free hand to rub her bare arms. I continued: "Why did everyone at The Cup know about it?"

"Didn't August tell you about our record?"

"She mentioned something about it. She said it was a CD though."

Spring laughed at that. I assure you; it was quite involuntary.

"August would. She is a stickler for semantics. Well, the money was going to go toward a small tour to support our CD. Especially if the record company didn't come through."

"The company doesn't pay for the tour?"

"Depends on the company. Right now, the label we're closest to getting signed with will only pick up distribution and manufacturing costs. If we start getting airplay in Savannah, and there seems to be an interest in us playing there, we have to get there ourselves. That's what the money was going to be for. We wanted to try and set up things all over the country. Bernie said he'd help us out, talk to other club owners."

"Did Bernie ever offer to fund your tour?"

"Right." Without a doubt, I believe I had just heard the most sarcastic reading of that word ever.

"But he was going to help you out?"

"Yeah, as long as it didn't cost him anything. A phone call was cheap and besides, I'd... we'd rather do it ourselves." She fell silent as the waiter set her omelet down.

I let her slip go, for now, but made a note in my book. Now, I needed to get back to the point.

"What about you and Jā? What happened there? August said she and you were friends since she got down here and now, you're doing her guy? Just doesn't seem very friendly."

She eyed the waiter as he set down her two tiny glasses of orange juice, wondering, I'm sure, if he was paying any attention to our conversation. If he was, he had a great poker face. I risked a glance around the restaurant. The place was packed. Odds are the guy had enough on his mind making sure his tables were happy than to worry about a silly little affair being discussed at table nine. Either way, I didn't care.

Spring Tyme did. She waited until the waiter had dropped all our food and confirmed there was nothing else he could get for us before she answered my questions.

"It wasn't supposed to happen. I met August at McCabe's on a Saturday afternoon. We were both in line. I was getting some strings and she was picking up the sheet music for Smells Like Teen Spirit. We got to talking and ended up going for coffee and then lunch and by the end of dinner we had decided to form a band together. I was the first person she met in LA. I grew up here, so I showed her around, helped find her an apartment and got her her first job. She became my best friend." She paused to eat. Personally, I was glad. Not because I didn't want to hear what she had to say, but the thought of the expensive meal sitting in front of her going to waste would have really irritated me.

I waited. She seemed to be doing fine and besides, I had just taken a big bite of bagel and my mouth was full.

"Then she met Jā." I was surprised the juice didn't go sour from the tone in her voice.

I was all ears. She didn't like Jā, that was obvious enough, but I had to know why. My pen was making inkblots waiting to write in the notebook. I made a quick note to get new pens then started a new line for her.

"When she met Jā everything changed."

"Changed how?" I was getting into the detective game in a big way.

"We used to hang out all the time. Music was the thing. No matter what else was going on, our music came first. When she started dating Jā, he took up all her time."

"So she didn't care about the band anymore?"

"She did, but it wasn't the same. We didn't work on songs together anymore or go out or anything."

"You mean this was the first time either of you had had a boyfriend since you met?" I found that hard to believe. Both of them were babes, no question. And I certainly wasn't being subjective. I knew, for a fact, Guantanamo would have dated either of them, despite his preference (this week) for sculptors.

Spring shook her head at me like I was an undisciplined child. "No, that's not what I mean at all. We both had boyfriends come and go, but nothing was ever this serious. Usually, for us, boyfriends were a game. Look at me, Mr. Poppe." I looked. She continued: "Do I look like I would ever have trouble getting a boyfriend?"

"How did they meet?" I asked, ignoring her question entirely. This girl knew she had something in her pants most guys wanted to get at and had no qualms about using it. I was not about to get into an argument about how women had been treated by men, because, frankly, I wasn't interested. But I didn't need to let her know it.

"He picked her up one night at The Cup. She was so excited. Thought he was the cutest thing since her last cutest thing. She told me all about him the next day."

"And when did things, as you say, change?"

"After a while, he was all she talked about. What films he was going to make, which movie stars she had dinner with. Eventually, she began including herself when she talked about making films. She was still coming to practice, but her mind wasn't really there. We weren't booking a lot of gigs and things were really falling apart and then, all of a sudden, Jā got us the regular spot at The Cup."

I was taking notes like crazy, putting things into place. "When was this?"

She had taken a cigarette out of her purse. She waited for me to light it for her. I let her wait. I had run out of things to write down, so I made a note to pick up some cat food for the neighborhood strays. Out of the corner of my eye, I saw Spring make a move to get some matches. I pretended to notice her, finally, and grabbed my Zippo. I flicked it open and held it for her.

She took a couple of drags, blowing the smoke over the dog's head. "About eight months ago."

"Was that the first time you met Jā?" I coughed, turning my head when the ocean breeze blew the smoke back in my face. Contrary to popular belief, I don't smoke. Any more.

"Hell no," Spring said, smiling slightly at my discomfort. "I'd met him long before. He had shown up at rehearsals a few times." She sucked in another lungful of smoke.

I nodded. "When did you start sleeping with him?"

She exhaled in my face. I coughed again, exaggerating so it sounded like I was hacking up a lung. She apologized. I didn't forgive her.

"About six months ago."

I looked at my notes. "Six is more than a couple, isn't it?"

"It's three couples, in the right company. Yeah, so it was more than a couple of months. So what?"

"Why?" This was really the question.

"Why not?" She snubbed her cigarette out. Even when I did smoke, I don't think I ever sucked one down to the filter that quickly.

"Look, I don't want to be here any more than you do, but if you answer the question, you'll really be helping out Bernie. And you said you liked him." I seemed to strike a chord. She pulled out another cigarette. This time I lit it right away.

"Fine. But this goes no further."

"As long as you didn't kill Jā."

"I didn't kill him. I fucked him because he was bad news."

"What the hell does that mean?" I was thoroughly confused.

"It means he started coming on to me, telling me how much he wanted me."

"Why didn't you tell August then?"

"She wouldn't have believed me. Not then. I thought if I slept with him, I could get the proof I needed to prove to her that he was no good."

"Why didn't you like him?"

"I just didn't. You know how there are some people you know, instinctively, you just don't like?"

Boy, did I.

"Well, Jā was like that. The more I got to know him, the more I didn't like him. He was always talking about these grand schemes of his, the 'films' August had been telling us about since they'd met. And in all that time, nothing ever materialized. He'd borrowed money from her. He even hit her once. But she was so devoted to him it was sick. She once said it was all forgivable because when he made it big, he was going to take her with him. The only thing that could shake that faith was another woman. Another woman was the only thing she feared."

"And you didn't believe him? You didn't think he would take her with? That's why you slept with him, out of love for her?" Was I being too hard? I didn't think so.

"I knew he wouldn't. Riding his coattails was the same pick-up line he'd used on me. He was a manipulative bastard." She was almost done with cigarette number two. I wondered what she'd done when LA passed the law about indoor smoking. Probably held a vigil. Or just ate at restaurants with patios.

"Why wouldn't she have listened to you?"

"Because I'd been telling her for a while that I didn't trust him. She said it was all in my head."

"Was it? Did you ever see him hit her? Was she ever bruised?"

"I didn't need to see it. I could tell. And if I'd told her he was coming on to me, she would have said I was just jealous because I didn't have anything like that in my life. Like I said, things between us weren't good." She thought about getting another stick from the pack but changed her mind.

"Why didn't you tell her after you'd slept with him?"

"I was going to. I really was."

"What happened?"

"Nothing. Every time I thought about telling her, the timing wasn't right. After about the fourth or fifth time, Jā had figured out I was going to tell her. He said if I told her, not only would it hurt her, which neither of us wanted, but that he'd tell her it was all my idea. That I had seduced him."

"So you kept sleeping together?"

She changed her mind again and stuck her third after-meal cigarette between her lips. I lit that one, too. Then she nodded.

"What made you change your mind? Just the blackmail?"

"Isn't that enough?"

I shrugged. I guess it was a good enough reason for now.

"I think I've finished eating, Mr. Poppe. I should probably get Jack back on the path." She had artificially softened her voice, making her tone seem light and airy. "I wouldn't want him to get fat and lazy now, would I?"

I acted hurt. I knew she wanted me to feel that way, so the least I could do was oblige.

"Thank you for lunch, Skids. Good luck in your search." She left the table, dragging her beautiful dog along behind her. I watched her go. She passed the waiter on the way out, who immediately swung by to drop the check on the table. I don't know...talk of affairs and me wearing yesterday's shirt, maybe he thought I couldn't pay.

I checked the bill against the contents of my pocket, saw it was the waiter's lucky day. I had enough to cover it, plus tip, and still had enough left over to walk across the street to The Cow and grab a cup of coffee. I was feeling like J. Paul Getty's bastard son.

A few minutes later I was back in my element, sipping a cup of really strong mocha and re-reading my notes. When I finished my cup, I looked up at the clock above the glass display case of expensive cigars. It was already getting close to four and I still had a couple more calls to make before it got too late.

Sunday Evening

Guantanamo was on the phone when I finally got home. I knew I had at least twenty minutes until I could use it. And that was only if I got on his case now.

"Get off the phone!" I mouthed loudly. True, I didn't actually make a sound, there was no reason to disturb the call, but he got the point. He nodded and walked away from me. I sat down at my desk and made a list of people I needed to talk with before I went to bed. First up was Doc. I knew he did some work for the police from time to time as a sign language interpreter and figured he might have a little bit of insight into this whole investigative biz. Even if he didn't, he would certainly enjoy hearing about me doing it. As far as he was concerned, I was a great source of entertainment.

When I opened my laptop to get an e-mail ready to send him, I found Guantanamo's note. For some reason, my sidekick has a huge problem with the idea of leaving me a message where I might actually find it in a reasonable amount of time. Then again, he knows me well enough to know one of the first things I do is check my computer. Maybe he's not as out of touch as people think he is.

Today's message was from August. The note said she'd called, had a great time last night (at which point Guantanamo put in his own nudge nudge, wink wink editorial) and I should call her.

I put the note aside and wondered what was going on. It hadn't been one day, let alone the good girls required three. Either I had made a great impression or there was something going on. As much as I wanted to believe it was the former, I had a pretty strong feeling I was wrong. And since August was already on my list of things to do, albeit not for a day or two, I drew a little arrow up to the top of the page with a star on either side of her name.

Next on my list was Accountant Marty, and then Bernie's girl, Gina. I thought about it. I was pretty certain Marty's number was for his office, which would be closed today. That moved Gina to the top of the list. Right after August.

I tapped out my message to Doc and as I finished, I heard Bey finish his conversation, wrapping it up with an exuberant "Fuck you, too." He must be talking to 'Happy' Ellison, an old army buddy of his. I'd met Ellison once. He was the saddest, most morose motherfucker I'd ever met. It seemed perfectly natural to me that he and Guantanamo had teamed up in service.

"Here's the phone," he said, handing me the cordless. "You have messages."

"I know," I said, waving the paper at him. "How's Happy?"

"Depressed. August is last night's girl, huh?" I nodded. "Sounds nice on the phone." I nodded again. "She didn't waste any time in calling you, huh?" I shrugged. "You sly dog you." He chucked me under the chin and left the apartment. He was going out to watch the sunset. I never got the chance to ask him why he wasn't at the movies.

August hadn't left her number when she called so I grabbed her card out of my book and dialed her up. I don't know if personality types can be determined by how quickly one answers the phone, but I'm sure it's an indicator of something. Me? I usually pick it up on the second or third ring. Guantanamo, contrary to what you'd think, answers it immediately. I've even seen him knock things over in his rush to say hello to whoever is calling.

August took her sweet time. It rang three and a half times and I thought for sure I'd be leaving a message when she finally answered. Her place wasn't large, so I guessed she was kind of like me, she'd get it, eventually, but it wasn't crucial.

"Hello," she said.

"August?"

"Skids?"

Well, at least we weren't sure about each other.

"Yeah, it's me." We both said it at the same time.

Silence.

Okay, so it wasn't the best start for our first phone conversation but at least we knew it could always get better.

Before I could break the silence, she did.

"You got the message I called?"

"Yeah. What's up? I was going to call you anyway."
"You were?"

I could hear her voice smile. I know, that sounds kind of cheesy, but if you've ever heard someone's voice change like that, you know what I mean.

"I was." My voice smiled back. "So why did you call? I thought good girls waited three days? Not that I'm complaining, mind you."

"Good girls are allowed to break the three days rule on special occasions. The first is if they're calling boys who pretend to be not so good."

I let the "pretend" go for now. Bringing it up could only send the conversation into a different direction, not as good, direction. "And the second?"

"The second is if they have something important to tell the not-so-good boy about the good girl's dead ex-boyfriend. The rules are rather specific."

"I can tell. So what news does my good girl have?"

"Your good girl? Rather presumptuous, huh?"

"I understand not-so-good boys have that right. So 'fess up. What news?"

"I found a key to Jā's place. It was on the key ring I used for my carks. I completely forgot about it."

"Carks?" I was confused.

"Sorry, car keys. Carks is just an abbreviation I made up. But anyway, I don't drive anymore because I don't have a car. I had to sell it when it stopped running and I couldn't afford to fix it. But when I did, I couldn't find the keys. I keep them on a separate ring from my house keys. So I had to give the guy who bought it the spares and today, when I was looking to see if I actually did have the sheet music for 'The Night Chicago Died,' I found the original keys which had Jā's house key on the same ring. So, if you wanted to get a copy of Body Mechanics, we could probably go over there and grab one. I know where he kept all that stuff."

"August, you are amazing. Can we go tonight?"

"When? I haven't eaten yet..." She let the words trail off. I got the hint.

"Can I take you out for dinner and we'll hit Jā's place afterwards?"

"Sounds great, but we can do dinner afterwards. I'll be ready in a half hour."

"I'll be there in forty-five minutes. Have a place picked out for dinner."

"I already called and made reservations."

"Already? Rather presumptuous, huh?"

"Good girls are entitled. It's in the manual. You really should read it before we have more of these misunderstandings. Our table will be ready by the time we've gotten the script." If it was possible, her voice smiled wider.

"See you in an hour," I said.

"What happened to forty-five minutes?"

"I got my own manual. And I gotta get you your own helmet."

I hung up and called Gina.

Gina and Bernie had been going out for a while, maybe eight or nine months. That doesn't sound like much, but in Bernie's case, it was one of the longest relationships he'd ever had. I had met her a couple of times up at the Rock Store. The first time he'd brought her, she seemed very out of place.

The Rock Store is a biker hang-out buried deep in the Santa Monica Mountains and while there is no prejudice about what kind of bike you ride, there is if you don't ride a bike at all. Gina looked so uncomfortable riding in on the back of Bernie's bike, we could tell right away she wasn't a biker. It took a few minutes before we would even acknowledge her presence. I'm sure it wasn't all that comfortable for her, either, meeting her new boyfriend's old riding buddies (not to mention the famous Skids Poppe) but she hung in there like a trooper and at the end of the day, when she disappeared into the bathroom, we all gave Bernie the thumbs up.

Once she was accepted, she didn't have to show up all that often, so she didn't. All told, I think we'd seen each other face to face two or three times at the Rock Store and once, Bernie took me out for dinner and she had come along. I was pretty sure she'd remember me, but I had my little "I'm Skids Poppe, the guy trying to save Bernie's ass" speech all prepared for when she answered the phone. As it turned out, I didn't have to worry about it. She never picked up. I left a message on her machine, using a shortened version of my speech which ended with my phone number, and asked her to call me.

My next call, to Marty the accountant, was pretty much the same. I was right. The number I had was an office, so the machine wasn't unexpected.

I had a few minutes to kill before I had to leave so I thought about my lunch meeting. With all the things I asked, and the things she told me, I realized I hadn't asked the most important question: Where were you Thursday night? The more I thought about it, the more I thought there must have been a reason I didn't ask. I looked back through my notes.

There it was. August said she had been playing Thursday night so Spring must have been with her. I flipped back another page and saw Bernie had said he had been at the club on Thursday night because a band had been playing. There was no reason for him to be there if the band playing was his house band. Maybe he had been lying. No. He wouldn't do that. He knew I needed to know everything. Suddenly a light bulb flashed in my head. I ran back to my room and grabbed the piece of paper I had taken from The Cup.

Damn. There it was and I had missed it last night before bed. Airheads of State had played last Thursday and unless my dear August had joined their band, there was something she wasn't telling me. I would have to ask her about it. I'd wait though, until after we'd gone to Ja's house. Why ruin a perfectly nice dinner until the last possible moment?

Oh shit. Nice dinner. She had said she had made reservations someplace. Any place around here which needed reservations was bound to cost more than I had on me, which was precisely thirty-eight cents.

I grabbed my spare helmet from the closet (I keep one for just such an occasion as a date) and headed out, knowing I had to stop by the bank first. I hate using debit cards if I can avoid it and never actually carry one unless I know I'm going someplace I'll need it. The bank qualified.

I made it to August's place early, flush with cash. She must have heard me pull in because she was locking up before I could kill the engine. She looked great. Tonight, she was decked out for motorcycling: A nice cotton shirt tucked into a pair of faded Levi's. The jeans tapered and hid themselves in a pair of fashionable riding boots. As she walked towards me, she slipped on a fringed leather jacket, zipping it up halfway to show off breasts already in danger of introducing themselves.

I handed her the extra helmet, and she let me help her lock it on. Then she slid behind me, her leg lifting high to get over the back of the bike. Her arms came around my waist and pulled her close to me. I could feel the balance of the bike shift as she pulled her feet up and placed them on the back pegs.

"Ready," she said softly. I could barely hear her over the low grumbling of the engine.

I pulled out of her drive, heading to the bridge. As I crested the second bridge, the one under which Jasper Alweighz had been found, I leaned my head back and yelled, "Where to?"

She directed me south on Lincoln to Sepulveda and from there to Pacific Coast Highway. Redondo Beach was the last of the beach communities before you hit the Palos Verdes Peninsula. It was way the hell out of the way if you were working in Hollywood or even Venice. No wonder Jā had often crashed at August's place.

Jā's place was about three blocks from the beach. August pointed it out as we drove past and I parked a couple of buildings down. I certainly didn't want to have my bike seen in front of a dead guy's building. It wouldn't do my reputation any good. I got the key from August as we walked up the stairs to Jā's second-floor apartment.

The door was sealed with several pieces of yellow tape reading "Police - Do Not Cross." I reached between the bands and put the key into the lock. It clicked open.

"Should we be doing this?" she whispered in my ear.

"These things," I said, grabbing a piece of the tape, "never meant all that much to me."

We ducked into the apartment. I stepped into the middle of the living room, using the light from the door to guide my way. I stood still for a second, trying to let my eyes adjust to the darkness so I could see into the rest of the place. A moving shadow told me August had come in behind me.

"Eyes," she said softly.

Before I could ask her what she was talking about, the room flooded with light. I involuntarily squeezed my eyes shut against the seventy-five watt sun.

"I tried to warn you," August whispered.

"Why are you whispering?" I asked. My voice sounded abnormally loud in contrast.

"We're breaking in," she answered in her throaty voice. "Aren't we supposed to whisper so we don't draw attention?"

"As opposed to turning on the lights?" I could tell by her face she hadn't thought of that and she was very sorry. "Don't sweat it. Just act normal. It's the clipboard rule. If you carry a clipboard and act like you know where you're going, no one's gonna stop you. If we just get what we came for and leave, no one will bother us. Now, where's the script?"

August led me to a back bedroom. Jā had it set up like an office. A huge desk dominated one wall and rows of storyboards plotted out the film on a second wall. File cabinets and a closet took up any other space.

"No bed?" I asked.

"Two bedrooms. He slept in the other one."

August opened the top drawer of the desk and pulled out a thick pile of paper with a red cover held together with two metal brads. She handed it to me. Sure enough, Body Mechanics was written in big black letters across the front. Perfect. I looked around to see if I could find a crew list or anything which might be interesting. I flipped the power switch on the desk's computer and thumbed through some files while it booted up.

"I'll be right back," August said. "I have to go to the bathroom."

I grunted to let her know I heard and kept looking.

When I heard the first scream, I thought it was the computer, making a noise to let me know it had finished booting up. The second scream was louder and coming from the bathroom. It was also yelling my name.

I ran into the bathroom and immediately at least one question was answered. The reason Gina hadn't answered my call earlier was she was here, quite dead, with a gaping hole where her heart had once been.

My first thought was I'd seen worse. You don't spend significant amounts of time with people who are accused (and acquitted) of violent crimes without seeing things which make John Carpenter movies seem tame. My second thought, which immediately followed on the first, was to stop August from screaming.

She had been screaming for a solid thirty seconds and

if she thought talking loud would cause suspicion, it was nothing compared to blood curdling, high pitched wails. I grabbed her around the shoulders and turned her around. She didn't fight it. She turned into me, burying her head in my chest. Her screaming changed to quiet sobs punctuated by mournful "Oh my gods" and once a "How could someone do that?"

I led her out of the bathroom and back to the living room/kitchen area. I took a second to look around, since I hadn't really done it when I'd first come in, and decided the best place for her was the over-stuffed love seat. We maneuvered over and when I let go of her, she collapsed into the cushions. I knelt down in front of her.

"Are you okay?" I asked. I had to ask three times before her eyes focused enough to answer me with a slight nod. "Good. Do you want some water or something to drink?" Again, she nodded.

I patted her knees and went into the kitchen to find something to give her. I opened the freezer to see what Jā had on ice. I made the assumption she wanted something alcoholic as opposed to South Bay tap but Jā had nothing in the freezer except a couple of steaks and a box labeled "Kodak." The fridge wasn't much better. A couple of bottles of Budweiser wasn't going to cut it for what ailed August, but I kept it in mind in case I couldn't find anything else. I quickly opened the cabinets surrounding the fridge. Dishes, glasses, and dry foods galore. I grabbed a tumbler for when I found something. There was no way a guy who works as a bartender wouldn't have at least something hard to drink, especially since he had beer in the fridge.

Then I had a thought. My hunch was Jā didn't cook. I wouldn't if I worked at a pub which served food. I opened the door to the oven. Pay dirt. It was like a very expensive mini bar in a four-star hotel. I rummaged through until I found an open bottle of Captain Morgan, my remedy of choice for these kind of situations (and believe me, I've been in enough to have tried a variety of cures) and poured a healthy dose into the plastic glass.

All of this took no more than a minute, but by the time August was putting the cup to her lips, she had calmed down considerably. I had to give the girl credit. If nothing else, she was doing a great job of convincing me she hadn't killed Jā.

I set the bottle down next to her, making sure she knew where it was, and went into the bathroom to figure out what had happened.

There were two things I was sure of when I went back in to look at the body. The first was she was definitely dead. The second was it was definitely Gina. She was sitting on the can, fully clothed. Her legs were splayed open and her head rested to one side. If she'd only had a cigarette dangling from her flaccid lips, she would have been the perfect caricature of all the photos ever taken of strung-out rock stars.

Whoever had killed her had gone to great pains to make sure she was easily identifiable, though. It wasn't just the fact she was shot in the chest, at close range, leaving her face serenely intact. No, it was the fact they had rummaged her purse, which was sitting on the tiled floor next to her, and left her driver's license in the sink basin. The final touch was the thin stream of water running from the tap, cascading over the laminated ID.

I thought about shutting the water off but figured I should leave everything exactly the way I had found it. Without touching her, I examined the body.

She wasn't killed here, but that was easy to get. There was no blood on the wall behind her, or anywhere else in the bathroom for that matter. I got up close and inhaled deeply. No smell, at least no really bad smell, at least not yet. There was some kind of perfume lingering, but nothing which smelled like rotting person. She hadn't been dead long. That ruled out Bernie as a suspect. Or at least as a trigger man. I knew for a fact he was in Vegas. Unless he hired someone to do the job, he was clear of this one.

I mentally cleared Bernie completely. No sense keeping the job if I thought he did it, therefore he was innocent. Of course, this meant someone was going to a lot of trouble to frame him (point two in me declaring his innocence) and I, by sending Bernie to Vegas, had unwittingly helped them along. If he couldn't be found, he could be charged.

I figured if whoever killed her had rummaged her purse, I could probably get away with it as well. There was nothing unusual. Maybe she had a few too many fast food coupons, but who's counting? At the bottom of the bag was her key ring. Attached to the ring was a simple gold wedding band. I figured she used it when she was out by herself to avoid getting picked up. Lot of good it did her. I left it. Wedding rings leave a bad taste in my mouth. I took the keys, though. You never knew what might come in handy later on.

I left Gina and went back to see how August was doing. She had refilled her glass, at least once, and was breathing normally.

"Is she dead?"

"She's dead." I figured I didn't have much time left alone here. August's screaming was bound to have drawn some sort of attention and I wasn't sure how this neighborhood would react. If this was my neighborhood, people in the building could be beating each other with wooden canes and no one would call the cops, hell they would probably take odds on the outcome (when it happened a couple of months ago, I got ten bucks out of Guantanamo). In the beautiful, sleepy seaside community of Redondo Beach, people may actually decide they like their peace enforced with armed response. Who was I to judge their lifestyle?

"Dead?" August took a large swallow of her re-filled tumbler, draining about half of it. Until I had confirmed it, she was ready to believe the woman with the hole in her body was just playing a cruel Halloween prank. "This isn't good," she said.

I agreed and went back into Jā's office. The computer had finished booting and I stumbled around his desktop until I found a file labeled "Body Mechanics." I flipped on the printer, loaded it with a stack of three-hole-punch paper from an open ream and set the machine to print everything in the file. I could sort it all out later.

As soon as I saw the first sheet feed through, I went back into the bathroom. Gina was where I'd left her, her purse still looking rummaged. Not much I could do about it now, though. August had regained enough of her composure to stand and said she was going to see if some of the clothes she was missing were here.

"Don't touch too much," I cautioned. Then I set about looking for anything else I could find on the bookshelves.

Mostly, he had film books. Everything from history to theory to actual production guides. Biographies of filmmakers stood next to three copies of the Raiders of the Lost Ark script. Holding up one side as a bookend were back issues of American Cinematographer, Filmmaker, and the DGA Journal. This guy took his business very seriously. Good for him. I think I had four books on my shelves about writing, and two of those were Strunk & White's Elements of Style. I don't even own a dictionary.

There was almost no fiction in the place, unless it was a movie adaptation. Nothing the other way around. I saw no Crichton, Grisham or King. I began to think this guy was seriously obsessed. I went to a second, smaller shelf. This one covered a different subject, but with the same obsessive nature. It seemed the subject du shelf was gambling and Las Vegas.

Again, there were biographies, but of gaming legends and mobsters this time. Half a dozen books on blackjack crowded the space with pamphlets on how to win at craps, which was a completely random game. Fiction here (can you tell I look for the story?) was limited also. The only novel I recognized was Last Call by Tim Powers. It was an edition I didn't have, the hard cover, so I grabbed it. I figured it as my fee for walking in on a crime scene. That kind of thing I never do for free. Nicholas Pileggi's Casino was there as well, but I didn't think it counted as fiction. Nothing else seemed to jump out at me as possible clues, so I went to check on my printing.

I waited until the printer thought about printing something else, then decided not to. I took a look at the last page completed to see if it stopped at a reasonable place. It did, so I took out the stack it had generated, squared it up, and grabbed the copy of the script I had snagged earlier. I loosened the brads and put my new pages in between the last few script pages. If anyone looked, I just had a really fat script. And if they knew anything about Hollywood, they'd know it'd never get produced, but that's all they'd know.

And I did it just in time.

I had heard the sirens coming closer for a few minutes now, but, as is my wont, I blocked them, knowing there was nothing to be done. Now, though, the Doppler effect of them getting very shrill then fading away in the distance wasn't happening. They got shrill, but then they stayed there. August ran into the office holding a couple of shirts, a pair of lacy underwear, and a day-runner.

I was most interested in the panties. Not that the organizer didn't hold a fascination, but since I was new to the detective biz and well used to being a guy, it was the frilly unmentionables which did it for me. I would get around to the day-runner later.

"Are those sirens for us?"

"I'd say so." I was calm. Like I said, I'd been in these situations before. Besides, I was Skids Poppe, esteemed member of the third or fourth or whatever estate it was I was a member of. I had the credentials to prove I had a right, an obligation even, to my reading public to be there. I grabbed the phone to call 9-1-1 just to back up my case.

"Why? Who called them?" August was panicking.

"We did." I punched the last 1.

"When?"

"Right now." I held up my hand to quiet her down as the emergency operator answered. "I'd like to report a murder. Can you send someone right away?"

My timing couldn't have been better. A loud banging sounded on the door, followed by the sound of several large, heavily armored men trying to be quiet. I jerked my head to tell August to open the door for them.

"Never mind, they're here. Thanks." I hung up. The police stormed in, all talking at once. I ignored what they were saying and pointed to the bathroom. All but one of them ran past me to see. The one who stayed turned to look at what was going on but moved slightly to block the door. He didn't want us to leave. Fine with me. The only thing concerning me was if August could keep up with me. I was betting an awful lot on the hope she could follow my lead.

After a few minutes, they started filing back into the living room, one by one. As they came in, I checked to see if I knew any of them. Of the five with August and me, I didn't know a single one. I still had a chance with the guy left in the bathroom, but somehow, I doubted it.

The one in charge started organizing the crime scene. He delegated others to call it in, get a photographer out here, and generally destroy a night's sleep for the rest of the neighbors, no matter that they still had a while before their normal bedtime. These guys would be here until the wee hours, or, as August would put it, until it got early. Then he turned his attention to us.

"My name is Sergeant Etra and you may as well sit

down. You're going to be here a while."

We sat. It was interesting. After knowing each other all of twenty-four hours or so, we moved like a unit, sitting on the love seat together, close, but not touching. Our hands in our respective laps.

Then the questions started.

"Who are you and what's going on?" Simple question, really, but a lot depended on the answer. August's hand reached out, her fingers wrapping around my forearm. It was a show of support, a show of affection. It was perfect.

I told you, I'd been dealing with various law and security people for most of my life. This was nothing. August, on the other hand, was freaked. This was a girl who had probably never ditched school in her entire life and now she was about to be questioned, for the second time in three days, about a murder. Her second. I wondered if the folks back in Portland would hear about this little incident. To ease her discomfort, I answered for the two of us.

"I'm Skids Poppe," I said. I paused to give him time to recognize the name. "The young lady is August Everywhere. As to what's going on, we have no idea. We came in and found a dead woman in the bathroom and called 9-1-1."

"How'd you know she was dead?"

This guy was never going to make detective.

"You're never going to make detective if you couldn't tell at first glance she was dead. She has a hole in her chest you could drive a sidecar through." I was already getting bored. "Is there a detective already assigned to this case?"

He ignored my comments. "You know this is the apartment of Jasper Alweighz, whose murder is already under investigation? You are trespassing into a restricted crime scene."

"Oh," I feigned surprise, "is that what the yellow ribbon across the door meant."

"How did you get in?"

I covered August's hand with my own. I'm sure we looked like a rather cozy little couple. "Miss Everywhere is an old and dear friend of Mr. Alweighz, and since he is now dead, she felt he no longer had any need for her undergarments." She held up her panties right on cue. "She asked me to accompany her since the thought of tip-toeing through a dead man's apartment gave her the willies. As for how we got in, Miss Everywhere has a key. They were that close." I winked at the cop.

"And what are you in all this, Mr. Poppe? Yes, I know who you are, and I don't particularly like you, so just watch yourself."

"Me? You don't like me? Why-ever not?" I could be a real asshole when I wanted to be.

"Fuck you, Skids. I read the column about police brutality and you happened to nail a few of my friends."

"And your friendly attitude is to ensure I write about you the same way? Thanks. Next month's column is shaping up nicely. So, who is the dick...I mean detective, assigned to the Alweighz case? You gonna get him out here at some point or are you going to take credit for fucking this up all on your own?"

"Detective Collins is handling the case and I'm sure he'll want to talk to you as badly as you seem to want to talk to him. What are you doing here, Skids? What connection do you have with this thing?"

I grinned like a cat with feathers in his mouth. "She's my girlfriend." I looked at August. She smiled right back at me. I was gonna hear about this later.

"Girlfriend? So, what? You killed the ex to get the girl?"

Damn. Even he got the "ex" part down the first time. "Now, now, Sarge, you know I can't answer any questions like that without my attorney present. Anything else you want to know?"

"Be smart, Skids. Tell me what I want, and I won't have to arrest your ass."

"You won't arrest any part of me, and you know it. The most you could hold me on is trespassing and even that is flimsy. If you ask, I'm here researching a story about police screw-ups. How did you spell your last name?"

That was when he slapped me. It was almost too easy. "Fine," I said. "I'm done talking to you. I'll wait here for Detective Collins, thanks."

Etra turned his attention to August. "Don't let him bluff you. He's going downtown and you're gonna go with him if you don't answer my questions." She squeezed my arm tighter. I'd have to check later to see if her fingernails broke skin. When I looked, she was still wearing her rictus-like smile. "Why are you here?"

I felt obliged to answer for her. "Miss Everywhere reserves the right to answer questions only in the presence of an attorney." She nodded.

Etra was pissed. He knew he was stuck and there was nothing he could do about it. He went into the bathroom under the pretense of checking progress there.

I looked over at August. "Sounded pretty good, huh? I saw that last phrase on an old episode of Perry Mason." I was feeling full of myself.

"Skids, what are we going to do? We broke the law coming in here and the police already questioned me about Jā and now with Gina dead in there... it looks like I had something to do with it."

"Did you?"

"No!" She was shocked I'd even think to ask such a question.

"Good," I thought. Then I made a mental list of things needing to be done. First up, I'd have to call my attorneys, Skip and Scott. The law firm of Towne and Freigh had been representing me for years, ever since the incident with that TV newscaster. I still say I was innocent and merely exercising my right as a journalist, but that's now a sealed court record so there's really no need to bring it up here. Then I'd have to figure out a way to tell Bernie that Gina was dead. Wait a second...

"... How did you know her name was Gina?" I finished my thought as a question to August.

"She's an old friend of Jā's." Now it was my turn to act surprised. "He introduced me to her a couple of months ago... said she had just gotten in from some place back east and was now living out here. They knew each other through school or something."

"Did she ever come into The Cup?"

"Once, maybe twice. Why?"

"So you didn't know she was dating Bernie?"

"My boss Bernie?"

"That would be the one."

If we had been playing the surprise game, the one where you keep trying to top the other person with the most outrageous true statement you could muster, I would have jumped way ahead in the point standings. Even the Romanian judges would have given me points just for the look on her face, if nothing else.

"But... but..." August started. I put a finger to her lips to shh her before she sounded too much like a little kid doing a bad impression of a motorboat. She was losing it.

"I need you to stay calm, just for a little while longer. Do you think you can do that?"

She nodded, her lips moving up and down my finger. Under different circumstances, I would have gotten extremely turned on. As it was, I knew we had to wait until this Detective Collins showed up before anything could change.

It didn't take long, in police terms. August and I sat on the couch, chatting amiably about anything not related to Jā or the body in the bathroom for an hour or so. I carefully avoided drinking anything, knowing that if I had so much as a glass of water, about forty-five minutes later I'd be wanting to defile a crime scene investigation and also knowing they wouldn't let me. So I didn't drink, and we talked.

I learned she liked British comedy shows and the reason her folks were so adamant about a 'fall back' career was her dad's life-long job as a theatre manager. He'd seen too many performers fail, and wouldn't let it happen to his oldest child. On the other hand, she learned about my eclectic cinema tastes; that I would see any movie with John Cusack made her laugh.

She was amazed I liked ancient sculpture. I offered to take her to the Getty Museum and give her my own private tour (with a motorcycle, you don't even have to have a reservation). She almost left when she found out I not only had seen Styx in concert, twice, and was proud of it, but I had also worked as personal security for Tommy Shaw during his Damn Yankees phase. Actually, Guantanamo had been the one hired, but I went along for part of the tour. It was one of the cheapest ways I've ever found to get across the country.

Just as we were getting to the psychological analysis of my fascination with Lewis Carroll's Alice in Wonderland books, Detective Collins showed up. Hell of a guy, he was. He made Sergeant Etra look like the Good Housekeeping Neighbor of the Year award winner when it came to liking me and my writing. I had a feeling this was going to be a long night.

As it turned out, the night wasn't nearly as long as I thought it would be. Collins came in, said three words when he saw me sitting there on the couch ("Fucking Skids Poppe" to be precise) and then went to talk to Etra.

Evidently, as much to my surprise as anyone's, I was right. There really wasn't all that much they could hold us on. My story checked out, pretty much. They wanted to look through the few things we were taking out of the apartment, just to make sure we weren't trying to swipe anything which might become evidence later on. I looked for a pair of size 12 Bruno Magli shoes, but couldn't find any. August's panties and other articles of clothing got by unscathed. My script got a nice thumb through, but evidently not enough of one to notice the extra pages I had inserted. Or if they had, they didn't know what they were looking at, so eventually they let it go as well.

All told, we were there another 20 minutes. We each gave our addresses and phone numbers (mine was the magazine - it's good for Publisher Steve to get calls from the cops every now and again...keeps him honest) and then told not to leave town. I was pretty sure we had no intentions of doing that. I didn't know then I was wrong.

Leaving the apartment, I ran into Cricket. She was coming up the stairs, camera gear in hand. We passed each other near the top landing.

"Hi, Skids," she said, stopping. She readjusted her Minolta, as if settling in for a long conversation. "How are ya? Haven't seen you since Friday at the canals. Dead people holding a certain fascination for you, or are you just pining away for me?"

"Cricket...you were on my list to call." I was uncomfortable, sure, but I knew I could handle it. Until August slid her hand into mine, definitely marking her territory. The effect wasn't lost on Cricket, who suddenly remembered the dead girl in the bathroom.

"I have to get to work," she said. "Go ahead and call. If you get the machine, just leave a message. I'll get back to you."

She passed us and stopped just before entering the crime scene. "It was nice meeting you," she said to August. "Shame Skids is so bad at introductions, I would have loved to know your name."

She left before either August or I could say anything. I wasn't disappointed, but I knew August would have something to say about that later on as well. I could wait.

"So... what was that all about?" Evidently, I didn't have to wait long.

"An old friend?" It was worth a shot.

"Good try, but it ain't gonna cut it."

"A girl I went out with a few years ago. She took my picture once and we keep running into each other at crime scenes and police benefits."

"You? At a police benefit? The only benefit you could be to the police is if you stopped writing."

I don't know how it was intended, but I took it as a compliment. I smiled. "Thank you." We'd gotten to the bike and I put my script and her unmentionables into one of my saddlebags. "Can we still make dinner?" I asked.

"Don't think I'm letting you off this easy about the camera girl."

"What are you? My mother?"

"According to the police reports, I'm your girlfriend. I think that gives me the right to at least ask questions."

"Fair enough. Here." I handed her a helmet. "Put this on and let's see if our reservations are still good."

She looked at her watch. "It's almost eleven. No way we'll make it before they close."

"Then pick another place and you can buy me dinner." I put on my helmet.

We ended up at Edie's Diner in the Marina, which is one of those faux '50s places with bad Formica and red leatherette cushions. Dinner was typical blue plate special and the conversation ranged from high school art teachers (hers, not mine) to juvenile delinquency reports (mine, not hers).

The more we talked, the more I liked her. She laughed so easily it was hard not to. I found myself with a growing distaste for Jasper Alweighz. A couple hours after we had finished dinner and split a sundae, our waiter brought the bill and pointed out there was no one else in the place and if we were to leave now, they wouldn't make us help clean up.

When we left the restaurant, I still wasn't ready to go home. I asked August if she was.

"Not yet. Could we just go someplace and walk around? I just know I'm going to have nightmares if I go to bed before I'm ready. I'll lay there and try to force it and all I'll be able to see is her face. I need to get so exhausted I fall right to sleep."

"Are you always like this during traumas in your life?"

"I was like this for the two weeks before I moved out here. Drove my little sister nuts. We were sharing a room and I'd come in and crash so hard she'd think I was dead the next morning. I think she was glad when I finally left. She was able to get a good night's sleep."

So, we were off for a late-night walk. She told me I had to choose where we went though, because she chose last night. Since we were already close, I took her around the Marina to Fisherman's Village. All of the shops in the really tacky imitation of a New England wharf town were closed, but I wasn't there to shop.

I live by the ocean because I love the water. I feel at

home walking around boats; almost as much as being around a group of Harleys, but in a different way. I think boats and bikes both offer a unique sense of freedom you can't get anyplace else. That and I've been told by more than one psychic along the Venice Boardwalk that I lived a past life as an infamous marauder of the sea. I told you, I'm a pirate from way back.

There was a tall ship docked in the harbor, set up as a floating museum. I impressed August with my knowledge of the sail structure and the history of the boat before I came clean and told her I'd done an article on it for another magazine Publisher Steve runs. See, whenever he needs filler, Publisher Steve calls me in to do write-ups for any one of the six or seven rags he publishes, not just the biker stuff. I'm his best writer and he knows it. Sometimes it gives me a warm feeling inside. Mostly it just keeps me in beer and laundry detergent. Well…at least beer money.

As we started down to look at the rest of the boats, August slipped her hand into mine. We walked in silence for a bit. I wasn't sure who was supposed to start the conversation today. Last night, I knew it was me. I had an objective. Today? Who knew? It had been a long time since I'd been out on a date where I didn't know the outcome in advance. I was out of my element.

"You were great back there," August said.

That was when I came clean about the article research.

"No, that's not what I was talking about," she laughed. For some reason that laugh made me feel as sparkly as good champagne. "I mean back at the apartment. The way you talked to the police and made it seem like we did nothing wrong. You took care of it and let them know I wasn't involved. You took care of me." She stopped walking. Since she was holding my hand, I stopped along with her. "You were wonderful!" Then she kissed me.

It was hard and forceful at first, like she was trying to gain footing. As soon as she had it, she backed off. Her kisses became tender and tentative. Her tongue ran along my lips, probing my mouth. I kissed her back, my fingers tightening on hers. Her free hand snaked up around my neck and wound itself into my hair, not pulling me in, but not letting me pull back either. In the distance, I could hear a ship's bell ringing five chimes.

When the bell rang six, August decided it was time to go home. We had spent the last half hour standing against the rail, our hands exploring each other's bodies, never breaking contact.

Walking back to the bike, she nestled next to me, her head tilted onto my shoulder. She shivered as a breeze suddenly sprang up, chilled by the ocean's mist. My arm circled her waist, holding her, keeping her warm. Aside from the minor incident with the police, this had been the perfect night.

Back at her place, August got off the bike before I had a chance to kill the engine. She walked around to the front of the bike and handed me her helmet.

"You'd better go home," she said.

I stopped, not sure of my reaction. When she had said it was time to go home, I naturally assumed she had meant together. There would be some serious frustration tonight if I went back to my place alone. I think my confusion was obvious.

"If you come in," she explained, "I only have one bed, which means we'll both have to use it and if I'm lying next to you, there's a very good possibility we'd have sex."

"And the problem with this is... ?" I thought

"And I don't want to do that, not yet." There was hope. "If we make love, I want it to be right and special. I'm tired of just fucking. I did that for too long with Jā and I'd rather go without than do it for the wrong reasons. I mean, this is only our second date and in the mood I'm in, if you walked through my door, I'd sheath you senseless and then what kind of a girl would you think I am? You understand, right?"

I nodded, anticipating a long, hard night ahead.

"I knew you would, which is one of the reasons I can't. You act tough, Mr. Poppe, but deep down, you are a really good guy and something real is better than something real good, at least for the moment, right?"

I nodded again. I knew if I spoke, my voice would crack.

"You're the best." She leaned down and kissed me on the lips. A nice, sweet kiss. "Will you call me tomorrow?"

"Not later today?"

"Is the sun up yet? No. Therefore, it's still today. Call me tomorrow." She kissed me one more time then turned and bounced to her front door. I watched her unlock and open it. Just before she went in, she turned back to see me watching her. She smiled.

"I had a great time tonight, Skids. Even with the police." She shut the door.

So she hadn't forgotten about Gina. For my part, she

hadn't been out of my mind, either.

I crested the bridge over Linnie Canal and the question of where August had been playing Thursday night popped into my head. Dammit. I had to remember to let the detective work come first. Or at least second. I may be having fun, but Bernie was paying my tab. I had a job to do.

When I got home, my mental self-scolding was put on hold. August may not have forgotten about Gina in the bathroom, but she had forgotten about her clothes and Day Runner sitting next to the Body Mechanics script in my saddlebag. I left the underwear there and took the rest inside. I had research to do before I slept.

Guantanamo was sitting on the floor, watching some T&A film on cable.

"What's on?"

He shrugged. "Tits."

"Cool. I'm going to bed."

"Where's dead guy's girl?"

"I dropped her off at home."

"Date didn't go well?"

"Smashing, actually. After the police thing it could only go uphill."

"Do I want to know?"

"I don't think so."

"I think you're right."

I left the room. In all that time, he never looked away from the screen.

In bed, I faced the moral dilemma of the evening. To read or not to read, that was the question. The Day Runner sat, taunting me. I knew eventually I would look, see what was written down for last week. The only question was how long it would take.

"She was playing a kids birthday party last Thursday night," I said to myself.

Evidently, it didn't take me all that long. The entry said she was doing a kid's party with someone named Leo the Loon and there was a phone number. I could confirm it anytime. I guess, technically, she hadn't lied. She said she was playing, and she was. She just wasn't singing for Bridesmaid's Protocol. I could forgive that.

As long as the planner was already open, I thumbed through it. The Loon seemed to be a relatively steady source of income over the last few months. Afternoon gigs, mostly.

She wasn't anal about entering every meeting, though. It seemed it was just paying gigs and important things. I couldn't tell you if she saw any movies in the last four months. Although about three weeks ago, she did pick Jā up from the airport. This was written in big bold letters. Underneath it was an address for him while he was away. The address was in Las Vegas.

Monday

Monday Morning/Afternoon

"Well whadd'ya know," I thought. "The alarm on that clock really does wake you up in the morning."

This was the first time I'd ever had to use the alarm, although I'm sure that was the original purpose in my receiving it. The clock had been a gift from Publisher Steve after I'd missed yet another staff meeting. I think he was trying to tell me something. All it really told me was if I kept missing meetings, I'd get free parting gifts.

But when the alarm finally did sound, I knew it was time to give the day a running start. Or at least a brisk walk down the beach to The Cow for a morning coffee-tutional. Eight a.m. was too early to be running anywhere. Some people passed me on the beach who didn't believe me, but I just can't be responsible for the world, you know. At least not anymore.

Sitting outside on the green-tiled bench, letting the

mocha work its magic, I thumbed my enhanced copy of Body Mechanics. After re-organizing the pages so my stolen production notes were all lumped together at the end, I worked my way through the story. It was a nice little action drama, which, if cast correctly, could probably be quite good.

I had the major twist figured out about two thirds of the way in, but I write about and watch a lot of movies. I had a feeling the average viewer wouldn't catch on until the end.

As I was reading, I thought about what I knew of filmmaking, which was mostly based on articles in Filmmaker or Empire or various websites. According to them, this would be a good script for a low budget film. Not a lot of characters, (I counted only four major roles) mostly daytime exteriors (which saves money on lighting equipment) and the few inside shots could be done in someone's living room. The only other expenses I could see were some small explosions and a bullet hit or two. All in all, if everyone worked for free, you could probably get away with not spending too much money.

Of course, not too much money is a relative term. "Not too much money" for a film could buy you a nice house in Los Angeles and a mansion in my sister's neighborhood.

And while the script itself was a good read, it was nothing compared to the rest of my pages. I had breakdowns of where all the locations were and what kind of deals were struck to use them. Cast lists with home numbers and addresses were there, along with shooting schedules and scene breakdowns. I was fascinated. This was my first look at how movies were actually made and I felt like a kid at Disneyland.

This didn't spoil the magic for me at all. In fact, it was like watching Penn & Teller explain a magic trick. The explanation made it all the more impressive. If I was correct, according to this schedule, they were actually shooting not far from where I was today. I could go home, make a few calls, and hit the set around lunch time.

Then I hit the most fascinating thing of all, and the particular paperwork which made the whole trip last night worth it: The budget.

Flipping through it page by page, I could see exactly where Jā was spending his money. When I got to page fourteen, about two hundred and twenty-eight thousand dollars had been spent, with the remaining twenty-two grand set aside for overages and incidentals. There it was, all of Bernie's money laid out nice and neat. And then I turned the page and the budget started over. This version took four more pages and cost Jā another five hundred thousand.

I knew Bernie was going to have to buy me another mocha before I started comparing them.

It seemed the second budget was the more realistic for the project, but when I looked at them both side by side, there was money being spent for things which weren't in the script. I didn't recall any locations outside of LA, yet Jā had budgeted in a location scouting trip with plane fare and hotel accommodations. Picture car rental in a film where the main character is afraid of driving also seemed a bit extreme. I could forgive the cost of catering for the crew, I know an army travels on its stomach and a film crew doubly so, but the price per head seemed rather high. I wasn't very good at math in my head (I usually left that for Guantanamo…it was amazing how much figuring he had to do to blow something up completely) but without my sidekick or a calculator, I guessed Jā was padding his budget by a cool two and a half bucks. About the total of what Bernie had given him.

I looked through the rest of the stuff to see if there was a list of investors. There wasn't. I guess that would have been too easy, huh? I looked at the cast list again. Following it was a crew list. I went through each name and checked it off with what I knew from years of reading the credits.

Cast wise, I recognized all four major characters from the script, plus a couple of minor characters. The crew list started with Jā as director and went on for two pages listing grips and electricians and camera people. Marty was listed under production accountant, and the number listed was the same office number I had for him. Most of the others should be on the set when I got there. At the very bottom of the list was Bernie's name, with The Cup's address, listed as Producer.

As far as I could tell, there was nothing unusual about any of this. There were no hidden meanings or subliminal messages. I guess I was gonna have to really work for my money.

By the time I got back home, Guantanamo was awake, if not up, and it was now a reasonable hour to make phone calls.

"You got a call," he told me from his berth on the couch.

"Who was it?"

"How the hell should I know? I didn't answer the phone."

"Then how do you know it was for me?"

"Who's gonna call me?"

He had a point. I don't think anyone knew he was here. And odds are, anyone that knew probably wouldn't be calling. I highly doubt he'd given sand girl this number.

"How long ago did the phone ring?"

"Twenty minutes. It woke me up."

"I feel so bad, truly. Of course, now that you're up, you can go to work. Oh wait, that's right, you don't have a job." It was an old routine. Anyone listening in would have thought I was mad. I wasn't. I went into the bedroom to see if I could get the answer machine to give up its message.

Guantanamo yelled after me. "It's a full-time job just being your sidekick. And the dental sucks."

"I bought you a toothbrush, so just shut up," I yelled back.

After a couple of tries, my machine told me Marty had returned my call. Well, now was as good a time as any to call him back. I walked back into the living room to grab the cordless phone so I could pace while I talked. It was a bad habit, but hey, it worked for me.

I flipped the "talk" button and waited for the phone to find a channel and give me a dial tone. I didn't get one. I hit the "channel" button to see if it would help. Nothing. I looked at Guantanamo. "The phone's not working again. I can't get a dial tone."

"Mr. Poppe?" The voice came from the receiver.

"Who's asking?" I said cautiously into the phone.

"This is Detective Collins, LAPD. I'd like a few more words with you."

Well, that explained why I couldn't get a dial tone. "What can I do for you, Detective? I thought we had this all cleared up last night?"

"We did, Mr. Poppe. And I was hoping I wouldn't have to see you again, but then I went to Miss Acton's house. You remember Miss Acton, right? She's the woman you found dead last night. Well, when I went to her apartment, I checked her answering machine and, stop me when this starts to sound familiar, I heard your voice telling her to give you a call. Something about being the guy trying to, let's see here, 'save Bernie's ass.' You wanna tell me about it now or should I send a car to bring you to my place?"

I was fucked, and I don't mean that in a good way. But I learned early on in my career (and feel free to fill in the blanks as far as which career I'm talking about) that the easiest way to deal with anyone, is to be straightforward and try not to lie. You don't always have to tell the whole truth, but if you lie, you will get caught. General rule of my thumb and you can have it free of charge. "What do you want to know, Detective?"

I think I stumped him. I'm sure he was expecting me to hem and haw (which I've never been very clear on how to do to begin with) and here I was ready to answer him, willingly. If there's one thing I know how to do, it's keep people off guard.

"Let's start with Bernard Hamilton."

"Who?"

"Bernard Hamilton? Your friend who owns 'The Cup of Fools?'"

"Is that his last name? I always wondered."

"Do you know where he is?"

"Nope." It was an honest answer.

"You understand he is wanted for questioning in an ongoing murder investigation?"

I nodded, realized he couldn't see me, and said "Yes."

"And if you interfere, you could be charged with obstruction of justice at the very least?"

"And at the very most?"

"Accessory to murder, harboring a fugitive." He didn't wait for me to continue. "When was the last time you saw him?"

"Saturday. He bought me breakfast."

"You haven't seen him since?"

"Sorry."

"So what about the message? Why were you calling Miss Acton?"

"Bernie told me someone was stealing from the bar. Now, I'm sure you've read my columns and you know I've done a bit of strong-arm work in the past, so he asked me to look into it for him. I told him I would. That's what breakfast was about. He figured if it was me, no one would get suspicious."

"He must trust you."

"Everyone trusts me. I'm Skids Poppe."

He laughed, slightly. I was getting to him. "Alright, Mr. Poppe. Like I told you last night, don't leave town for a little while, please. You're not under investigation…yet, but I want to be able to get hold of you if I need to, okay?"

"You got it, Detective. And you can call me Skids."

"Thank you, Mr. Poppe. I'll be in touch." He hung up.

I clicked off the phone.

"Police?" Guantanamo asked.

"Yup."

"About the dead guy?"

"Yup."

"You sure we're not going to South America?"

"I think so. I'll let you know after lunch."

"Where we going for lunch?"

"I'm going to a movie set. Don't know where you're going."

"Sure, desert me in my hour of need." If there was any less sarcasm in his voice, I might have believed him. Naw.

"Then I'm gonna take off now," he continued. "I think I'll head up the coast and have lunch in Ventura. There's this waitress up there in a little place in the marina…mmm." I just couldn't keep track of his women. "If I'm not home by ten, I won't be home till morning."

"Have fun," I said, as he walked out the door. Then I sat down to call Marty back.

His secretary answered the phone. It was her voice I

had heard yesterday on the answer machine. I asked for Marty. When I told her who I was, I was put right through.

"Marty Haifisch here, Mr. Poppe. What can I do for you?"

He was very formal. I made a snap decision then and there this would never work on the phone. "Hello, Mr. Haifisch. Do you have a few minutes today when we could get together? Your cousin Bernie asked me to look into some things for him and he said you could help me out. Whaddya say?"

"Can I meet you for lunch?" he asked.

"Where and when?"

"One o'clock looks open. I'm in Santa Monica, so anything in the area is fine with me. Do you know the Crocodile Cafe?"

I did. It was a nice little place on Santa Monica Boulevard. They had an oven roaster which put a nice, woody flavor on everything they ran through it. I'd done a restaurant review on them about six months ago for Publisher Steve's food magazine.

I agreed to meet Marty there but asked if we could push it back to two so I could have a little bit of time on the set, which I still wanted to hit today. That and I always like to set the time when I meet someone. I know, it's a childish power ploy, but you gotta look at the source.

Marty said, "Fine, two it is. If I'm late, wait at the bar. I'll know you, don't worry. Bernie speaks very highly of you and I've seen the infamous 'haircut' pictures."

"Great," I said, not really meaning it. "I'll see you there."

I hung up, mortified Bernie had shown those pictures. He and I were going to have to have a little talk. If you don't know about them, good. I doubt you ever will.

I looked at the backwards clock hanging on the wall, decided it was too early to try and read it straight and looked in the mirror across the room. Ten after ten. I could make it to the Body Mechanics location by ten thirty if I hurried. Ten forty-five if I took a shower. I opted for the shower.

While going to The Cow doesn't require cleanliness (they know me there), meeting people for the first time requires a little bit of deodorant and shiny hair. There is absolutely nothing worse than living up to the "biker" image when you need something from someone else, and while I wasn't about to look like a corporate American middle-manager, I still felt I shouldn't smell really bad. Besides, if things went well, I might be able to hook up with August later. Just the thought of her lips on mine made me re-adjust the water I was running for the shower to make it a little colder.

By ten thirty-five I was squeaky clean and strapping a helmet over my wet head. As I walked out the door, I grabbed a bandanna, knowing if my hair dried with the helmet on, I would have a really bad hair day. The bandanna was just a pre-emptive strike.

The last two things I needed were an extra helmet (for August, just in case) and my Body Mechanics script. I already had my notebook stuffed into my back pocket. Now, I was prepared. I locked the door behind me and headed off to visit my first film set.

Today, they were filming at a park up on Rose. I remembered the scene they were shooting: It had the main characters involved in a pick-up basketball game. The scene came about half-way through the film and was a metaphor for the action which surrounded it. According to the schedule, they had blocked off three-quarters of the day to shoot the three-page scene. After that, they were headed to a house to do some of the interiors. I figured I would still be able to catch them at the park.

I was right.

There is one thing about a film crew; no matter how big or small, they take up all available parking. Down in Venice, where I live, people are filming all the time. Every season, I walk by some crew shooting a new show in the Baywatch vein; you know, hot girls in bikinis solving crimes. Happens eight or nine times a year. And then there's the news remotes and the foreign TV shows and the UCLA student films (USC students shoot in Malibu). All told, it's a sad week in Venice when I don't see a film crew and the one constant is they always take up way too many parking spots.

Today was no exception. I knew where the crew was by the three huge trucks lined up single file, electrical cords dangling between them like elephants holding each other's tails. There was a bustle of activity in one of the trucks. When I peeked in, I saw two guys opening blue metal boxes, frantically looking for something. While I watched, two more people came in, one a girl. The girl was the first one to speak. When she did, it was not a happy sound.

"Have you found the lens yet?" She asked.

One of the original duo answered her.

"Not yet. I know it's here because I packed it up myself, but I can't find it."

"Well you better find it. I don't have all day to get this fucking shot off. I know we lost a director, but that doesn't mean I'm losing a goddamn day of filming. Do you understand me?"

She turned and stormed past me, yelling into a walkie-talkie about making sure they were ready to shoot as soon as the camera was in place. I figured she was the first A.D.

I read a book once which explained all the jobs on a film set. I figured it would help me to better understand what everyone did so when I didn't like something in a film, I could have someone to blame it on. And, let's face it, I loved this business. I read a lot of "making of" books and I'd always wondered what it was a gaffer did anyway. This book had explained a first A.D. (assistant director) was the person responsible for making everything on the set ran smoothly. They got to be the asshole so the director could be brilliant. The girl now walking away from me had that air about her. I figured if anyone knew what was happening on the set, it would be her. I turned and ran after her.

When I caught up to her, she was in the middle of yelling at a costumer to get the sweat stains right. I interrupted.

"Excuse me?"

"Who the hell are you and what do you want?" I'll

tell ya, there is nothing like having that kind of fury unleashed in your face. And people wonder why I got divorced.

"Skids Poppe," I answered her.

That stopped her for a second. It wasn't that the anger dissipated or anything dramatic like that, it was just she stopped yelling for a second. It took her that long to formulate her next question.

"Skids Poppe, the journalist?"

"That's me," I smiled. I hoped it would be enough to have her smile back, invite me to meet the cast and crew and maybe take me home for Thanksgiving. But then, fame can only go so far.

"Who gave you permission to be here? This is a closed set. No press allowed. Now if you'll excuse me..." If she said anything else, I didn't hear it from behind her back as she walked away again.

I stood there, stunned. Now I had a few options. I could run after her again and try to explain the situation. Somehow, as I looked in the direction she had gone and saw her standing in front of a group of obviously cowering people, I didn't think this was my wisest course of action. Next, I could go talk to the guys in the truck and see what was up with them. Then again, they didn't seem all that bright. Besides, they were working. I figured my best bet was, at least to start with, people who weren't working. At least that made the most sense logically.

I scanned the crowd for anyone who didn't seem to be involved in a greater purpose. Found one.

He was sitting alone in one of those folding canvas-backed chairs reading a magazine. All around him people were active, moving like excited electrons around a nucleus. He was calm and still. I approached cautiously.

My dad, Pop Poppe, used to say to me, "If you can keep your head while all about you others are losing theirs…you probably don't know the extent of the problem." I let this be my shield as I waded through the crowd. Odds are this guy didn't have a clue. The closer I got, the more details I could make out. The magazine he was reading was The Hollywood Reporter and he had a couple of pieces of tissue paper tucked into his collar, protecting it from the make-up on his neck.

I made a mental note to call Pop and add an addendum to his saying: "If you can keep your head while all about you others are losing theirs…you probably don't know the extent of the problem…or you're an actor." As soon as I realized this, I walked more confidently. If anyone here was going to talk to me, it would be him.

I approached from the front, not wanting to scare him.

"Hi," I said, putting out my hand slowly, giving him time to get used to me being there. "I'm Skids Poppe."

He was cautious, I'd give him that. But he took my hand anyway. I must be someone important if I had the balls to come up and introduce myself just like that.

"Wallis Michaels," He said.

"How are ya?"

"I'm good." He was gaining confidence, getting more sure of his surroundings.

I'd worked with actors before. Doing interviews

for Publisher Steve to fill the gaps in my movie-review column had taught me a lot. Hell, all celebrities are the same, really. They just wanted to know you weren't going to hurt them and then, as soon as they were comfortable, they'd open up and you couldn't get them to stop. And the lower down the ranks they were, the easier it was to put them at ease and get them to tell you things they wouldn't tell their own mothers. This guy was going to be fun.

"So, Wallis, you're playing, who? Chris?" I took a guess. There were two male leads, Chris and Steve. Chris was the better of the two roles. Even if I was wrong, it would be an ego stroke for this guy.

"That's right," he said. "You've read the script?"

"I have. Chris is certainly the better role. Congratulations." He nodded. On him, it looked more like a mini bow. "How's filming going?" I asked.

"Well, we had a bit of a setback last week, but now we're back on track. I think it's some of the best work I've done."

I acted surprised. "What kind of setback?" I reached into my back pocket and pulled out my notebook. This might be good.

"Our director disappeared."

"He disappeared?" I scribbled something down. Nothing about what this guy was telling me.

"Are you a reporter?"

"Not really. I do entertainment features for…" I stumbled for a second. "For Hollywood Insider. You know, 'Getting the Outsider In'?" It was the first thing I could make up.

Wallis nodded sagely. "I've seen you on the newsstand, but I've never picked up a copy. Maybe I should."

I gave him a "don't worry 'bout it" wave.

"I'll send you a copy." I said, eliminating all fears he'd upset me. Then I thought I should tell Publisher Steve about it. It probably wasn't a bad idea for a real magazine.

"I'm supposed to be here doing an article on stars of low budget films, which I can see I have the perfect subject for," I said, and his eyes lit up. "But, you know, maybe I can swing a second article about disappearing directors? What do you say? What else can you tell me?"

He thought about it for a second. Maybe less. "I probably shouldn't say anything…but he and the D.P. were arguing pretty heavily the last few days he was here."

"D.P.?" I asked. I knew the answer, but people always like to think they're teaching you something. It puts them at ease.

"Director of Photography. He's the guy who does all the lighting and figures out which lenses should go on the camera. Between him and the director, they figure out how to get the best shot."

"And they were fighting? I would think that's fairly common if you have two creative people trying to do their best."

"It is, but not like this. I've been on a dozen sets and sure, you always get Director/D.P. arguments. Like, if the Director wants a long shot and the D.P. thinks it would work better as a medium two. Or the lights aren't set and the Director has us actors rehearsed and ready to go. Arguments over that kind of stuff. But an argument isn't a fight. With Jā, he and Ian were at it like cats and dogs. At one point they started brawling so bad we thought they were gonna break something other than each other."

"What was the fight about?"

"Who knows? I know it had something to do with funding. I didn't want to get involved but what I overheard had something to do with money promised and not delivered. Jā told Ian he was lucky he still had a job and then Ian mentioned something about some girl not being able to fuck her way out of this mess. Then the fists flew. And Ian's a big guy. Jā put up a good fight, but when it was over, he had taken a huge pounding." Wallis had gotten out of his chair and was acting out the fight for me. "When Jā got up, his face was already starting to puff up. He screamed he wanted him off the set, that he was fired."

"What happened?"

"We were close to the end of the day anyway, so Kristen, she's the AD," he paused, "Assistant Director?" I nodded. "She called it for the day and both Jā and Ian stormed off."

"When was this?" I was scribbling notes like mad in my little book.

"He didn't show up on the set on Thursday so it must have been a day or two before that. Yeah, it was probably Tuesday."

"Tuesday? So, what happened Wednesday?"

"Nothing. When I got to the set the crew was setting things up and Jā and Ian were laughing like old friends. But it didn't look right."

"What do you mean?"

"I mean you can't fool an actor. Someone had a talk with at least one of them Tuesday night. These guys were never close, and now, after one brawl, they were best friends? Nope. That's too 'Simpson/Bruckheimer' for real life."

I wasn't even going to ask about that last one. But there was one question nagging at me.

"And who was the girl?"

"No idea. I didn't catch her name."

I was going to ask him more, but someone came over, obviously sent by Kristen, She-Wolf of the A.D., to fetch him to the set. He said we could talk more after he shot the scene, but I knew I was gonna have to split fairly soon so I just got his number and told him I'd be in touch.

This was getting rather interesting.

I walked over to where the bulk of activity was happening. I assumed it was the set. As soon as I saw the camera, I knew I was right. It was a nice camera, with Panavision written across the side in big letters. I'd never seen one up close, so I went to take a look.

As I got closer, I could feel more and more people looking at me. By the time I was close enough to touch the rig, one of the guys I'd seen earlier in the truck was standing next to me, offering his help.

I introduced myself and repeated my line about being with Hollywood Insider. At least he had the honesty to tell me he'd never heard of it.

"But then again," he said, "I really don't follow the business all that much. You know, it's just a job. Personally, I'd rather be driving a race car."

I agreed with him. I find in my line of work, whatever my line of work happens to be at the moment, that agreeing with people is one sure way to get them to trust you. If they think you understand them, you must be an okay guy. "I feel the same way about writing for this magazine. I'd rather be racing my bike. But you have to go where the money is. Sad truth of life."

He was warming to me. "Certainly is. You ever do any work on race magazines?"

"Once." I smiled at him like it was the best moment of my life. "I interviewed Angelle Sampey once."

"The drag racer?" He was impressed.

"The very same."

"You're that Skids Poppe?"

"I didn't know there was more than one of me."

"I read that article. A friend sent it over. It was great. You really understand what motorcycles are all about."

"I try." Now was the time to ask about things. "So, what happened here last week? I heard there was some problem between your director and some of the crew?"

He looked at me conspiratorially. "Not all the crew. Just a few guys, mostly crew heads. I'm an electrician and my boss, the gaffer had no problems with Jā, but Ian the D.P. did. And since, officially, I'm part of his department I figured it was best company policy to stick with him. After all, I've worked with the big guy before and if he keeps hiring me, I'm gonna side with him regardless. We all did. You know what I mean?"

I did and I told him so. I pressed further.

"What really happened?"

"Really?"

I nodded.

"I guess what it comes down to first and foremost is the check bounced."

"So, he didn't get his money?"

"No, it's not that at all. Ian was brought in by one of the producers when Jā's first D.P. fell through. I don't know what their deal is and it's not my business to know it. I just know Ian does good work, even if he is a bit of a handful. I'm not saying nothing here, and you better not repeat any of this, but Ian does need a bit of handholding sometimes. I mean it's not unusual for him and directors to not get along, you know? From what I've heard, he'll be up half the night working out a shot sequence, real insomniac, and then the next morning, the director would change it all around on him. But like I've said, I've worked with the guy before and the images he captures on film make all the angst bullshit worth putting up with… at least I think they would if I was a director, which I'm not and I really don't want to be, but you know what I'm saying, right?"

I nodded again.

"So yeah, it wasn't his paycheck that bounced. It was the check to one of the suppliers. I don't know which one. But if you don't have supplies, you can't make a film. So anyways, that was the start of it. It went from there to Ian complaining about some girlfriend of his, or some ex-girlfriend, whatever. Eventually, they went to blows. I'm sure if we were a big-budget film and it was Johnny Depp and Gore Verbinski, The Hollywood Reporter would have splashed it on the front page and TMZ would have done a featurette on the whole incident. Since we're not, we get you, no offense, and we all got sent home early. I got to take my girlfriend out for dinner and the next day someone had smoothed everything over."

"And that was it? No one knows what else it was all about? No details?"

"Yeah. I guess it would be better for your story to have more details. Maybe you should talk to Ian."

"Maybe I should." I looked at my watch. It was getting late. I was going to have to meet Marty for lunch soon. I doubted I would have time to talk to the cinematographer before then. Damn. I quickly looked over my notes to see if there was anything else I could ask this guy before I split. I found it. "Do you know which producer hired Ian?" I figured this would be a gimmee since Bernie was the only producer I knew of on this film. And if he hired Ian, I could at least get a handle on the big guy from another angle.

"I only know one producer of this film, although someone said there were a few. Some guy named Dave."

"You don't happen to have number for him, do you?"

"All I got is a fax number where we were all supposed to fax in our rate sheets and signed deal memos. Will that help?"

"Couldn't hurt."

I wrote the number down in my notebook, thanked him and left so he could go back to work.

As I walked back to my bike, I thought about this guy

Dave. I'd have to fax him something and check it out.

I got back to my bike and spun around to head down to Lincoln and then into the heart of Santa Monica. I looked over at the set as I passed, and wouldn't you know it but Kristen the A.D. was conferring with Ian the D.P. and pointing at Skids, the owner of the H-D.

I wasn't close enough to read the expression on their faces, but I'd be willing to bet my next date with August they weren't smiling. Oh well. I mean, you make enemies in this biz just as often as you make friends. Although with the way my averages were going, I was due for another friend about now. At least I felt that way. I'm sure whoever was tallying things up would have given me extra credit for August.

I smiled at the thought and popped my bike into third, letting the clutch hang just a little, enough to bring the front wheel off the ground when the gears finally did engage. Stupid shows of speed were really beneath my status as a journalist. Still, it felt good.

Rose Avenue is the border between Venice and Santa Monica. At Lincoln, it adds Mar Vista to the mix. You can tell. There are definitely three classes of people living in the three different cities bordered here, even if Santa Monica was the only real city. The other two were just municipalities of the greater Los Angeles area. Didn't matter. On the beach side of Rose/Lincoln, some very nice people lived in some very shitty low-income housing generally referred to as "The Hood." I'm not saying it's a bad place, just that I wouldn't walk through there at night if I didn't look the way I did.

Yet right across the street, you have the template for suburban America. Mar Vista is homes and yards and kids with dogs named Sparky and Rex. And none of that touches the great Santa Monica. The revival of Main Street was good, but the homes up near this intersection (and the golf course just up the road) have never been out of style, or in my price range. It always amazed me how much difference one street could make.

That was the street I turned off of as I headed into the Oz of the West side.

Several miles of increasing real estate prices passed before I crossed over the 10 freeway. This was really the entrance, the point of no return. Main Street Santa Monica was on the Venice side, so we could forgive it, but once you crossed the interstate, you had to be ready for anything. At least I did. Back before the haircut incident I would get hassled as a biker and an unwanted element. Now, it was just my personality I had to watch out for.

I turned left on Santa Monica Boulevard and drove toward the water. The Crocodile Cafe was on the corner of Ocean, the last street before you hit the cliffs overlooking the Pacific.

Past the Santa Monica Library is the only redeeming feature of the city: The Third Street Promenade. Third Street was renovated right around the same time as the canals and Main Street. I guess when the city council gets a bug about something, they really go for it.

I wasn't going to complain. Since the renovation, they've opened seventeen new movie screens in three theatres. Nothing beats THX sound and then stepping out for some good Italian two doors away. Between that and The Spilled Ink Bookstore, which recently moved off the Promenade and around the corner, I've wasted many an hour on the three-block-long open-air mall. Okay, I also dig the topiary dinosaurs. And since the street has been closed off to car traffic with barricades just the right size to slip an 883 through, it makes for a great little escape route (not that I would need anything like that in my current line of work, mind you, but it's nice to know it's there).

Anyway, I found a spot right near the front door of the Crocodile Cafe between either a Lexus or an Infiniti and an Infiniti or Lexus. I can't tell the difference anymore. All I know is they both had out-of-state plates and my bike would be safe.

Leaving my helmet dangling on the handlebar like a fishing lure, I went inside.

The girl at the small front counter wanted to know if she could seat me and if I'd be dining alone. I told her no on both counts and looked around for a Jewish accountant.

The Crocodile Cafe is nice in that there is an outdoor patio to enjoy the summer breezes and bikini-clad women, a bar for after-dinner or before-lunch drinks and a main dining area which smells of wood-fired pizza. A nice selection of seating plans.

At the bar, a guy with glasses, dark wavy hair (thick where it wasn't receding) and a slightly larger than average nose seemed to fit the bill. I walked up to him. He was wearing a suit which looked like it had been slept in, more than once. Not the best look for a financial consultant, but he was a relative of Bernie's so who was I to judge?

"Marty? Hi, I'm Skids Poppe." I put out my hand, trying to be friendly.

He looked at me, confused. "My name's not Marty, Mr. Poppe."

Now it was my turn to be confused. "It's not?"

"'Fraid not. My name is Walter Johansson, Mr. Poppe, and as long as you're here and your friend Marty isn't, I'm assuming you're supposed to be meeting him here for the first time, am I correct in that, of course I am, anyway as long as he's not here yet do you mind if I take a few minutes of your time? It'll certainly make the wait go faster. I was just about to leave but you stopping me like this may prove beneficial to both of us and I think after a few minutes, you'll agree with me. You see Skids, it is Skids, right? Do you mind if I call you Skids? Good. Now Skids, that's a rather odd name isn't it, unique, like you. You're a unique individual and I can sense that."

"As opposed to a unique member of a pack," I said. Well, I would have said it if I could have gotten a word in edgewise. I looked around, hoping the real Marty would show up soon. No one seemed like a likely suspect. I glanced at the clock above the bar and saw that I had six minutes before Marty would be officially late. I hoped he was an early to punctual kind of guy.

Meanwhile, Walter Johansson continued talking at me.

"I guess what I'm really getting at Skids, is protection. Do you feel you have enough?"

At last it was my turn to say something. I motioned for Walter to come lean in. Now, like I've said in the past, I'm not a big guy, nor particularly violent and when I have Guantanamo around, I look positively tiny, but that doesn't mean I can't be imposing when I want to be. Right now, I wanted to be.

"Walter. Can I call you Walter?"

"Of course you can Skids. We're friends, right?"

"No, Walter. We're not. Look at me, do I look like the kind of guy who needs protection?" I lowered my voice. "Walter, I'm going to buy myself a drink and see if I can flirt with the hostess, if she hasn't been scared off by the fact I was talking to you. You are going to continue your original plan of leaving here and not talking to me anymore. Okay?"

He looked up at me and opened his mouth.

I put a hand up and stopped him before he got out more than a syllable. "Uh. Not a word to me. None."

Walter looked at me, knew I was serious, and walked away without saying another word. As soon as he was gone, you could feel the atmosphere lighten up. I ordered a Red Seal Ale as I stepped up to the bar. The bartender set the mug down in front of me.

"How much?" I asked, reaching into my pocket.

"That one's on the house. Anyone who can get rid of Walter Johansson gets his first drink on the house. Your next one's on me, as a personal thank you."

I lifted my glass to him and took a drought.

"Skids Poppe."

The voice was assured and confident. I turned around

and found myself facing an impeccably dressed man in his mid-thirties. Looking at him, I knew that what Walter had been wearing was a cheap suit because what this guy was wearing wasn't.

"I'm Marty Haifisch, Mr. Poppe. Shall we get a table?"

"Tell me about Body Mechanics." I started the questions once we'd ordered.

"It's a script for a low budget film which Bernie invested in. It was being directed by a bartender who works for him."

"An ex-bartender you mean?"

"Of course. That was an unfortunate incident."

"Unfortunate? The guy's dead and they think Bernie did it."

"Absurd. There's no way he could have done it. It's just not in his nature."

Were we talking about the same Bernie? It had certainly been in his nature in the past. I didn't think Bernie did it, but that didn't mean I thought he was incapable of it. "You don't think so?"

"I don't. In fact, I've been trying to get in touch with him so I could tell him the same thing. I have a lawyer standing by to take his case as soon as he turns up. You don't happen to know where he is, do you?"

I thought about it. Bernie trusted this guy but look where trust got him. Me, I trust no one but Guantanamo and I've successfully avoided any major indictments. As Pop Poppe has said Just because you're paranoid doesn't mean they ain't out to get you. My dad is quite the philosopher.

"Not a clue. He asked me to do some investigating for him. He said he'd call me every so often to see how I was doing."

"And why would he do that?"

"Obviously, if I don't know where he is then he'd have to call me, wouldn't he?"

Marty was getting bored. I could see why people trusted him with their money. He was no-nonsense, no-humor, and probably played golf. "I meant why would he ask you to check into things?"

"I'm an investigative journalist."

"No, you're not. You write a fairly amusing column and every now and again some witty celebrity profiles and bland movie reviews. Somehow I don't see you breaking a story which would take down a President."

"I write those articles under the name Woodward. I get more respect that way."

A smile. Hah, a crack in the façade. I knew I could get him to open up and warm to me. I was ready to plunge ahead.

He beat me to it.

"No, really. Why did Bernie ask you to investigate?"

"Honestly, I have no clue. For some reason he trusts me and thinks I can find out something the police can't."

"Like what?"

"Like who the real killer is."

"And who might that be? Do you have any…what do they call them in the movies? Leads?"

"A few."

"And what makes you think the police will believe you when you discover the real killer?"

"Don't you think Bernie is innocent?"

"I certainly do. But I also think he should have professional representation. I think trusting his future to someone like you is a big mistake."

"You do?" I was flabbergasted. Who the hell was this guy to lump Skids Poppe into the 'someone like you' category? Now I was determined to get to the bottom of this just so I could tell this waste of air to fuck off. Forgive me, I get angry when I get lumped into a group my worst enemy (or my ex-wife) would put me into.

"Yes, I do. I assumed you wanted to meet with me to verify Bernie's alibi and yet you haven't even asked me about it."

"Asked you about what?"

"Where Bernie was on Thursday night when this murder allegedly took place. Instead you open your line of questioning wanting to know about the film."

"'Allegedly?' It did take place on Thursday night. Or damn early Friday morning depending on your semantics."

"Granted. But you still haven't verified Bernie was with me on Thursday night."

"Was Bernie with you on Thursday night?" This was news to me.

"He was. Does this satisfy your curiosity?"

It didn't, but before I could tell him that, our food arrived. I grabbed a slice of my BBQ chicken pizza and stuffed it into my mouth. At least keeping my mouth full of food would give me a chance to think without looking awkward. Marty poked around his Caesar salad (with lightly grilled chicken breast, diced, not sliced and tossed - this guy had more specifications than Clinton had girlfriends) and looked out over the ocean.

It's amazing how dry your mouth can get when you're eating pizza (not to mention trying to get information out of someone who doesn't want to give it to you). A slurp of beer and my mouth was significantly moist enough to begin talking again.

"What were you two doing Thursday night? Where?"

Marty kept his eyes focused on the end of the Santa Monica Pier. "Still asking questions? Fine. We were going over his finances. He'd told me about the missing hundred and fifty-eight thousand and wanted to know what to do about it."

"What did you tell him?"

"I told him he was stuck. The account was in both names and Jā had every right to take it out. If he wanted it back, he'd have to ask Jā."

"You told him to get it back from a guy who later on shows up dead? Don't you feel the slightest bit guilty?"

"About what?"

"You're the one who set the deal up originally, aren't you? Didn't you recommend that Jā have access to the account?"

"It made sense from a business standpoint. If Bernie had to sign every check, okay every transaction, nothing would ever get done."

"But if Jā didn't have access, none of this would have happened."

"You can't guarantee that. In fact, I told Bernie Thursday night it was the best thing for him."

"Losing $158K is best?"

"It is from a business standpoint. The loss would offset his earnings for the fiscal year. Especially since we set up the film company as a division of the club. Losing the money was probably the best way to save his investment."

"But the film is still being made."

"Artists will always fight to keep a project alive, won't they? It'll end as soon as they run out of money."

"Unless they find another producer to pick up the slack."

He looked at me, hard. Again, that's one of those things which unless it's happened to you, you don't know what I mean. It wasn't just intense. It was like he was trying to figure me out from the inside. Finally, he spoke. The entire thought process took maybe a second and a half.

"Where would they find another producer?"

"How the hell should I know?" He didn't know about the other producers? This Alweighz guy was pulling a hell of a scam. But it wasn't my responsibility to inform Bernie's accountant about anything I found out, was it?

I continued, "People usually don't tell people like me anything they wouldn't tell you, right? Maybe you should ask someone on the set?"

"I just might do that."

A thought struck. "Are you hoping the film won't get

made?"

He stammered. "Why would I want that?"

"Just wondering. I mean, you weren't all that shook up when the money vanished." I searched my memory. "You said it was the only way to come out on top or something like that. It just seems like as far as you're concerned it was okay that Jā had disappeared with the money."

"I wanted the film to get made, don't get me wrong, but from a business standpoint it would be good to show a loss."

"Was Jā an acceptable risk?"

"What?"

"You interviewed him, right? Met with him to advise Bernie? You must have thought this guy was okay. At least okay enough to give him control of a quarter million. All I'm asking is, was he a good risk?"

Marty Haifisch threw his napkin down on his plate and signaled for the check. The waiter rushed right over.

"Listen, Skids. I really don't know why Bernie has asked you to look into things. If he had asked me, I would have advised against it. You're sure you don't know where he is?" I shook my head even though I knew it was a rhetorical question. "In fact, as his representative, I'm going to ask you to stop looking into this matter. I'm sure you and your line of questioning could not only not help, but might, in fact, hurt his case."

"Can't do it. Sorry."

"Why not?"

"I need the money."

"Money? He's paying you? I handle all his finances. How much did he offer you? I'll write you a check right now." He actually reached into his pocket for his checkbook. He had it out on the table, pen poised over the amount box before I said a word.

"$158,000. And that's Poppe, with three Ps." I smiled.

He looked up and didn't smile back. The waiter set the check down, looked at Haifisch, and told him they didn't take checks. Marty nodded and handed him a credit card. He took it and left. Marty now focused on me again.

"Seriously, Skids. How much?"

"Seriously. I can't quit. He paid me in cash and besides, I've already had cards printed up." I handed him one.

He looked at it and set it on the table, face down. The waiter came back with the credit card receipt. Marty signed it. Then he took his yellow copy and the bottom off the original bill - you know the perforated part you keep for tax reasons - and stuffed them both in his pocket.

"Skids. This is the last time I'm going to ask. If not for me, then for Bernie, stay out of this. You could get him in a lot of trouble."

"More trouble than he's in now? I don't think so. But if I do decide to chuck in the detective towel, you'll be the first to know."

Marty got up to leave. I stayed where I was.

"Thanks for lunch," I yelled after him, then finished my pizza, alone.

Monday Evening

I sat in the park and wrote down some notes from my meeting with Marty Haifisch. Not a lot of notes, really, but hell, that's what I was being paid for so I figured I should do my job, right?

Of course, those of you who know me are wondering what I was doing sitting in a park. I'll tell you. I was waiting for Ian the D.P. to finish what he'd called a "set-up." Yeah, something about the film was nagging at me and I knew if I didn't find out what, I'd never be able to get to sleep. So, after lunch I descended back into the world of Venice/Mar Vista and low-budget filmmaking.

As soon as I got there, I was greeted like an old friend. It seems word of my last visit had spread in the 90 minutes or so I'd been gone. By the time I'd made my way over to where Ian was sitting, he was waiting for me.

"So," he said, letting it hang in the air as if he were

expecting me to grab it from him. He had a British accent, but I couldn't tell you if it was from London or Liverpool or one of those places with way too many vowels. Someone once told me English accents where so specific that if you could tell them apart at all, you could pinpoint, to the neighborhood, where the speaker was from. I bet Bram the copy-shop guy could have told me where Ian was from. When I didn't respond, he continued. "You're Skids Poppe?"

"I am," I said, feeling like a Neil Diamond song.

"And I suppose you want to talk to me about, what was it? Disappearing directors on low budget films? For The Hollywood Insider?"

I nodded, feeling slightly uncomfortable. Not because the guy was calling my bluff about my cover story. That happens more often then I care to remember. No, I was nervous because I was standing and he was sitting and we were eye-to-eye. Now I knew why the grip had called him 'The Big Guy.'

"Okay," he said. "I'll talk to you. But I have to finish a set-up first so we can get a shot off. Wait here and I'll be back as soon as I can."

He got out of the chair and I knew it was delighted. He walked away without giving me another glance.

So here I was, sitting in a chair in a park waiting for a guy. After I'd finished writing down what I remembered, I played myself a best-of-five series in tic tac toe and narrowly avoided an upset. Then I was bored. I looked over towards the set and saw Ian - let's face it, he was hard to miss - yelling at some kid. They were standing next to a big, shiny, silver board and it looked like Ian was trying to show the kid how to position it so the sun would reflect onto the actors. The kid just wasn't getting it. Eventually, Ian positioned it himself, called someone else over to stand guard and sent the kid away. I watched him talk to a few more people, who then went scurrying on their assigned tasks.

A minute later, he was back talking to me.

"I don't have a lot of time, so what do you want to know?"

I stood up and offered him the chair. I wanted to be on level ground when we started. Thankfully he accepted, and the chair's arms parted like the Red Sea to give him room to sit.

"What happened?"

"Jasper Alweighz disappeared, then turned up dead. I would have thought you'd know that."

"I do. I want to know what you think happened? I mean, I'm reasonably certain first-time directors who get their big break don't usually walk off their set then go swimming face down in reclaimed swamp water. But then that's just a hunch."

"First off, this isn't anybody's 'big break.' It's a piddly little half-million-dollar film and most of the crew are working for a fraction of their normal rate."

"Not even the director or writer? I get the idea it's not Avatar, but it's got to have something if you and everyone else are working for nothing?"

"I liked the script," he softened. "Yeah, I suppose for Jasper, he considered it his big break."

"Then why would he walk away from it?"

He thought about it. "I don't know."

He was lying but I wasn't going to say that to his face. "What about the fight you two had?"

"What fight?"

"C'mon, Ian. Work with me here. I know you two had a fight a couple days before he walked off. Rumor has it you were even fired. Yet here you are, back at work."

"Yeah, he fired me. But it was stupid. We talked about it later that night and everything got worked out."

"You mean the bills got paid?"

"Who've you been talking to?"

"I had lunch with one of the producers. Dave. He told me."

"No, you didn't. He wouldn't have mentioned the bills to a reporter." The way he said it made "reporter" sound like a bad thing. "And he's not in town at the moment. So how did you hear about things not getting paid?"

"Does it matter? I heard about it, that's all. Is that what the fight was about?"

"Part of it."

"And the other part had to do with the girl?"

"Oh, they mentioned Spring to you as well, huh? Listen, mate, I don't know where you're getting your information or what you're really after, but I don't think we need to speak any further. Get off my set."

"I thought the set belonged to the director?"

"I am the director. Now go."

By the time I got home, it was past 5 o'clock. I didn't see Guantanamo's bike parked out back so I figured he was still up in Ventura or wherever he was going today. I was slightly disappointed. Guantanamo and I have been best friends for years and sometimes it's just nice to have him around to bounce ideas off. He's helped me through a couple of patches of writer's block and now, I could have used his unique viewpoint on all this new information. Oh well, I was on my own.

I grabbed a beer out of the fridge and sat on the couch. Then I got up again to throw some music into the CD changer. For good, thought-provoking music I chose my new Driftwood Messiah, an early Elvis Costello and the Misplaced Childhood which had just returned to my collection. I hit "random," then went back to the couch. Popping the top off the beer, I flipped the cap into the kitchen, hoping I'd gotten somewhat close to the garbage can, and then sat looking through my notes.

Five songs later, I was reading along with the lyrics, hoping they'd give me a clue. Nothing. My mind was mush. Finally, sometime around 6:00 or 6:30, I gave in and closed the notebook. As soon as I put it away, I opened it up again and found Spring's number. She answered on the second ring.

"Spring? Skids Poppe here."

"What?" She didn't need to add the "do you want" to get her point across.

"How's Jack?"

"He's fine. Can I do something for you?"

"Where were you last Thursday night?"

"I don't think it's any of your business."

"Aw, c'mon. I got money riding on it. A ten spot. I say you were with Jā and my sidekick thinks you were with Ian.

It's worth five bucks to you to say Jā."

Silence on the other end of the phone. I waited until just after that point where it gets uncomfortable and they think you've forgotten how to talk. "Damn. He was right. You were with Ian."

"Fuck you, Skids. Don't ever call here again."

I hung up quietly, just to counterbalance the way she'd slammed the phone down. Well, that really didn't answer anything, did it? Okay, so it let me know she knew Ian, which I'd gotten from him, and that she didn't deny being with either one on Thursday night. Shit. This was getting complicated.

Outside, the sun was just beginning to go down. One more thing and then I could hop on my bike and cruise along the coast, figure some things out.

I opened my computer and typed out a little note to producer Dave. I said I was looking for work as a runner on a film set, was new to LA and Ian had given me his number. I signed it Mark Phillips, a name I use when Skids Poppe isn't appropriate, and emailed it off. The number I left as a contact was at the magazine. It was answered by the girls with a simple hello and they had a list of all the names all of Publisher Steve's writers used when researching stories. They knew about Mark Phillips and would let me know if there were any calls.

After it was sent, I remembered Ian had said Dave was out of town. Oh well. Maybe he was calling in for messages or his secretary would forward it. Not that I was really expecting a call, but you never know.

Now I was good to go. I grabbed my thoughts, a cold

beer, and my helmet and was just about out the door when my phone rang. Was Producer Dave returning my fax ever so promptly? A police psychologist once accused me of being the biggest optimist she'd ever seen. Come to think of it, that was after I'd expressed an interest in sleeping with her. And in retrospect, my optimism at that point had been well founded.

I dropped the helmet to the floor and put the beer in my pocket before getting to the phone. I got it just before the machine would have, presuming it was working.

"Yeah."

"Skids, it's August."

This was even better than Producer Dave calling. "Hi. What's up?"

"Nothing except it's getting close to seven and you haven't let me know what our dinner plans are."

"We have dinner plans?"

"Don't we?"

I paused.

She didn't let it get anywhere near the uncomfortable point. "We either do or we don't and you'd better make up your mind soon because I'm hungry and you've --"

"How could I have forgotten. Of course we have dinner plans."

"I thought so. When are you picking me up?"

"I was just about to walk out the door."

"I'll be ready. Bring my helmet."

"Already on the bike."

Now it was her turn to take a pause. "Really?" she asked timidly.

"Really."

"You were thinking of me today. Don't tell me where we're going, it'll be a surprise. I'll see you in a few minutes." She hung up much nicer than Spring did.

Back out the door I went, putting the beer down when I picked up my helmet. No need to bring my own refreshments if I was taking the fine Ms. Everywhere out for dinner.

I thought about what she said as I locked up and flipped on the porch light. I had been thinking of her all day. I mean I really had put the extra helmet, her helmet, on the bike in case I got the chance to hook up with her. Then why didn't I think to call her and ask her for dinner?

Because I was unsure, that's why.

My bike roared to life under me.

What was I unsure about? Thursday night. No matter how I looked at it, everything came down to four nights ago. I still didn't know where she was or if she had been telling me the whole truth. And the more people I met, the more complex the whole thing got. That was why I was going for a ride, to sort things out in my head and figure out where to go next.

Except I wasn't.

I sped down Pacific and turned up Venice. I could have gone all the way around to Washington but somehow, I felt like breaking the law. That, and it was quicker.

No matter what, I still had blood rushing to all the right places whenever I thought of her.

I turned right on Dell, past the "Do Not Enter - One Way" signs, and hugged the right side of the road as I crested the first hill. No cars that I could see, so I proceeded with caution up and over the next, turning left onto August's street.

I was expecting her to be waiting outside by the time I pulled up. I would have bet on it. Thankfully, there wasn't a bookie between my house and hers because I would have lost. I pulled into the driveway, not worrying about the Ferrari since it wasn't home, and parked the bike.

I thought about honking but two things stopped me. First, Ma Poppe always told me you should knock on the door and treat the girl with respect. Honking was for your friends. I agreed, but that wasn't why I didn't honk. Not really. No, I stayed silent because there is nothing more pathetic in the world than the honk of a motorcycle. The reason the Harley Davidson motorcycle has such a glorious roar coming out of the tail pipe is to make up for the high-pitched squeal coming from the horn. When I first started riding, I honked at a guy in traffic who'd cut me off. He laughed and told me to let go of the rat's balls. I kicked in his tail lights and haven't used my horn since.

I got off the bike and walked up to the door. But I'd like my mom to think it's because she raised me right. She gets such few pleasures in life.

I knocked.

"Skids, if that's you, come in. If it's anyone else, I'll be right there."

This was a girl who had never lived in the rough part of a big city. Without checking my ID, I knew I was Skids, so I went in. She was nowhere to be seen, but the phone cord disappeared behind her Chinese curtain. In a second, I heard her voice.

"No, Dad, I'm fine. You don't have to come down. Everything is okay, really."

She came out from behind the partition, phone wedged between her chin and shoulder. She was holding a shirt up over her front. She looked at me, her eyes asking for my opinion on the top. It was a shiny, silvery thing, too small for her chest. I nodded my approval. She indicated she'd be right back, then raised her eyes while pointing to the phone. I understood.

I flipped through her CD collection while I listened to her tell her dad, again, she was fine and not to worry. She had a nice collection, stocked with all the albums one really should have; Blonde on Blonde, Sgt. Pepper's and a numbered copy of The White Album, Synchronicity, Born to Run, Armed Forces, an Otis Redding compilation and Gabriel's So. Then some more off-beat bands came up: The Pixies, Mike Oldfield, Pulp. I forgave her the Duran Duran and Rick Springfield discs, chalking them up to youth. Obviously, she went through a punk phase. Transformer and Never Mind the Bollocks were stacked next to London Calling. The number of '70s and '80s compilation discs was a bit scary but it is the cheapest way to get the hits. Personally, I prefer getting the whole record because they almost never play the best song on the radio.

I was looking through the track listings of Graceland, reminding myself I had to replace the copy the ex-wife took, when I heard August say good-bye and set the phone down. It clicked and August let out a long breath.

"Everything okay?" I asked.

"Just fine. I'll be ready in a minute. Mom called just

after I hung up with you, so I didn't have a chance to finish getting ready. I didn't know what to wear since I don't know where we're going. I've changed clothes three times since Mom put Dad on the phone. Is this okay?"

She came out from behind the barricade. I was speechless. She had put the silvery top on and had changed pants. She now had on a pair of leather trousers, form-fitted, and cowboy boots. Where this woman shopped...

"Well? Will I fit in wherever we're going?"

I nodded. "Oh yeah."

"So where are we going?"

"I haven't the faintest idea."

She laughed like I was lying. I followed her out the door and stood aside as she locked up. As we got to the bike, she turned to me, suddenly remembering something. "Did I leave my organizer with you? I couldn't find when I got back."

I did my best to act like I wasn't expecting the question. "Oh damn!"

"What?"

I unlocked the extra - sorry, her - helmet and handed it to her. "You did. I took it out of the saddlebag because I didn't want to leave it out overnight and I forgot it back at my place."

She was momentarily stymied before she found a silver lining. At least I hoped that was what the look on her face meant because the next thing she did was put her arms around me, kiss me on the cheek and explain it was as good an excuse as any to end up back at my place at the end of the night.

"I thought you wanted to wait?"

"Doesn't mean we can't go back to your place at the end of the night, does it?"

I couldn't think of a witty answer so I shrugged and got on the bike. I backed it out of the drive and started her up before I told August to get on. I know, you must be thinking me rather rude for not letting the lady get on first, but I have to say if you've ever let the passenger get on the bike first, and then done it again a second time, you're a better man than me. Personally, I think it's just as gallant to start the bike and get it ready for the girl first. And if you ever meet my mom, tell her you agree.

I pulled out and re-ran the same route I'd used getting there. The sun was still in the sky, but barely. I still wanted to see the sunset over the water and I hoped August wouldn't mind.

"Where're we headed?" August yelled when we stopped at the light on Pico.

"Next left. Up P.C.H. for a bit. I want to watch the sunset." The light changed and I gunned it. August squeezed tighter and a few seconds later there was nothing between us and the ocean but sand.

A few seconds after that and there were houses between us. I was going to have to get closer to Malibu if I wanted a nice, clean view of the horizon. Traffic was heavy, but then, that was one of the advantages of driving a motorcycle: lane-splitting. Sure, it's not the easiest thing to do on a fully kitted out Fat Boy, but on my Sportster, I knew my limitations and it'd been years since I'd scraped leather or tarnished a stud. For August, though, this was a new experience. She just held on tighter, always a plus in my book, as we zipped past cars and made our way to the front of every red light.

As we passed Sunset, I checked the crowd situation at Gladstone's-4-Fish. That's what the sign says, I swear. It wasn't crowded, but then, I didn't expect it to be at 7:30 on a Monday night. I made a mental note, just in case we didn't find any place further north to eat.

I stopped the bike about a mile later, pulling off the road to join a long line of cars parked in the dirt on the ocean side of the road. On the other side of the cars, their owners were standing around, preparing for their nightly ritual: Each guy in a wet suit, unzipped and folded all the way down to the waist. The ocean becomes the great equalizer and no matter what they did during the day, as soon as their surfboards hit the waves, all was forgiven. Go rent Point Break if you want to get the full picture.

Personally, I never understood the fascination. I mean, riding a Harley through LA traffic is enough to get my blood pumping. I don't need to worry about sharks or whales or oil slicks or whatever. Nope, for me, the ocean was purely for looking. I didn't even like swimming all that much.

While she wasn't used to driving through traffic, August was fast becoming an expert at getting off the bike. She was on the ground, helmet in hand and heading for the sand by the time I had the kickstand down and my own helmet hanging from the handlebar.

"C'mon, you're gonna miss it."

I wasn't. But I was touched by her enthusiasm. I pocketed my keys and followed her down to the beach.

I finally caught up with her, sliding my hand into hers.

"You know," she said. "If you'd told me we were going to the beach I probably wouldn't have worn these boots. Completely impractical." She stopped and looked at my feet. "Although not nearly so impractical as yours. What are those? Combat boots? When's your birthday? I'm gonna get you a pair of shoes you can wear for walking on the sand."

I looked at my feet. Guantanamo had gotten these for me before he'd been asked to leave the service. They'd served me well.

"My birthday? I can think of plenty of other things you could get me for my birthday other than shoes."

She turned her back to the water and kissed me on the lips. Then moved closer to my ear. "Oh yeah? Like what?"

"Watch the sunset."

She nibbled my earlobe. "I've seen it before. This, however, is new."

I stared out over the water, running my hands over her back. She whispered in my ear, just loud enough to be heard over the surf. "You go ahead and watch the sun go down. I'll still be here when you're done."

I did. She was.

It was close to 10 when we left Gladstone's and headed back down the coast. I hadn't done a lot of thinking about the case, but I did have a topic for my column; The Multi-Purpose Biker Boot. August was great. I was falling for her big-time. And just in case you're wondering, the only people having "sex on the beach" were those in the bar.

We had gone to the seafood place not long after it got dark. See, in California, there is no such thing as twilight.

It's sunny, then it's night. And the difference between the two takes all of about 10 minutes. In the film industry, that's called the magic hour. Don't ask me why. The people who named it are probably the same guys still out there surfing.

The meal was nice and I was glad for the company, but the ride back towards the city brought back all my questions about Bernie and what I was going to do about getting him off the hook. August had mentioned, off-handedly, my conversation with Spring. Sunday's conversation, that is.

She said Spring thought I was competent and that Jack seemed to like me. For August, that was a good thing. She thought Jack was a good judge of character. I didn't have the guts to ask what Jack had thought of Jā.

As soon as we got off the highway, August reminded me about her organizer. Like I could forget. I nodded and headed home. I turned left and went the wrong way down the one-way alley which ran behind my place, pulling into my usual spot next to the dumpster. I didn't see Guantanamo's bike, so my guess was things were going rather well for him in Ventura and I wouldn't see him until sometime the next day.

I caught up with August, who had jumped off the bike and was busy examining my building.

"You live... here?"

Now, I know my place isn't as nice as a place on the canals, but it is home. And I told her as much.

"I didn't mean anything bad, I swear." I could see in her eyes she meant it. "It's just I would have expected you to live someplace else. I don't know, someplace more... criminal. I've read a lot of your columns and stories and I've listened to you talk for the last few days and I just would have thought you lived more in the hood. I'm kind of glad you don't, though."

"Thank you... I think."

We walked through the little corridor between my building and the one next to it. The automatic light came on and showed us the stairs leading up to my floor. I motioned for her to go up first and followed right behind her. When we got to the second floor landing the motion sensor light downstairs went out and I fumbled with my keys in the darkness.

I was prepared for this, though. See, I keep all my keys organized and different ones on different key rings. My bike keys, for instance, are on the keychain with the Harley logo (a thank you gift for a nice review of their clothing line). My house keys, along with the keys for the office and my post-office box, were on the chain with the Hogs and Hooters emblazoned bottle opener (a Christmas giveaway for subscribers one year). So it was that key chain I had in my hand in the dark.

To make things even easier, I knew if I were to hold the whole thing by the tag and let the keys dangle, my house key was the one on the right end. It was a system I devised to help me get into the house after a night of drinking too much. So far, it's worked. Tonight was no different.

I explained all this to August while I fit the key in to the lock. "See, works every time."

She slapped her hands together in a poor imitation of a golf clap. "Very good, Mr. Poppe. I just have one question?"

I turned the key, feeling the door unlock. "Yes, Ms. Everywhere, what is your question?" I pushed the door open.

"Why don't you just leave the outside light on?"

The door was pulled out of my hands by someone on the inside and at last I knew what was wrong; I had left the outside light on.

August screamed as I was pulled inside. A second later, she was inside as well and the door was slammed shut behind us. I had just enough time to see her get thrown to the sofa before the first solid punch connected with my face.

"Shut up and stay down," said a voice, not the one attached to my attacker. It wasn't a voice I recognized.

I tried to get to her, but as soon as she was down on the couch, her dancing partner decided he wanted to do a double with my guy.

"You know," one of them said. "I would have thought you'd be tougher, Skids. Judging from your stories and all." He was using his fists like punctuation marks.

I sucked in a lungful of air. "I'm much more a strategist," I gasped. "Like McArthur." A rock with the weight of Gibraltar behind it connected with my stomach.

"Funny. You should be more like Napoleon and know when to retreat. Asking the wrong people the wrong questions could get you hurt."

"Thank God," Oof "this is only hypothetical."

Now the thing about fighting is knowing where you are at all times. I'm told the same is true for trapeze artists, but I wouldn't know. All I do know is that in order to win a fight, any fight, you have to know three things: what your strengths are, what you can use to help you and (this is the most important part) be willing to fight dirty.

Poppe Culture

I guess a close fourth is knowing how to take a hit. In this case, I took the hits as well as possible, trying to roll with them until I could strike back. His next blow hit my face. I staggered back, my hands scouting the landscape for a safe landing. I didn't find one. I hit the cabinet hard and CDs exploded all around me.

Then, I found something better. A few years ago, for my birthday, Guantanamo gave me a heavy plaster figurine as a birthday present. My left hand grasped the statuette. It did me no good there. I'm right-handed.

Thankfully, I'd landed on my stomach so a quick push to the side and a twist and I was on my back, a weapon now firmly held in my right hand. I groaned, to let my attacker know I was injured. Remember kids, information is power. If he thought I was down and I wasn't, I had information he didn't and therefore the ball was in my court.

I waited until he was standing over me, looking down. I guess in the dark room, he couldn't tell if I was really hurt or just faking it. I groaned once more for effect. This gave him pause. He kicked me once in the side, just to be sure I was out. I wasn't expecting this, and it hurt, but it also positioned his leg for me. I knew exactly where he was. So as soon as he sucked in a big breath (always a sign they think the fight is over) I attacked.

My right arm swung upwards, aiming for his groin but settling for anywhere in the upper thigh region. Luck was with me. I hit the upper thigh but in such a way as to guide me home to the balls. The chunk of plaster I'd hit him with weighed in at a good eight pounds and since I had the floor to push off against, I'd say I hit him fairly hard. I didn't think he'd argue. Especially not right then.

He screamed, grabbed his crotch and backed away all in a single move that would have made Michael Jackson proud. Now there's a myth which is propagated all the time in movies and on TV that when you get hit in the sack, very hard, you immediately begin talking in a higher register and continue fighting. Not true. Really what happens is you double over in pain and, if the hit was hard enough, vomit. In this instance, Guantanamo was going to have to rent a carpet cleaner very soon.

As he backed away, I stood up. Bad guy number two rushed over to help but by then I was ready. I know my apartment better than anyone else and I could hear him tromping through the magazine jungle trying to reach me and help his partner. As soon as he stepped within reach, I swung, connecting with his head.

There is nothing quite like the sound of bone breaking. Invariably, when you hear it coming from somewhere inside yourself, especially during a fight, it's a demoralizing thing. On the other hand, the feel of bone breaking, especially when you are the person causing it (point of view is everything), is a reason for celebration.

In my case, it was a reason to keep hitting. Because, unlike getting hit in the 'nads, having your cheek crushed by a man swinging an 8-pound plaster object is not necessarily enough to stop you. Slow you down, sure. I took advantage of the slow-down and hit him again. This time, I angled my attack a little further back, connecting just above the ear. And I hit him hard. I was able to cock my arm and bring it all the way around for a full-velocity effect. It worked.

When the guy woke up (and I seriously doubted it would be before the sun) he would have a major headache, probably a concussion.

Attacker number one was still trying to decorate the middle of my floor. By this point it was dry heaves, so he wasn't having much luck. I staggered over to him and gave him a quick slug to the back of the head. He was out before he was horizontal.

Now it was my turn to inhale sharply. As long as there was no one in my bedroom, this fight was definitely over. I stepped over a body and found the light switch.

"Lights," I called out, trying to be polite. Then everything was bright.

August was on the couch, shaking. The apartment was a mess, although if you'd been there this afternoon you wouldn't have really been able to see much difference. The thing was, I knew what was in which pile and now the piles were scattered randomly.

"What's that?" A small voice from the couch asked. I looked down at my hand, my weapon now splattered in blood.

"The Maltese Falcon."

August was into her second rum and coke when I collapsed on the couch next to her. I was nursing my first, finding it difficult to open my lips to let the alcohol in. Although the more I got in, the easier it became.

August spoke first. "Who are they?"

"How should I know? It's not like I have a calendar with mugger rotation schedules on it."

"You think they were muggers?"

"No, I think they were sent here to beat the crap out of me, which they did. They weren't supposed to get themselves taken out in the process, so demerit points are inevitable."

"What did they want?

"Presumably, my fine china and seventeen years' worth of Sports Illustrated Swimsuit Editions."

"Really."

"I don't know, really. They could have been after anything. It's not like I'm everybody's best friend." But even I didn't have enemies who would break into my house and attack me. At least I didn't think I did. Then again, I'd never investigated a murder before.

"Do you think it has something to do with Jā?"

"The thought had crossed my mind." Just.

"What do we do now?"

"Well," I said, heaving myself off the couch. "Let's roll 'em for ID and change."

I winced in pain as I brought the two unconscious bodies together on the floor and laid them out nice and neat. Then I started looking through their pockets. No identification, but a grand total of one hundred thirty-eight dollars made its way from their balance-sheet to mine. I left the sixty-seven cents in nickels, dimes and pennies on the floor. I don't keep anything below a quarter. There was also an indeterminate Ford car key. I know there are guys out there who can tell you what model or year or color or anything like that based solely on the key, but I ain't one of them.

I was just about to get back to it when the phone rang. I answered quickly; for some reason I was hoping it was

Guantanamo. I could always count on my sidekick to help this kind of stuff make sense.

"Guantanamo? That you?"

"I'm afraid not, Mr. Poppe. I'm sincerely glad my employees have left your hands free to answer the phone. Will you please put one of them on?"

"Which one? The sleeping one or the unconscious one?"

There was a long pause. "I see," was all he said. I didn't hear him hang-up, but he must have because a minute later a recorded voice was telling me if I'd like to make a call to please hang-up and try again. It was then I realized we'd lost a minute of time.

"C'mon. We gotta go. These guys' older brothers are coming and they ain't happy."

I ran into the bedroom and before I could forget it again, I tossed August's organizer into my "bug out" duffel bag and then grabbed a roll of scotch tape. "Do you mind if I crash at your place tonight?" I asked.

"Do you always keep a bag packed?"

"Always. Never needed it before. Besides, it gives me the time to do this." I knelt down next to the bodies.

"Do what?"

I grabbed eight pennies from the stack on the floor and taped two to each eye of my sleeping attackers.

"What's that for?"

"Inflation."

I grabbed her and pulled her out the door. I even bothered to lock up after us.

Monday Night

I took the long way to August's place, going up Venice to Ocean and around to Washington. I thought about taking one of the foot bridges and skipping a whole section of the journey but decided against it. In retrospect, I guess it's a good thing I did.

Coming back around Dell Street, I made the right turn onto Linnie. August noticed the sedan before I did. Good thing really. We probably would have been in a lot of trouble if she hadn't. Then again, I probably wouldn't have been there if it wasn't for her, so I guess it all evens out.

I hit the kill switch on the bike as she pointed to the piece-of-shit beige four-door monstrosity parked in her driveway. Instinctively, I knew it didn't belong to any of her friends, or to friends of the Ferrari people. Therefore, by order of elimination, it had to belong to some of my friends. Or at least people who wanted to kill me. Some days it was tough to tell the difference between the two. That's why I killed the engine. No sense in letting everyone in the neighborhood know we were there.

We coasted past the car and I had enough momentum to get most of the way through a U-turn before we stopped. I pushed forward until we were again next to the car, but this time pointed in getaway direction. August got off and put her hand on the hood.

"Still warm," she said. "They must have just got here."

I was amazed. I thought that only worked in the movies. She looked at me for guidance. "What now?"

"You don't happen to have a bag packed already, do ya?"

She shook her head.

"Is there anything inside you can't do without for a couple of days?"

She thought about it. "Contact lens fluid?"

"Unless it's some special brand you can only get in Britain, we can get more on the road. Anything else?"

"They're after you, right?"

"And by extension, you, but yeah."

"So, they won't tear up my place and gut my teddy bear?"

"Odds are against, but I'll sew him up myself if they do."

I heard a noise inside the house and motioned for August to get back on the bike.

"Do you know how to sew?"

"I'll learn," I yelled over the sound of the engine coming to life. I could see shadows being thrown by August's porch light getting longer and then figures were coming around the corner. I hurt my wrist opening the throttle as wide as I could.

In my rear-view mirrors, I could see them coming out into the alley, shouting after us. I couldn't hear what they were yelling but the gun shots came through loud and clear. I dropped my right foot to the ground to balance as I took the corner without braking. The great thing about gyroscopic action on a bike is that once you get up to speed it's hard to fall over as long as you have traction. I prayed for no wet spots and kept the throttle at full.

The people in my rear view had been replaced by their car as we turned east on Venice Boulevard, South. We were well ahead of them as we passed Abbot Kinney's Memorial

Library but by the time we were speeding across Abbot Kinney's Boulevard they were getting closer.

The Chevron station on the corner reminded me to check my fuel level, which isn't as easy as it is in a car. I looked at my odometer and calculated how many miles I'd gone since my last fill-up. I sighed as the math came up, for once, in my favor. Usually, I always ran out just before a date. But since I hadn't made any trips to the Valley to go to the office, I had at least thirty miles left. And if this chase kept up, I was going to need them all.

The light at Oakwood was red, and I slowed only enough to make sure it was safe. The guys with the guns didn't even bother. For me it was self-preservation. If a car slammed into us, we had no metal protection around us. These are the things you never worry about in a car. Of course, what it meant to our current situation was that they were closer, and they were shooting.

Thankfully, they were stupid and trying to shoot out the tires instead of trying to shoot us. I figured that out as soon as they got close enough that I could see where they were aiming. Thing is, you can't shoot out a tire of a moving vehicle without a lot of work. The spinning will deflect the trajectory of the bullet, which I knew courtesy of Guantanamo and his demolitions training. On the other hand, their shooting was causing August to squirm behind me, completely throwing my balance off.

"Stop moving!" I shouted. If she zigged when I was trying to zag, the guys wouldn't have to do much work and we'd still be road pizza. Maybe they weren't so stupid.

The light at Lincoln was red. No way through. Cars

were lined up, waiting for the green. I judged my route as quickly as possible. A hard median on the left made my choice easier. I cut to the right. August pressed her body into mine and moved with me.

I cut towards the far right lane across the front of the sedan. They tried to stop me, hitting the brakes hard to make the angle. Too close. Their back tires lost traction, sending them jack-knifing into one of the stopped cars.

I cut back to the left, splitting between the two outside lanes. I looked, didn't see any cross-traffic. I prayed. Then gunned it straight through the red.

I didn't pray loud enough. August screamed, pointing to the left at a lime-green Miata heading straight for us. A little car like that is usually not an issue. But at this speed, even a Mazda could hurt.

I downshifted for an extra burst and cranked my wrist all the way back. The jelly-bean car slid sideways, trying to get us out of its line. I didn't look back. August did. She twisted around and there went our balance. Suddenly, the car wasn't our biggest problem.

I jammed the rear brake and threw the bike into a slide. My left foot hit the ground and kept us upright. "Sonofabitch!" I yelled as the pain shot through my ankle. At least my scream caused August to straighten out.

I got the bike under control just as the Miata passed where we would have been, the piss-ant driver yelling obscenities at me like it was my fault.

The light behind us was still red. I popped the clutch and gunned the engine. I straightened up, the bike shot forward, and got us out of the intersection.

I smiled to myself. No way a sedan could follow Skids Poppe.

When we got to Ocean Park with no sign of our chasers, I relaxed a little and eased off the gas. I pulled into a gas station on Olympic and filled up, putting it on Publisher Steve's card.

I thought about it. Was it just that afternoon I had come down here to have lunch with Marty? Wow, what a difference a day makes. Topping the tank took a little more than ten bucks (which is why Publisher Steve gave me a gas card) and I asked August if she wanted anything from the store. She didn't.

"Were they shooting at us?"

"Yeah."

"Why?"

I took a guess. "They wanted to kill us?" It sounded right.

"Did they succeed?"

"Nope. You sure you don't want a quick soda before we hit the road?"

She shook her head no.

"Okay. I'm gonna get a Dr. Pepper and then we're off."

"Where are we going?"

"Someplace safe."

She stopped me with the tone in her voice "Skids."

I turned slowly. "Vegas."

About two hours later, we were pulling into the McDonalds at Barstow Station. I don't care what anyone says, riding for long periods of time isn't good for any part of the body, especially the kidneys. Especially after downing a Dr. Pepper in record time about two hours earlier. I'd had to pee since Victorville, but I figured if August wasn't complaining, who was I to stop by the side of the road? Of course, by the time we'd hit the halfway mark of Barstow, if I didn't stop, I would have exploded.

Before the engine had started ticking its cool-down, August and I were racing each other to the bathrooms.

A minute later, I felt a whole lot better and was waiting for August in the gift shop outside the women's toilet.

Yes, I said gift shop. The Barstow Station is a throwback to the small town's roots as a water stop on the Western railroad line. Barstow Station was designed like a train station, with a McDonalds using the old railway cars as dining areas. I was contemplating the purpose of a ceramic cowboy boot stuffed with toothpicks when August snuck up on me from behind.

"Boo!"

"Feel better now?"

"Yep."

"Hungry?"

"Yep."

I ordered us a couple of Big Macs and had them supersize the fries and drinks, just to load up on calories. When I found August, she was sitting in the far end of one of the dining cars, close to an exit and two booths away from a mother trying to force chicken McNuggets into two screaming children. As I walked up with the tray, I questioned her with my eyes. She responded by looking out the window. From where we were sitting, we had a direct view of my bike in the parking lot. Her choice made a lot more sense now.

We ate and discussed Barstow and the trip so far. As we were sorting through the last of the fries, the big question came.

"Why are we going to Vegas?"

I knew it was coming. I'd known it was coming since before I'd mentioned it, but that still didn't mean I was ready to answer it. I stuffed my mouth full of fries and took a big swallow of Coke. That was my standard diversionary tactic number three. I was proud of it. It had worked in the past with publishers and parole officers alike. Obviously, neither of them had ever taken lessons from August Everywhere's teachers.

"Go ahead, talk with your mouth full, I don't care. But I will tell you this, Skids, I'm not getting back on that bike until you tell me why we're going to Vegas."

I was caught. I came clean with diversionary tactic number five: Don't answer the question asked.

"Because people are trying to kill us," I said.

"Actually, people are trying to kill you, they were just waiting for me. We don't know they were trying to kill me. I think my folks would prefer to think they just wanted my cooperation in tracking down a vicious killer. Either way, though, it still doesn't answer the question why we're going to Vegas."

"It doesn't?"

"Nope. I mean why Vegas? We could stop here for the night and hide out amongst the locals."

"Well, first off, look at you. You would never pass for a local. Way too sophisticated and beautiful." I was trying out the compliment as a new diversionary tactic, but somehow I didn't think she was the right person to try out new tactics on.

"Bullshit. Nice of you to say so, and I really think you mean it, but bullshit. There's a specific reason we're going to Vegas. What is it?" She spoke a little too loud for the room and her voice echoed around the almost empty train car. That and her choice of language caused the McNugget lady to look up. There is nothing quite like a mother of two infants trying out the disapproving mother stare on you. Because at that point they haven't quite gotten it right and sometimes they balance too heavily on the guilt and not enough on the what-have-you-done-with-your-life. This woman was giving it all she had in the your-father-and-I-are-disappointed-in-you department. I felt sorry for the two kids. They were in for a rough life. At least Woody Allen would have two new fans.

I tried a last ditch effort. "I have family there."

At this point, August wasn't buying anything.

"Fine," she said. "You don't want to tell me, that's okay. Give me a couple of bucks and I'll get a hotel room. You can pick me up on the way back." She stood up and held out her hand. I freaked. Just for a second, I flashed back to my ex-wife. I broke down.

"I sent Bernie there on Saturday to hide out. Jā also went to Vegas a few weeks ago. I just figured as long as we had to leave LA, I might as well keep working. And I really do have family there. It's where I grew up."

"How did you know Jā went to Vegas a few weeks ago?"

I knew the right answer would get me into a lot of

trouble so I fumbled for anything that sounded right.

"Spring told me?" I said meekly.

"What did she say?"

"She said Jā went for the weekend. She said she'd asked to go with, but he said no because you were driving him to the airport." Whew. Clean getaway.

August was slow in responding. That was okay. She was digesting the information. Her friend wasn't on the up and up and she needed to get used to that. Fine with me. I didn't like the girl anyway.

"I see. So, after he made the phone call from my place which informed him he needed to go to Vegas immediately and after he booked the ticket from my house but before I took him to the airport, she called him and asked to go with? Is that about right?"

Man, I hate it when I'm wrong. Clean getaway my ass. She'd just shot out my tires better than any real bullets could do. I stuttered for a minute, sounding like a defective whoopee cushion. Thankfully, she didn't let me spin for long.

"How'd you find out, Skids? He was only gone two days, didn't miss work and as far as I knew, I was the only person who knew about it. So, tell me, how'd you find out? I promise I won't get mad."

Never trust a woman who says she won't get mad. If there were rules of life, I'm sure that would be in the top ten.

"You're just saying that so I'll tell you, but you'll still get mad."

"True. But the sooner you tell me, the sooner I'll get over it."

I thought about the logic in that and decided I was better off just telling her than trying to figure it out. I'd fucked up and now it was time to come clean.

"It was in your Day Runner. You were picking him up from the airport and the address you had for him was in Vegas."

Well I certainly felt better.

I wish the same could be said for August.

"Excuse me?"

Silly me, I thought she wanted an answer. "I-"

"Now is not your time to talk."

"You asked."

"Yes, I did. And you told me you found the information by going through my Day Runner. What were you looking for? Where I was Thursday night? You wanted to see if my story held up? See if maybe I'd written, in ink, I bet you thought, lessee, Thursday, 'Kill Jā.' I would certainly want to plan that ahead of time, make sure to get my hair and nails done beforehand, just in case I got caught. How am I doing so far?"

This time, I wasn't saying anything. I'd learned my lesson last time.

"Well? Aren't you going to answer me? What gave you the right to go through my date book?"

I was lost. Was I supposed to answer her or wasn't I?

"Where is it now? Do the police have it? Is that who was after us? It wasn't anyone trying to kill us, was it? It was actually the producers of the Jerry Springer show wanting to know about my sordid life singing at children's parties!"

She trailed off and took a second to breathe. I figured

this was my opportunity to jump in and say something redeeming.

"Calm down. I think now you're being silly."

On a scale of one to ten of things not to say to a woman who is upset at you, 'you're being silly' ranks right around number two. Number one would be 'you're overreacting.'

"Silly? You think I'm being silly? You, who has spent every minute since you met me charming me completely and calling yourself my boyfriend, you go through my date book, snooping for some sort of clue in this weird pseudo-investigation of yours, and you call me silly?"

I tried to be the calming force my parole officer told me I could be. "Don't overreact." Oops.

"I won't overreact you little fuck. You violate my personal rights and spy on me and you think it's okay? Well fuck you. I'd rather go back to LA and take my chances with whoever it really was at my apartment. At least those guys were straightforward about what they wanted to do to me. I deserve that kind of respect."

She turned and walked down the length of the dining car, leaving me to smile feebly at the family of three sitting near us.

I left our food trays sitting on the table and went out to follow her.

I looked by the bike first. I'd had a few dates (the number isn't really that important) where my date wasn't too enamored of me at some point in the evening. She would storm out and be waiting by the bike, expecting me to take her home.

I had a feeling August wasn't that kind of a girl. No, if

she was walking out on me, she was self-sufficient enough to walk all the way out. One of the reasons I was crazy about her.

Still, old habits die hard. I could see she wasn't waiting for me, but I went all the way to the bike just to be sure. There was an off chance she had taken the thirty-or forty-five-second head start I'd given her and written me a detailed note, with illustrations, giving away her hiding place because she secretly wanted me to find her. Call me an optimist.

Call me wrong. No note, no nothing. Of course, now her head start was getting bigger and for as small as Barstow was, I certainly had no idea where she could have gone.

Finally, after another few minutes of barging into the women's toilets in the surrounding gas stations, hoping to find her crying in one of the stalls, I hit upon the obvious answer. Walking back to my bike, I remembered what she had said. She had said she'd rather go back to LA. It was a dumb move, if you asked me, but she hadn't.

I gunned the engine, revving it high, past 6500. I wanted her to know, just in case she was hiding somewhere nearby, I was starting up and I'd leave her if she didn't come out right now. No go. I let the revs fall back to normal and stepped into first.

I found the on-ramp back to the coast and headed down the incline onto the highway. I made a mental deal with myself to go no more than five miles before I decided to go five more. I figured if she had gotten a ride fairly quickly, there would be no way to find her. On the flip side, it was midnight, families at McDonalds notwithstanding, and there wasn't a lot of traffic. I just hoped I was right. And, as long as I was right, I hoped I wasn't too late.

It's a great feeling, sometimes, when luck is with you. She was up ahead, maybe 300 yards, on the shoulder, walking backwards. Thumb out. I'll tell ya, if it had been daytime, she would have been picked up in an instant. A girl looks like that, she don't walk long. I pulled up on the shoulder. I kept the bike idling to keep up with her as she continued to walk backwards.

After a few aborted attempts to talk, I yelled at her to stop walking. She glared at me, hard, but her feet stopped moving. I turned off the key. And there we sat, for what must have been years.

"What?"

"You can't walk all the way back to LA."

"That's what you came out to tell me?" She turned and started walking in earnest, just to prove me wrong. I jumped off my bike and trotted to catch up with her.

"Stop a minute, would you."

"Why?"

"Because you really can't walk all the way back and people are trying to kill you and while I may not have been totally honest, at least I'm not trying to do permanent damage."

"No, you're just setting up a pattern for dishonesty in our relationship which, at the worst, could be more damaging than death."

"Not to your folks. They may not like me, but at least you would still be around." That got her attention.

"Don't you dare bring my parents into this!"

"Listen. You left your date book in my bag and I thought it might give me some clues--" She tried to interrupt me. I barreled right over her protests. "Which it did. And yes, I was curious as to what you were doing Thursday night. You told me you were playing and when I found out there was another band at The Cup on that night it certainly raised a few questions. Your ex-boyfriend is dead and my friend is on the hook for it. At least he was. I'm willing to bet yours truly here is now a prime suspect since the police saw our little love-birds act and you're probably wanted as an accomplice either before or after the fact so can you blame me for wanting to know all the details?"

I could see her trying to come up with a good response. She false-started a couple of times and by the time she did speak, it was back at a level which wouldn't arouse suspicion among passing motorists.

"You could have asked."

"I did. I mean you told me everything about baby-sitting for your producer, I couldn't figure out why you would lie about Thursday night."

"Because I saw Jā that night, after I did the kids party."

"Oh," I said. There wasn't much else to say, was there? Then again, I've never been one to follow convention. I kept right on talking. "I see."

I realized I had looked away for a minute, because when I looked back, she was staring at me intently, her eyes were scared and hurt. She opened her mouth to talk but had to wait until a truck passed before actually speaking. I think she needed the time. "Are you mad at me?"

"I'm going to ask you this once: Did you kill Jā?"

"Oh God, no!"

"Okay. I believe you. But we have a lot of talking to do and I-15 is not the place to do it. Get on the bike and let's go to Vegas. I know a great place for 99-cent steak and eggs where you can tell me all about it."

I turned and walked the half-mile back to my bike. I didn't look back until I got there. If she hadn't followed me, I'd have known she was guilty.

I'll spare you the suspense. She was behind me, just a few feet. Far enough to seem apologetic but not close enough to be completely innocent. I was confused.

I know, confusion is a typical situation for me, but I'd never felt confused about a woman before. I mean, even the ex-wife was never confusing. She was either around or she wasn't. When we split, it was me who did the leaving.

Now here I was involved with a girl who could very well be a killer. No. I didn't really believe that, did I? Although the way she tells it, Jā wasn't a saint and she had every reason in the world to want to cause him harm. But dead? I don't know.

And what about Gina? She couldn't have killed Gina and left her in the apartment for us to find together...except for the fact she was the one who suggested we go to Jā's place when we did, when we'd be sure to find the body. But she looked pretty shook up when she saw her. It was all too much.

It kept going around in my head like that for the rest of the ride to Vegas. She held on behind me, but only loosely. She was putting as much distance as she could between the two of us while still staying safe. I barely noticed the various landmarks which were ticking off the passing miles: The huge thermometer in Baker, the oasis of Stateline (which for some reason was now called Primm, as if it were a real city), and Jean, the home of the Southern Nevada Correctional Center (not to mention several casinos). It's amazing to me what money can build, especially when I think of the time I spent at that correctional center at a time when the only thing around there was a dinky place called Pop's Oasis.

I was still trying to figure out what I was going to do when we rounded the big curve and saw the lights of Vegas spread out like a jeweled carpet across the desert floor. And then, just to keep things in perspective, I saw the sign: The next two miles are cleaned courtesy of the Southern Nevada Harley Owners Group. I felt truly home. I loved those guys. So civic minded. I'd like to think it was because of one of my articles, but who knew for sure?

Soon, I could feel August squirm in her seat, looking around as we passed the big hotels of the fabled Strip. It really is an around-the-world trip, starting with the pyramids of Luxor and ending about three-and-a-quarter miles later back at the Sahara. It was August's first time in the American interpretation of "The City of Lights." I hoped she was impressed.

If we'd been talking, I'm sure she would have asked if we were going to spend any time touring. As it was, she didn't say a word. I changed from I-15 to the 95 and headed to the North part of town.

"This is a great place for 99-cent steak and eggs?" August asked as she got off the bike and looked around the residential area we were parked in.

"In the morning," I said.

I grabbed my stuff from the saddle bags and headed towards a house a couple of doors up the street. August followed.

"Where are we going?"

"Here," I pointed to the front door of the house we were in front of. "My sister's place."

"Does she know we're coming?"

"Not officially."

"It's 2:30 in the morning. Won't she be mad?"

"Probably."

We'd reached the front door and my finger hovered over the doorbell.

"What are you waiting for?"

"Just planning my strategy." I took a deep breath, held it, and pressed the button.

Nothing. I exhaled and pressed again. Silence. I hit it like I was firing at asteroids in an arcade. Still nothing stirred inside. Finally, I gave up and started banging on the door itself.

A minute later, a groggy Brandy opened the door and let us in. "Hi Skids."

"Brandy. This is August."

The two girls said hello to each other. Brandy walked us through the house, pulling out blankets and pillows as she went. She ended up in front of the couch and threw her linen load down on top of it. "The couch pulls out into a bed or you can sleep on the floor, whatever you want. I have to work in the morning and I hope I don't wake you. Sometime between when I get home and when I go to bed, I will want an explanation as to why you are in my house. Good night." She disappeared into her bedroom and shut the door on any comments we might have made.

I looked at August. "Where do you want to sleep?"

"The bed is probably more comfortable than the floor."

I shook my head. "I've slept on that bed. Not comfortable at all."

"Then the floor it is. Why'd you ask if you knew the bed was so bad?"

"I just wanted to know what you'd say."

August grunted and set up a bed for us. Meanwhile I rummaged in the fridge for a beer. I found one and August and I split it without saying anything.

I gave August a shirt to sleep in, promising to go shopping for her in the morning. She got under the covers and rolled over, away from me. I killed the light and crawled into bed next to her.

It was an odd feeling. I wanted nothing more than to sleep with this girl but not like this. Now it was just uncomfortable. I was just starting back on the "Killed him: did she or didn't she" treadmill when I fell asleep. At least in my dreams I could still have sex without remorse. And I did.

Tuesday

Tuesday Morning

I don't know what it is about my sister. The girl makes a good living but still, in all the time she's had this house, she has yet to put blinds on the living room windows. I mention this only as a way to explain why I was awake and squinting into the rising sun.

I rolled over and tried to block the sun out, but it was still reflecting off the back of August's neck. Suddenly, I discovered another reason for having drapes. I was hot. Very hot. I kicked off the covers from my side of the make-shift bed and let the still-cool air outside wash over my sweat-soaked body.

I tossed and turned for a few minutes and finally came to the conclusion I wasn't going to get back to sleep, especially after I started remembering the dreams I'd had - the ones which involved both me and August being hot and sweaty but for entirely different reasons.

I got up and carefully replaced the blankets so August wouldn't know I was gone and went and puttered around in the kitchen, trying to figure out what was next.

I fixed myself a turkey-ham and cheese omelet and sat at the dining room table to eat it. It wasn't nearly the same as the Sidewalk Cafe, but sis keeps a kosher house. I was breaking the rules by grating the cheddar on top of it, but if I washed up before she got home, no one would be the wiser. Besides, I always was the rebel of the family.

By the time I'd finished, I hadn't come any closer to deciding what to do now. I looked at the clock. It was just past 8 a.m. I grabbed the cordless phone and dialed home.

Calling home was a mixed bag. It could go well and no one would answer, which could mean Guantanamo wasn't around or just wasn't answering. Or he could be injured. No. He hadn't been home last night when we were there, and there was no reason for the bad guys, whoever they might be, to think we'd go back there, especially after the chase from August's place. The other possibility was he would answer and then I'd have to explain what was going on and his overprotective nature would want to step in and try to fix things and I've seen hurricanes which leave less damage in their wake.

He answered on the first ring and sounded totally awake. "Skids, I hope that's you."

"It's me. What's going on? Why are you up so early?"

"Me? What's going on with me? Where are you? No wait, don't tell me. The phone may be bugged. Just tell me if you're all right."

"So far I'm fine. Why would our phone be bugged?"

"I'm going to go out on a limb and say you haven't seen the news yet."

I wasn't even sure where my sister kept her TV. It certainly wasn't in the room I was in so I couldn't even have one of those movie moments where I flipped on the tube and instantly saw what my sidekick was talking about. Nope, no easy answers here. I had to rely on his story-telling capabilities.

"No news. I'm gonna have to rely on your story-telling abilities to fill me in."

"You are all over the news. Or I don't know, maybe the news is all over you, depending on how you look at it. Either way, we have the van from Channel 6 parked outside the place waiting for me to come out and give a statement. The police have already been and gone and how come the place was such a mess?"

I was lost. This was Guantanamo's way of telling me something, but I just wasn't sure what it was. I asked. "What are you trying to tell me?"

For the first time in his life, he answered plainly. "You're wanted by the police for questioning in some murder."

I took a moment. I may have taken more than a moment, I'm not sure. It seemed like a moment; I know that much. Okay, so it was a long moment. Moments are relative, aren't they? At least they are like relatives since you never know when one is going to show up or how long it's going to stay. This particular moment felt like a distant cousin who spends all his time at family functions pointing out how much better he is than you while telling you he's just the same, even if he does drive a brand new 'Vette. I guess this moment was lasting a bit longer than intended because I was still taking it when I finally registered Guantanamo's voice screaming my name in my ear to snap out of it. I did. Sort of.

"What did you just say?" I asked him.

"If I tell you, are you gonna drift away again?"

I thought about it, decided I didn't know and told him "No."

"You're wanted by the police on a murder rap."

"Last time you said questioning."

"I knew you were paying attention. I just said that to soften the blow. What the news really said was 'In connection with,' which in my experience means they think you did it."

"Mine, too." Another moment came along and knocked at my brain. I made the conscious choice not to let it in. Instead, I asked another question. "Did they say whose murder?"

"A couple actually."

"A couple? Like a husband and wife?"

"No. Like a couple of people. Two. You know that chick reporter you like who took out the restraining order against you?"

"Schyler Huntfeld?" She and I had been playing reporter tag for a few years where she would say something mean about me in her editorials on the news and I would do the same in my columns. A year and a half ago, when I was going through the divorce, we'd met at a movie premiere, gotten drunk and slept together. For a week. In

Cancun. On her expense account. One morning I woke up, she was gone, leaving only a return plane ticket. It was almost an Al Stewart song. When I got back to LA, she wanted to pretend nothing had happened, which she never mentioned to me. When I saw her at some local food fair and tried to say "Hi," I met the fiancée and the next day I was legally compelled to stay more than a hundred feet away from her. Ah...life in the big city.

"Yeah, that's the one. She says you're dangerous and the prime suspect in a recent rash of southland slayings."

"Nice alliteration on her part."

"I thought so. Anyway, she says, unconfirmed mind you, that you are involved in the death of a bartender found floating in the Venice canals and some girl found in the dead guy's apartment."

"I'm wanted for both? I can accept that."

"And that you are armed and dangerous and are in the company of the dead guy's girlfriend. Huntfeld's personal comment was it was probably a lover's triangle and that you were known to be a jealous man. Then the guy she shares the desk with laughed and said something like you should know and then he talked about baby condors hatching. Or something like that."

"Great."

"My thoughts exactly. What will my mother say when she finds out I'm involved with a felon?"

"You haven't talked to your mother in years."

"Precisely. And now is not the time for a reconciliation, thank you very much." He took a breath, adjusting to the fact I had just ruined another possible attempt at a mother and child reunion (no offense to Paul Simon), then continued. "So, anyway, don't tell me where you are, in case the phone is tapped. Just let me know you're okay and when I can expect you home."

"I'm fine and we've been on the phone long enough that if they wanted to track me, they would be knocking on the door right now. As for when I'll be home, who knows? I guess I better figure out what's going on before I set foot in the old neighborhood. The way things are going, I could be the next victim of the southland killer."

"Is that who made such a mess in here last night? The real killer?"

"I can only suppose. I take it when you got home there weren't two guys lying there with pennies taped to their eyes?"

"Nope, just some vomit on the carpet and the CDs everywhere. And your Maltese Falcon statue was over by the door, bloody and with its beak broke."

"Sorry about that. I'll have it replaced or fixed or whatever when I get back. In the meantime, be careful. I'll call you soon."

"Okay. Oh, and Skids?"

"What?"

"Since you're not going to be around for a while. Should I drink the beer in the fridge before it goes bad?"

I weighed the possible advantages of explaining that beer doesn't go bad, despite the date printed on the bottle.

It would be cheaper to pay for the beer than to pay for the extra time on the call. I sighed and told him to go ahead.

August was folding our bed linen into a nice, neat stack when I went back into the living room and put the phone back on the charger.

"Who was that?" she asked.

"Guantanamo."

"Your roommate?"

"Sidekick."

"What did he want? I didn't even hear the phone ring."

"I called him." I then went on to explain, briefly, our conversation. August's response was about as expected.

"But you didn't kill anybody!"

"That's correct. Now do you want to keep your winnings or go for the bonus prize?"

"So, what do we do now?" My sarcasm was completely lost on her.

"We find out who did kill somebody. Well, specifically who killed Jā and Gina."

I heard a door open and instantly knew that in a scale of bad timed events, with JFK's trip to Dallas a nine, this was an eleven. Bernie was coming out of the spare bedroom wearing a robe and Garfield slippers.

"What was that about Gina? And what are you guys doing here?"

"Good morning, Bern. How the hell are you?" Tactically speaking, a good offense is the best defense. "You want an omelet or something for breakfast?"

"No, I'm fine, thanks. Have you two met?"

I've said it before and I'll say it again; Bernie is not that quick on the uptake, especially first thing in the morning.

I assured him that, yes indeed we had met, and August was here as my guest. Which brought us right back around to the original question of "What are you guys doing here?"

"I'm doing what you wanted me to, looking into Jā's death."

"He was killed in Venice."

"We don't know that for sure. He was found in Venice. He could have been killed here and transported. Never leave a stone untouched-"

"Unturned," interrupted August.

"Exactly my point. We found an address for him here in town, so we thought we'd check it out."

We had him. Bernie was with us. Not that we weren't telling the truth. We were. It's just I didn't want things to get back to the first part of the original question. There would be plenty of time to tell him about Gina and now did not constitute plenty.

"Makes sense," Bernie said, grabbing a seat at the kitchen table.

I remained standing. "In fact, we should get going. A quick hop in the shower and we'll be back on the case. August, why don't you go first? I'm sure Brandy left some clean towels on the rack."

August smiled and walked away. A few seconds later, water was running.

"She's helping you on the case?" Bernie asked.

"Yeah. A detective has to have some sort of girl, right? And she is definitely that."

"You know she used to date Jā, right?"

"I know."

"Do you know who killed him?"

"Not yet, although the police have a pretty good idea it was me."

"But you didn't kill anybody."

I thought about using the same line but having it fail twice in so short a time would devastate me. Instead, I went with the more traditional "Nope." and left it at that. For a little while we stared at each other, then Bernie grabbed himself a bowl and some Frosted Flakes. Before the ones in the bottom had the chance to get soggy, I was in the shower empathizing.

Twenty minutes later, I was slipping my wet head under a helmet, ensuring a bad hair day. August was in place behind me. As I let the engine warm up, she reminded me she hadn't eaten and I had promised a 99-cent steak and eggs feast. I acknowledged my culinary duty and headed off to explore the wonders of the Las Vegas Strip.

Just my opinion, but The Strip has changed drastically since the days I lived here. For one thing, it was impossible to get a 99-cent anything between the Tropicana and Circus Circus. The Sahara may have had something, but I'm sure things hadn't changed enough that they would let me back in there. So as long as I was going to pay, I decided on someplace a little more like home: The Hard Rock Hotel.

Poppe Culture

The Hard Rock is a fairly hip addition to the sights and sounds of Vegas. So hip, in fact, it's not even on the Strip. It's on Paradise, a block away.

The funniest thing about the Hard Rock is the attire. In a town where the Rat Pack are revered like gods it's not uncommon to see some jerk-off dropping half a million at Caesar's Palace wearing a pair of shorts and a shirt that was never in style. There, in the old-guard hotels, they don't care how you dress as long as you have the cash to back up your bad taste.

The Hard Rock, though, is completely different. There, where they have Sex Pistols and Jimi Hendrix slot machines and all the chips have the names of bands on them, you would expect to see Marilyn Manson clones dressed in cut-offs and sandals and yet, on any given night, the boys and girls betting their $5 Red Hot Chili Pepper chips are clad in formal evening wear. It does a poor old biker's heart proud to see we are, in fact, showing the older generation what cool really is.

August and I went in and took a seat in Mr. Lucky's 24/7 and she ordered eggs Benedict. I shuddered. Eggs Benedict is such a weekend food. To have it on a Tuesday morning just went against all my natural instincts. Me? I had a couple of pancakes with some bacon and a big Bloody Mary. What the hell, if she could have a Sunday breakfast, I could have a Sunday drink, right?

It wasn't until we were halfway through the meal either of us said anything worth mentioning. It was August.

"Sorry I didn't tell you about Thursday night."

"Want to tell me about it now?"

"Not really, but I suppose I should, huh?"

"I'm not going to force you to do anything."

She sat silently for a few more minutes. I let her. If she wanted to tell me, she would. Eventually, she did.

"Thursday, when I got home from my birthday party gig, there was a voicemail from Jā on my phone. He apologized for everything and said he really wanted to see me. Needed to, in fact. He left a number, but it wasn't any number I'd ever had for him before. I didn't know what to do."

"So, what did you do?"

"I called it. Some guy answered the phone, someone I didn't know, and when I asked for Jā he didn't say another word, just handed the phone over. Jā thanked me for calling and asked if we could meet. I told him I didn't think so, that it probably wasn't a good idea, but he said he had to see me."

"Did he say what it was about?"

"No."

"So why did you ultimately say yes?"

"We were together for eighteen months and had just split up. I don't know, maybe a small romantic part of me wanted him to come back and tell me it was all right. Maybe I wanted to tell him to fuck off in person. I don't know."

"Sorry. I'm new in the 'mixing business with pleasure' aspect of this job. What happened when you met him?"

She took a deep breath and shut her eyes, as if trying to remember all of it precisely.

"We met at the duck park around the corner from my place. I didn't want him coming over, I knew that much, but I also didn't want to be too far from home so I figured the duck park would be best." The duck park was a small green area in the middle of the canals originally established for the nannies of wealthy kids to take them on afternoon walks. Then, a few years ago, when we had the great duck blight of Venice (the details of which I don't want to get into for fear of getting a bit too pissed off) a group of concerned citizens decided to honor the dead ducks with a plaque in the park. Thus, it became the duck park. I knew it well, although I'd never been there at night. Ironically, it was just two blocks away from where Jā's body was found.

"And you don't know who answered the phone?"

"All I know is the guy had some sort of accent, but I couldn't tell you from where."

"When was this?"

"I don't know, around midnight, I guess."

"Around midnight when he called or when you met?"

"Are you going to let me tell the story?"

"Sorry. It's just I'm trying to piece this together as we go and -"

"I know all that," she interrupted. "But if I don't get this out now, I may not get it out at all."

I could understand that. I shrugged and put a forkful of pancakes into my mouth. If it was busy doing something else, it couldn't ask any more questions.

"Anyway," August continued. "Anyway, when I hung up the phone it was about 11:45. He didn't say how long he would be, so I just went there and waited. He was there about five, ten minutes after I was.

"He was really grateful I had returned his call, he even tried to give me a hug and kiss, but I held him back. Just the sight of him reminded me he had slept with Spring and what a bad guy he was. As soon as I saw him, I knew it was over and I had done the right thing. I was itching to go. I think he knew it, too.

"But that didn't stop him. He carried on like his life depended on it, which I guess it did." She laughed nervously at that. It was the first time I think she took a breath since she'd started. I didn't say anything.

"He told me he was in trouble, that he'd made some wrong choices and he needed a place to hide. I told him to call Spring and ask her. He said she was already in it too deep and they would look for him there."

I couldn't hold back any longer. "Spring already knew about it? What does that mean?"

August looked at me, scared. "I didn't know," she said. "But it sounded to me like there was more going on than I really wanted to know about. I was furious."

"What did you do?"

"I slapped him, as hard as I could. I wanted him to hurt. I…I…wanted him completely out of my life."

She stopped talking. Her eyes screwed shut and her lips pursed as if trying to hold something inside her head.

Then it came out. Her entire body shook with sobs and tears pushed themselves out through her closed eyes.

I didn't know what to do. Part of me wanted to cross the table and hold her, part wanted to hear the rest of her story and part wanted to order another Bloody Mary. I went with a mixture of parts one and two. I held her hands in mine, caressing the backs of her fingers.

"Everything is gonna be okay," I said. "So...what happened next?"

She took a minute to answer. It took her that long to get her breathing under control. The entire time, her head was bent down. I couldn't tell if her eyes were seeing anything other than that night. Finally, she spoke.

"After I hit him, I turned to walk away. He ran after me, angry. He grabbed me by the arm and stopped me, telling me I had to help him. I tried to get away, but he held me tighter. I told him to let me go, that I couldn't help him. He hit me, slapped me across the face, and told me I'd better.

"I tried to get away, I pulled but he wouldn't let go. Finally, I spit in his face. His hands went up to protect himself and when they did, he let go of me. I knew if I tried to run then, he'd catch me, so I kicked him in the balls. As hard as I could. He went down on his knees and I ran. Fast. All the way home and locked and chained the door behind me.

"For the rest of the night I shivered in bed, fully dressed under the covers, holding a kitchen knife in case he came back. He didn't. I guess I fell asleep at some point because when I woke up, it was daylight."

She stopped talking and drank some coffee. She was finished.

"That was the last time you saw him? Crouched down in pain?"

She nodded.

"Do you own a gun?"

She was puzzled. "No, why?"

"Just checking. That's a hell of a story. I can understand why you didn't want to tell that to the police."

"I didn't kill him, Skids, I swear."

"I know, kid. I know."

Now it was time for the Bloody Mary.

We rounded out the morning by playing a couple of hands of blackjack, all losses being dutifully written down in my little expense-account book. During our two-hour table layover, August and I had another discussion pertaining to our highway argument. Now that her confession was out of the way and we had determined she was probably the last person to see Jā alive, barring the possible exception of the killers, it was my turn to explain why I had gone through her date book.

"You know, you still had no right to go through my date book."

"I know."

"But would you do it again?"

I knew I was about to give the wrong answer, but I had to try.

"In the same situation, knowing what I know now, of course not."

"Bullshit. You would and you know it."

"All right, I would. But can you really blame me?

You left it in my bag, along with some of your panties, I might add."

This had nothing to do with anything but there were other guys at the table giving her the once over and I wanted them to know in no uncertain terms this woman was off-limits.

"And I'm sure you got into them too, right?"

Damn, that plan backfired. "No. And I wasn't really looking for anything about you. I was looking for something about Jā, which I found." I was trying to sound self-righteous.

"And if you had asked to go through my Day Runner, I would have gladly given it over to you. But you had to ask. That's the point. Didn't you and your ex ever have privacy issues?"

"My ex's version of privacy was 'If it's in the house it's mine to pillage.'"

"So you understand what that feels like. Get over yourself, Skids. I know you're doing something nice for my boss and your friend and I think you're a great guy who I might possibly have a future with but understand there are things even your cute little reporter act will not allow you to find out without asking. Do I make myself clear?"

I nodded sheepishly. Then realized we hadn't been dealt our new hand. I looked up at the dealer. He was staring at me.

"Skids Poppe?"

I nodded.

"This is great. I love your stuff."

I had fans everywhere. In the next ten hands I caught three blackjacks. And August had ordered me another Bloody Mary. Sometimes I just love being me.

There's this thing about Vegas. Okay, not Vegas specifically, I mean not the outlying regions, but the casinos in particular. See, when you're in Vegas in the middle of summer it can get pretty damn hot. In fact, it can get pretty damn hot no matter when you're there, but summer is worst of all.

To offset this, the casinos have used technology reverse-engineered from the crap they have hidden up in Area 51 to create one of the best air conditioning systems on the planet. This makes you as comfortable as possible while you're inside said casino.

The key word there is inside. Why do I bring this up now? Because as soon as we stepped through the doors after our nice winning streak, we hit the oppressively hot and dry air outside. Just for a second I thought about completely abandoning my search for Jā's killer and turning back around so I could live out my days inside the Hard Rock as an air-conditioned recluse. Stranger things have happened.

Thankfully, August was there to propel me forward. If she hadn't grabbed hold of my hand and pulled me towards the bike, I might be writing this little memoir on the backs of keno tickets and drink coasters.

"Where to now?" she asked as we strapped on our helmets.

"Let's go see where Jā was staying." I reached into

the saddle bag where I'd stashed August's date book the night before and handed it over to her. "You find the address."

She gave me a mean look but took the Day Runner anyway, flipping it to the proper date. "2713 Rochelle #J."

"Okay. I know roughly where that is." I went to get on the bike, then stopped. "August?" I asked.

"What?"

"Stupid question, really, but if Jā was only gone for two days, why did he give you an address?"

"He didn't, not at first. He called the first night he was there…uh, here? And had me FedEx some stuff out to him. That was the address he gave."

"What did he want you to send?"

"I don't know. It was a box, already sealed and ready to go. All I did was address it and ship it off."

"Fair enough," I said and swung my leg up over the seat. August slid on behind me and we headed for Rochelle.

The apartment complex that matched the address was fairly close to the university, making it a prime location for college kids. This was evident as we walked through the center area where the average age of the people marking time on the chaise lounges was maybe 19. And the average major, judging by the books piled up in stacks next to them, was hotel management.

I felt hideously old and overdressed as we climbed the stairs, going up through the alphabet until we reached the right door. I asked August if she wanted to knock.

"Why?"

"Your dead boyfriend, his mysterious past. I just figured you should have right of first refusal."

"I see. No, you go ahead."

Personally, I wasn't all that sure she should even be here, but that argument had ended back at the bike. Hey, we already knew the guy was a slime. How much worse could it possibly get, right?

I knocked.

The door opened and I found myself staring at a pair of barely covered tits. And nice tits they were, let me tell you. Now, just for the record, it wasn't my intention of starting an interrogation by staring at some girl's tits. Nope. Usually I save that for a third date or prelude to a barroom brawl. Here, I had no choice. The girl who opened the door probably had a good six, maybe eight inches on me and her perky nipples were staring me in the eye. I wasn't sure if I should look up; I mean if I'm the first one to blink, I could be blowing it for all men everywhere.

"Can I help you?" came a voice from somewhere above the breasts.

I swear I thought of something to say. It was right there, on the tip of my tongue…or rather the tip of my tongue was right there. Before it could do any damage, though, August stepped up to the plate.

"Sorry to bother you, but we're from the Skids Poppe Detective Agency and we'd like to ask you a few questions."

"Detective Agency?" This time I could have sworn

Poppe Culture

it was the tits themselves talking. "Do you have any ID?"

I guess I didn't respond quick enough because the next thing I know I have a sharp pain in my side and August's elbow was retreating to her side of the personal-space line.

"Ow! What? ID? Oh yeah, right." I reached into my pocket and pulled out one of my new cards, looking at it before I gave it to her to make sure it didn't say I was a famous writer.

She looked at the card and, for the first time, I looked at her face. She was young - older than most of her neighbors, I'd bet, but still younger than I. If I had to guess, I would have put her right around 23 or 24. And she was beautiful in a classic way. She would have felt right at home on the screen with Bogie or Cary Grant. And from where I stood, which wasn't far away, it all looked natural.

"Please come in, Mr. Poppe," the young woman stepped back to let me in to her place. "And Miss...?"

"Everywhere," August filled in. The woman held out her hand and August shook it.

"I'm Kim Goldman, please, have a seat. Can I get you anything to drink?"

I opened my mouth to ask for a beer, but August beat me to it. "Water" she said quickly. "For both of us." I was going to have to talk to that girl.

A few minutes later I had a nice cool glass of ice water sweating in my hands. The beautiful Kim Goldman had thrown a t-shirt on over her bikini top and sat down opposite us.

"What's this all about?"

"It's about Jā Alweighz."

"What about him? I haven't seen him for a few weeks at least. What has he done? Are you with the police?" She was defensive and uncomfortable, that much was sure. The big question was, why? I glanced over at August. She had picked up on it, too.

Did she know he was dead? I decided not to spring it on her yet.

"No, we're not with the police. I work for the man who was funding Jā's most recent film."

She relaxed completely. It was like she was a puffer fish, all tense and bloated and then she let out a breath and became normal again, ready for anything. "You work for my father?"

What? "Bernie is your father?"

"Who's Bernie? No, my father's name is Leonard."

"Leonard Goldman is your father?" That question came from August. She was much quicker at putting two and two together than I was.

Why did that name sound familiar?

"Yes, he is," she was getting confused. I couldn't really blame her. So was I. She, however, had the presence of mind to continue. "Isn't that what you came to talk to me about?"

"Well…" I started. It did me no good. She was on a roll. Her eyes had glazed over and she was trying to put things together in her head. I figured it was best not to get in her way.

"I knew Daddy wasn't happy about me seeing Jā, he always said to keep business and pleasure separate, but why would he send a private investigator around? He knows if he has any questions to just ask me. I'd tell him."

She directed this last bit at me, as if accusing me of putting the silly notion of distrust into her daddy's head. Let's face it, if I ever had a daughter and she looked like that, I'd have an armed guard around her twenty-four hours a day. I was just about to tell her that, too, when August stopped me.

"Well, Miss Goldman, as long as we're here anyway, do you mind us asking a few questions?"

"I guess not. But it's not going to be anything Daddy doesn't already know."

"That's fine."

I wondered what August was getting at. The answer came to me as she asked her first question.

"How long have you been seeing Jā and what is the nature of your relationship?"

Oh damn, the dead ex-boyfriend was wick dipping here as well.

"A couple of months, I guess. Maybe six or seven."

"That's more than a couple," I pointed out.

"True. Yeah, it must have been close to seven. We met back in January. He had interviewed a friend of mine for a role in his film, Body Mechanoids or something like that -"

"Body Mechanics," I said. It was like being on a game show, talking to this girl.

"Yeah, that was it. Anyway, my girlfriend is a drama major at UNLV and she dances with me at the Tropicana and she brought me along on one of the readings and Jā and I met there."

"Did she get the part?" August asked.

"No."

"Why did he come here for auditions, rather than LA?" That one was mine.

"I don't know. He said he was looking for girls who wouldn't be afraid to reveal themselves. I guess he thought someone who worked topless for a big Vegas show would fit the bill."

"And how did you two start going out?"

"He asked. And he was kind of cute and seemed to know a lot about movies and stuff so I said sure. Besides, like you said, he didn't live here. We certainly weren't exclusive or anything like that. For Christ sakes, he even told me about his wife."

"His wife?" Swiss timing couldn't tell you who said it first, me or August. Kim, on the other hand, didn't seem at all bothered.

"So I'm going out with a married guy. Big deal. He's not the first and he won't be the last. If his marriage was strong, he wouldn't need to go out with me, right?"

There were a couple of things there that puzzled me. No, I was not about to take the moral high ground, having cuckolded a few guys in my time (I love that expression) but the fact she was still "going out" with him meant she didn't know he was dead.

August excused herself to go to the restroom ("First door on the right") and left me alone with the other other girl in Jā's life.

"Is your friend okay?" she asked me.

"Yeah. She's fine. Her husband left her for a lion-taming magician and she never quite got over it. She'll be back in a few minutes. While she's gone, do you mind if I ask you a few more questions?" She shook her head. "When was the last time you saw Jā?"

"A few weeks ago. He was in town to meet with my father. I would have thought he would have told you about that."

"He stayed with you?"

"Like always."

"Right. And did he have anything delivered here?"

"I don't know about delivered, but he said he was expecting some important papers one day."

"Your father hasn't been very clear on what Jā did for him…?" I was grasping at straws and I knew it, but it was worth the shot.

"Jā didn't do anything for Daddy. Daddy did it all for him. And once they started talking to each other, neither one talked to me, which was just fine. I don't want to know about my father's business and as for Jā I couldn't care less." She leaned in, to take me into her confidence. "He was a nice roll, but that's all. Any man that would cheat on his wife, how much can you really trust him, huh?"

Between her and Guantanamo, I had enough logic flaws to make a Michael Crichton novel look plausible. I knew I wasn't going to get much more out of this conversation, so August's return from the john couldn't have been timed better.

"Thank you for your time, Miss Goldman. Sorry to

have disturbed you."

"No problem. But did you find out anything Daddy didn't already know?"

"Jā never mentioned his wife before, but like you said, if he's gonna cheat, how can you trust him with the truth?"

"Exactly!" As she shut the door behind us, I knew I had made a friend. August, on the other hand, wasn't doing so hot.

"You okay?"

"He was married?"

"We don't know that. He could have just told her that to get her into bed." She looked at me. All of a sudden, I felt like the know-it-all screw up in every bad asteroid film. I was trying my best to take out the big huge meteor heading towards earth, but all I succeeded in doing was turning it into littler stuff which caused just as much damage. Maybe more. Hooray for me.

"Skids, I know you're trying to help."

I was.

"Shut up."

I did.

Tuesday Afternoon

Twenty minutes later we were in a place called The Asylum drinking fortified coffees. Mine was Irish, August's was Mocha. As far as bang for your buck went, I'd say hers was stronger. The Asylum was a nice little place, reminiscent of a watered-down version of Van Go's Ear, but trying real hard. It was eclectic in a Vegas way.

The only other person in the place was a balding guy with glasses and a goatee who looked like a college professor. He was working on some poetry. At least I assumed that's what he was scribbling in his notebook. If this place had been in LA, anyone writing in a notebook is working on a screenplay. Anywhere else in the country and they're poets desperate to break out of their shells. This guy had already broken out and was having too good a time to be put back in. The scariest part was, I think I might have gone to school with him.

"Do you know who Leonard Goldman is?" August asked me.

"The name sounds familiar... but no."

"He's a big mob lawyer. He was indicted a few years ago, but nothing happened."

"How do you know this?"

"It happened during a criminal psyche class. We all had to follow it on the news."

"What else do we know about him?"

She looked sheepishly at me. "That's about it."

"He's also a fine art dealer, one of the best in town. No one knows exactly how he comes by his stuff, but if you want something, odds are he'll be able to arrange the deal."

August and I both turned. This new tidbit of information was supplied by the Professor.

He looked up and, noticing he now had our attention, continued. "He's also a supporter of the arts, donates to charities like End of the Rainbow Children's Theatre Group, and sponsors several local art competitions. First prize is a scholarship."

"Sounds like a real humanitarian," I ventured.

"No. Just expensive wish-fulfillment."

"Can I buy you a drink and you can explain your theory?"

"I don't see why not."

He moved over to our table and ordered himself a double latte, or, as he referred to it, another usual. Introductions were made.

"I'm Skids Poppe and this is my..." I stopped and

looked at August. I had no idea how to refer to her at this point. Thankfully, she jumped in to save me.

"August Everywhere. I'm fine without being his… you know."

Evidently, the professor did, because he just laughed and looked me up and down. Then he said something really scary. "Skids, you don't remember me?"

Damn! We did go to school together and I had no idea who he was. He stuck out his hand. "Geoffrey Stills. Junior High?"

I shook his hand. "Jeff Stills?" I was incredulous. I did remember him, but not like this. Back twenty years ago, he was a skinny kid with too much acne. He used to hang around with me and my friends. He was kind of a dweeb, but he was our dweeb, you know? If anyone else picked on him, we defended him. We were the only ones allowed to pick on him. And now look at him.

"It's Geoffrey now. I'm surprised you remember me."

"How could I forget? You got me through biology class. What are you doing now and how do you know so much about Leonard Goldman?"

"They're actually tied together. I'm a professor at UNLV, teaching literature, but that doesn't pay the bills. So, to supplement, I do a regular arts column for the Review Journal and a couple of small, but prestigious, local publications. And you? Last I heard, you were in jail."

I put my fingers to my lips, making a shh noise then tilted my head towards August. "She doesn't know."

"So it was true?"

"Depends on who you heard it from and what I was in for. If you ask me, I'll swear it was a freedom of speech issue, and the law disagreed. But that's ancient history."

"What are you doing now?"

"Same as you. I'm working for a magazine company doing columns and articles. In town for a few days to see the family."

"What brings up the topic of Leonard Goldman?"

"We just ran into his daughter. She knew a friend of mine from back in LA, that's where I'm living now. A guy named Jasper Alweighz."

"Alweighz? The guy who's making the movie?"

I was stunned. How did this guy know about the film? I mean, I've heard of small worlds, but this is ridiculous. All I could do, though, was tell him yes, it was the same guy. "But I didn't know low-budget movies made the high art news pages in Vegas."

"They normally don't. In this case, though, the film was supposed to glorify the mob, show how Vegas couldn't have existed without them. Alweighz was writing it, with the angle 'the mob as a philanthropic organization.' That's how he got Goldman interested. Goldman agreed to put up a good portion of the production money, totaling close to two million. So far, I think Alweighz is into him for about four hundred thousand."

"What about Body Mechanics?"

Stills was mystified. "What's that?"

"The film Alweighz was working on when he died."

"He's dead? That's news."

"It is?"

"It means the mob film is put on hold."

"I guess it does." We all thought about it while we drank our coffee.

August finished her drink first, slurping the dregs before she said anything. "Should we talk to Leonard Goldman?"

"I don't know if it would do any good," I said.

"I don't know if you could see him even if you wanted to," Geoffrey supplied. "He's not the easiest guy to get to. The best thing to do, if you wanted, would be to go to his gallery. It's in the Forum Shops over at Caesars Palace. Sometimes you can catch him there."

"Sometimes?"

"Better than never at his office."

"True."

We settled the bill and I gave Jeff - now Geoffrey - my number in LA. I doubted he'd ever call, but you never know. After good-byes, August and I headed back out into the heat and left him to his journal. I never did ask him what he was writing. With all he knew about the Alweighz situation, maybe it was a screenplay after all.

The Forum Shops is a mall attached to Caesars Palace hotel and casino. It's designed to look like a pseudo-outdoor Italian shopping district with a painted sky overhead that goes from day to night faster than they make films from John Grisham novels and it started the trend of themed high-end malls all the new resorts in town are sporting. Everything else there perpetuates the illusion, from reproductions of Roman statues to cobbled streets.

I looked at the map and found Goldman Galleries right down the way from the Vegas edition of Planet Hollywood and across from an ancient Roman Harley-Davidson shop.

On the way there, we passed a rotunda where animatronics of Roman gods told you how wonderful it was to be shopping here. Above them, lasers drew out the constellations and pointed the way to good sales. August wanted to stay and watch the show, so I went on without her.

Walking into Goldman Galleries brought back a flood of memories from every time we went to see my Aunt Gladys when I was a kid and I was told, repeatedly, not to touch anything and to sit still on the plastic-covered couch. Okay, so maybe it wasn't that bad, but this place certainly had a "Don't Look If You Can't Afford It" kind of feel. The artwork ranged from flat watercolors to bulgy oil landscapes to sculptures larger than my apartment and with more metal than my Harley.

I looked around wondering if there would be anything there I would like. The closest thing to being my taste was a multi-colored blob which, when I squinted with one eye and balanced on my left foot, sort of looked like an old girlfriend of mine. While I was looking at it, trying to see what the artist intended, a salesgirl came up to ask me if she could help. Actually, she didn't ask it, she sneered it. And it was more "What are you doing in my store" rather than "Can I help you," but I got the idea.

See, in LA, this would never happen, which is one of the reasons I live there. The other reason, of course, is that I'm wanted in several states on moving violations, things they'd never think to extradite for, but which make it uncomfortable to go back nonetheless.

The reason this would never happen in LA, is they have no idea who you are and don't want to risk offending anyone. Remember Pretty Woman? See, in LA, I could be just as grungy as I normally am (not like today, I took a shower, remember?) and nobody would know I wasn't a producer or director or someone with a last name like Damon or Affleck in disguise. For all they knew, I could be worth more money than God and I was just slumming to see what kind of cheap art I could get for my new 9.6 million-dollar summer cottage in Malibu. Then again, maybe they could see through my disguise and realize I was a poor writer living on whatever my skinflint-of-a-publisher could find to pay me. Either way, I put on my best "Don't fuck with me, I'm Skids Poppe" attitude and asked how much this particular piece was.

She responded by taking it off the wall. Great. She decided I wasn't even worthy of looking at the painting, let alone purchasing it. Thank God August wasn't here to see this.

"Hi Skids," said August, entering the gallery. Oh man, was I ever embarrassed.

"Hi August."

"Looking at paintings?"

"Uh... yeah."

The salesgirl was standing a few feet away holding my painting against her hip. She looked at me disdainfully then asked: "Are you coming?"

"Where?" I answered.

"The room." Duh. Then she turned, expecting me to follow. I looked at August and we both set off after the woman.

She led us into a very nice, very dark room, the kind where the owners would tell my Aunt Gladys not to touch anything. The salesgirl put my painting on the wall and adjusted several of the small lamps around it to make sure nothing else in the room got any light. Then she pointed to an overstuffed leather sofa.

"Please, sit." We did. "This particular piece is an original by a brilliant new artist from New Zealand who goes by the name of Zard. It's called Impression of Melanie. I've adjusted the light so you can see the piece as it would be displayed in your home. I'll be back in a few minutes and you can give me your own impressions then."

She left the room, obviously pleased with herself for the well thought out pun. I was not so obviously pleased with the thought that the ex-girlfriend it reminded me of was also named Melanie. August was just wondering what we were doing here.

"What are we doing here? What did you say to that woman? You're not planning on buying this, are you?"

"In order: We're here to see Leonard Goldman, all I said to the woman was how much is this and while she still hasn't given me a price, I'm reasonably certain publisher Steve will not let me put this on my company expense account. On the other hand, it is a nice piece."

August looked at me like I was crazy, a look, I might add, I was not unaccustomed to, and sat back to wait for the girl's return.

Finally, she spoke. "I've seen your apartment, you know. You have nowhere to hang this where it won't clash."

"I know. But she doesn't. Now come on, isn't it fun to pretend you're rich?"

"Can we have a fight about where it should hang and ultimately decide it's not worth having if all it's going to do is cause an argument?"

"As long as we can mention Leonard Goldman's name in there someplace, sure. We can have any type of argument you'd like." I did like this girl. Once she got into the swing of things, she really got into it.

Our salesgirl came back in, the opening and closing of the door to the room sounding like an airlock in a '60s sci-fi film. "Well, what do you think?"

I opened my mouth, but August beat me to the punch. "It's nice enough," she said, with just the right amount of contempt in her voice. "But I don't think it fits in with our other pieces."

"You always say that," I responded, congratulating myself on the witty banter. "Why can't I ever have anything I like. It would go in my study, after all." I wasn't sure if we had a study in our fictional home with our fictional other pieces, but I felt if we didn't, we ought to. "And besides, Leonard said he could help us out on any piece in the place we liked, and I like this one."

I pouted and turned away from her, so I was now facing the salesgirl, who still had no name. In fact, she was the one who responded.

"Leonard?"

"Leonard Goldman? He's a friend of mine -"

"Ours."

"Sorry, dear. Ours." I extended my hand out to the salesgirl. "I am sorry, I probably should have done this before, but I'm Skids Poppe, from Los Angeles, and this is my…companion August. Leonard said whenever we were here in Vegas to just stop by the gallery to see him. In fact, is he in?"

Our girl's whole demeanor changed. Suddenly, we were important people who might really buy Melanie's impression. "I'm afraid he isn't. In fact, he's in Los Angeles for the next few days. He's been there for the past week, working on setting up a new gallery."

"He didn't call to tell us. Usually, we have dinner whenever he's in town. He loves that we can get him into the Magic Castle," I told her conspiratorially.

"Can I tell him you stopped by?"

"Better idea. We're going back to LA tonight; we'll give him a call. Does he still stay at Shutters or did he buy that place in Malibu he was looking at?"

"I'm not sure…"

"No matter, we can try him there. Or, you said he was setting up a new gallery, right? Do you have the number there? That would probably be the best place to reach him. The way he works, he's probably there more than at the hotel."

"I'll be right back." Out again through the airlock and we were alone with Melanie.

"That was slick," August said.

"Thank you," was my response. I must have completely missed the sarcasm in her voice.

"And now she's on the phone to security telling them she's got two frauds in here, pretending to be friends of her big mob-lawyer, gallery-owning boss and they're going to throw us over the side of that big dam just for mentioning his name in public without a permit. Don't you think you could have been a little more subtle?"

"Joe Pesci is your personal anti-Christ, isn't he?" Before I could continue telling her I had everything under control, the airlock cycled our girl back in. She handed me the piece of paper she was holding in her hands. "Here you go. This is the LA office card, but the gallery's direct number is on the back."

I took the card and looked at it before putting it in the inside pocket of my leather jacket. "Thank you very much, miss…?"

"Kaye."

"Well, thank you, Miss Kaye, we'll tell Leonard how helpful you were."

"Thank you. Um…?"

"Yes?"

"What did you decide on the painting?"

I decided the truth would sound like the perfect lie. "Actually, I used to know Melanie. And, uh, I had the same impression."

August and I showed ourselves out of the airlock.

As we walked back through the Caesar's Palace Casino to where the bike was parked, August asked me what we were going to do now.

"Go home, I guess."

"Back to your sister's place?"

"Naw, back to Venice. Well, back to Brandy's to pick up our stuff and then home."

"But we just got here," she complained. "Back home people want to kill us."

"I'm still reasonably sure they just want to kill me. Even more so once Little Miss Kim calls Daddy and tells him we've been around."

"You think Leonard Goldman killed Jā?"

"Not exactly. But I bet he was involved."

"Are we at least going to see your parents before we leave?"

I stopped. "You want to meet my parents? Hell, I was married for two weeks before my ex-wife met my parents."

"I still want to meet them."

I looked at her. She was serious. She had no idea what she was letting herself in for, but hey, if you run with the wolves, you have to expect to be bitten every now and again, right?

"On the way out of town we'll stop by their store. But don't say I didn't warn you."

My parents moved to Vegas in the mid '70s for reasons unknown, I'm sure, even to them. But I'll tell you, there is nothing like celebrating 200 years of your country's independence in a town where the everyday display of neon is more spectacular than fireworks.

Growing up there, however, was something completely different. Where else can you hold your graduation ceremonies on the same stage where the night before you'd seen Iron Maiden play? Or have the girl who lives two doors down from you be one of the top showgirls in town with her nearly naked body gracing billboards everywhere you turn? Add to that the fact that Vegas is a twenty-four hour town and always has been and you have the makings for a pretty fucked-up childhood. It really is a wonder I made it out as well-adjusted as I did.

I just wish the same could be said for poor old Guantanamo. When his parents took him out of the south and planted him in the southwest, a certain something was left behind. But then, I shouldn't be complaining. I think it's precisely due to that lack that we're such good friends. We understand each other.

What neither one of us understands are my folks. Mr. and Mrs. Bey are easy. They're nurturing folk who try hard but somewhere along the line, they sort of lost touch, literally and figuratively, with our favorite Guantanamo. (Let's face facts, when you name a kid Guantanamo, how much touch are you in to begin with?)

My folks, on the other hand, are a bit altered. Aside from the obvious - naming their only son Skids and dropping him in the middle of the desert during his formative years - they did everything they could to ensure a normal childhood. And if there's one thing I hate, it's being pigeon-holed like that. I was a rebel from the get-go and yet, in everything I did, the folks were right there to back me. Do you have any idea how annoying it is to try and rebel against people who encourage you to rebel?

Do you think it's any coincidence I left Vegas, where I'd lived for the best portion of my childhood and did all my growing up, before I could legally gamble or drink? It would have been too easy.

So, I left and they stayed. Brandy stayed, too, but that's just because she was too young to come with me and by the time she was old enough she didn't want to. You try so hard to teach them and they still do just what they want.

I explained all this to August as we packed up at Brandy's house. To her credit, she did her best to look interested. Bernie stood by, drinking and adding impromptu comments as the mood struck him.

After I'd finished my little tale of woe, Bernie asked the most pertinent question: "What do I do now?"

"You stay here, for just a few more days."

"Fair enough. Your sister said she was going to take some pictures of me if I was still here when you left."

"You should let her. She's a great photographer."

"Her stuff rank with the 'haircut pictures'?"

"'Haircut pictures'?" August asked.

"You see the hair on top of our young man's head here? Well, it used to hang down--"

"And that's really not important now, is it?" I interrupted. "We're out of here and I'll call you as soon as I know what's happening."

"Great. What should I tell Brandy?"

"Tell her I'll call her, too."

I walked outside and strapped our bags to the bike.

Bernie and August followed me out. August was putting her helmet on, but Bernie looked like he was going to ask a question.

"Two more questions, Skids?"

I was close. "What is it, Bern?"

"Will you let Gina know what's going on?"

Damn. I'd forgotten he didn't know she was dead. August started to say something but I cut her off. "Done. Next?"

"How's my bike?"

August and I mounted up.

"You'll be riding it again in a few days." I started the engine and gunned it, letting the machine warm up. I couldn't swear to it, but I'd bet Bernie was saying something about me not answering his question as we sped away.

If you stay in Vegas long enough, at some point, you work for the tourist industry. The most prevalent form of this is in gaming. And they wonder why Vegas is one of the suicide capitals of the world. Anyway, Mom and Pop figured the best way to avoid daycare was to each work different shifts in a casino. This way, one was always home with us. All it really did was force me to be cleverer about my schemes. Thanks, guys.

As soon as I left town, though, they figured with only one child, they didn't need that anymore, so they decided to open their own business. A specialty bookstore with an espresso bar and poetry readings on Friday nights. The kind of place Jeff - now Geoffrey - frequented. Even though I'd been back to Vegas dozens of times, I'd only been to the store twice since they'd opened it.

Why? It just felt wrong. Like when your parents come to visit you at your place and find the Playboy. Yes, you're an adult and are entitled to have it, but it just gives you the creeps knowing that it's okay. Same with them and books. It would blow my image completely if they knew I stole not to support a drug habit, but a rare book habit. I guess I'm more like them than I care to admit.

Their store, Poppe Culture, is in a little pod mall off Tropicana Boulevard west of the strip. It's a nice last stop before you hit the 15 and make your way back to LA. At least it was for us this trip.

Luckily, there was a space open right in front of the door, and I idled the bike right up to the curb. Man, if there was some place I didn't want to go inside, this was it. It didn't matter. August was off the bike, helmet hanging off the handlebar, before I could back out. Thankfully, she didn't jump the gun and rush inside to introduce herself as my new girlfriend.

"Are you Mr. Poppe? Hi, I'm August Everywhere, Skids' new girlfriend." Damn, he must have come out while I was taking my helmet off.

By the time I looked up, the two were hugging like long-lost relatives. Not that that was, in itself, a big deal. Pop hugged everyone. If you came into his shop (and bought something) more than three times, you were considered family and invited home for Thanksgiving dinner. By the time I got my ass off the bike, they were already headed inside, and my dad was yelling for my mom to come meet Skids' new girl.

Inside, the place looked pretty much the same as it did last time I was there. They'd rearranged some of the shelves and I noticed they'd added a "Skids Poppe" section to their magazine selection. See, about a year and a half ago, they'd come to LA for something and insisted on meeting Publisher Steve, the man who "keeps our boy off the streets and gainfully employed." I think they worked out a deal where they would carry the full line so they could promote me.

You gotta love parents like that. I think dad even had T-shirts printed up once which read "Poppe's Pop and proud of it!!!" Yep, it even had the three exclamation points. He wore it to one of my arraignment hearings. It's that kind of loyalty and support I was rebelling against to begin with.

I heard noise in the back so I knew Dad had hauled August back to meet Mom. I made my way into the storeroom and joined the happy family.

"Skids!!!" That was Dad. You can always tell by the exclamation points. "How come you didn't tell us you were involved with this lovely young lady?"

"I tried to tell her you were dead, but she didn't believe me."

"How long are you in town for? Do we get the pleasure of your company for dinner or did you just stop by to borrow money? We know how much you like coming into the store. He hates coming into the store, August. Thinks it makes him look like a chimp in front of his friends."

"Wimp, Mom. And no, the reason I don't like coming in is that you keep embarrassing me in front of my friends. Besides, we really can't stay long. Have to get back to LA. Deadline, you know. This was just an in-and-out visit."

"You saved us for the 'out' part. I feel very special."

I buried my head in my hands and walked back out to the main part of the store. No one can cut to the quick as easily and efficiently as family, specifically a mother. It's a skill they probably have classes for in the maternity ward. There was no reasoning with her when she got like this. In fact, I was wondering what had got her like this. Usually, her embarrassing moments come more from the "Isn't he the smartest, most talented boy you've ever seen" drawer, as opposed to the file labeled "notes to the ungrateful son I carried in my womb for nine and a half months." I thought about it while I wandered over to the mystery section and browsed their Lawrence Block selection. I could really identify with his literary thief, Bernie Rhodenbarr.

Dad snuck up behind me, surprising me as I thumbed an early edition of Burglars Can't Be Choosers.

"What kind of trouble are you in?" he asked. If he hadn't been whispering, there probably would have been at least one exclamation point.

"What are you talking about? I'm not in any trouble. I'm just here to do a story."

"Really? What story?"

Damn. I should have known he'd ask. Now I had to think of an answer. I looked around the place hoping for inspiration. Nothing stood out from the shelves of books but Mom's collection of shot glasses from all over the world. She still had the one I'd gotten her from that trip to Sturgis; there it was, right up in front.

"Do you want to tell me what story? Maybe I can help?"

Great, now he wanted to help. "It's a drinking story, Pop. You can't help since you don't drink."

"Steve sent you here to drink?" If his tone was any more mocking, I could turn it into a bird and give it to my love.

"Oh yeah. I'm supposed to start at one end of The Strip and get each hotel's collector glasses with their specialty drink and then write a story about it." It was the best I could come up with on short notice.

"Is that the best you could come up with?" Dad knows me so well.

I shrugged. "You have to admit it sounds like my kind of story."

"I'll give you that. Now you give me the reason the police are looking for you."

"They're always looking for me?" I tried. It was a feeble attempt and I knew it. So did dad. He shook his head, raised his eyebrows and pursed his lips. Deadly combination of incredulity and disappointment. I gave in. "How'd you find out?"

"Your mother's friend Andee called. You know how she loves it when she can one-up your mother. She's in LA and saw you on the news. She called this morning to gloat that her boy had never been arrested at all, and here you were wanted for questioning in a double murder."

"What'd Mom say?"

"That as a big-time journalist, they probably figured you had some leads on the case and you were refusing to divulge them due to your incredible ethics and integrity."

"She did not!!!" Sometimes, the similarities between me and Pop are only visible on the page.

"Oh yes she did!!!"

We both laughed for a bit, then caught our breaths. "Do you think August is okay in there with her?" I asked.

"Oh yeah, she's fine," Dad assured me. "Now, what's the real story? Why are you in town?"

"I am involved in this thing, but I'm trying to figure out what happened. I was looking into it as a story, since one of the guys who died happened to do it in my neighborhood. Now, the police think I did it. So instead, I need to find out who did."

"Which means the best help we can offer is to let you get back to it and stay off your back until you let us know everything is okay?" He was serious. I guess I should have expected it, considering everything, but every once in a while, the folks can surprise you.

"Yeah. I'll call you if I need help."

"No you won't. You never have before. But that's okay. We'll still be here either way."

"Thanks, Pop."

He gave me a "don't mention it" gesture. "Honey," he called out. "Bring the young lady out here. She and Skids have to get going. He's got a deadline to meet."

I looked at Dad. Thanking him again would have been redundant and out of character. I think he knew.

We said our good-byes outside, hugging twice before and once after we'd put our helmets on.

"You know I hate you riding that thing," Mom said before the engine noise drowned her out.

We waved as I pulled out onto the street. They were still there, waving, as I turned onto the on-ramp. I bet we were crossing the Blue Diamond exit before they went back inside.

"Thank God for lane-splitting," I said as I parked the bike in an access alley in Marina del Rey. "If it wasn't for lane-splitting we'd still be sitting in that mess downtown."

"And I wouldn't be in now-perpetual fear of losing my knees every time I ride with you," was August's witty reply.

"Fair enough."

The ride back had been uneventful. Two gas stops (and still less than a double sawbuck) and a pee break for August put us into the city at what has become known, rather optimistically in LA, as rush hour. Lane-splitting is the quickest and easiest way to get through that snarl and is the God-given right of motorcycle riders everywhere.

The basic concept involves traveling along the dotted lines instead of in the jammed-up lanes, between the cars which are stopped (or moving slow enough to be mistaken for stopped). For me, it was reason number 3 for not owning a car. Numbers 2 and 1 respectively are: Too hot in the summer; and the all-important lemming factor ("if everyone else is doing it, so should I"). Granted, there is a certain amount of lemming factor involved with the Sunday cyclists who are buying Harleys these days but put me up against any three of them and I think we all know who'd win.

"Where are we?" August asked, looking around the expensive neighborhood.

"Bernie's place." I tried the garage door we were parked in front of but it wouldn't budge. "Probably be able to open it from the inside."

"Inside?"

"Safest place in a storm is watching it on the big screen... or something like that."

Technically, I'm not sure of the definition of shock. I've seen people in both agitated and catatonic states which doctors then explained away with 'shock.' Personally, I think if you were to look up the word in the dictionary, you'd see a picture of August's face right then.

"We're going in there?"

"I don't see a better place for us to hang out until all this blows over."

"But...but...but..." I don't care what people say, you don't sound anything like a speedboat when you can't figure out what to say.

"I know. Crazy ain't it?" I grabbed her arm and started walking up the back stairs. I'd never been inside Bernie's place - the only reason I knew where he lived was I had dropped him off here one night a few months back - and hoped there wasn't an alarm or anything like that.

"But how are we going to get in?" At last, August

formulated a thought. "And won't the police be looking for us here?" Two thoughts even.

"Second first," I said. "Police already checked this place for Bernie. No way they'll be looking for us here. Besides, I want to talk to them anyway. And it's not really the police we're worried about, is it? And first, I have a key."

"We're not worried about the police?"

I shook my head.

"Where did you get a key?"

Bernie had given me his keys when I put him on the plane to Vegas, but those were back at my place and August knew that. Instead, I pulled out a set of keys held together with a tag reading "B's place" in nice, neat, and decidedly estrogen-heavy handwriting and showed them to her. "Gina's set. I decided she wouldn't mind."

"You touched a dead body?"

I shivered, mocking her. "Ewww, no." I tried the key in the lock and it turned the first time. "I riffled a dead girl's purse."

"I applaud your integrity." She was now mocking me, but that was okay. I turned the door handle and opened the door slowly, waiting for an alarm to go off. When nothing happened right away, I swung the door all the way open and walked in. August followed me.

"What now?"

"I'd say make yourself at home and I'd ask you to fix me a drink, but I have no idea where he keeps his liquor. So how about you learn the layout of the house, and I'll figure out how to get the garage door open and my bike into it?"

Before she could answer, I was heading down some stairs in what I assumed to be the general direction of the garage.

Luckily, the garage door opened quite easily from the inside and my bike was still where I'd left it. I wheeled it in and unpacked the saddle bags.

August had all the lights on, and I could follow the noise of the TV all the way into the living room, which was just off the kitchen. A large tumbler of Captain's and Coke was waiting for me on the island in the middle of the kitchen. August was stretched out on the leather couch with a remote in one hand and a drink in the other. I noticed the bottles still out. Choosing for herself, August was drinking two fingers of a nice single malt.

Bernie's answering machine sat on the counter, its red light blinking like the window of an Amsterdam whorehouse. I couldn't resist. Personally, I think it was just the idea of hitting the "play" button and actually hearing the messages the first time. So I did. I turned the volume down so I wouldn't disturb August.

There were six messages in all. Three from the club filling him in on Cup details. Two from Marty, asking where he was and offering a good lawyer. The final message was from Gina.

"Bernie, I need to talk to you," Gina's voice said. She sounded hurried and quiet, as if someone in the next room might overhear. "I know you didn't kill Jā. Meet me at our special spot, tonight if possible."

Her special spot must have been Jā's place.

I grabbed my drink, shut the kitchen light and joined her in the living room.

"Your friend has a nice place," she said.

"Never been inside before, but yeah, I'd say he's doing all right." I stayed standing.

"What's our plan?"

I looked at my watch. "It's getting late to make any type of business calls, so I'll probably just check in with Guantanamo and see if I have any messages. You could do the same."

"Sure, but why would Guantanamo know if I have any messages?"

I scowled at her with a "you know what I meant" kind of look.

She smiled back with a "two can play at that game" response. "And then?"

"I dunno. I guess we should take it easy and rest tonight and I can start up again in the morning. I have a lot of work to do."

She patted the couch cushion next to her. "Do you think you could hold off on the phone calls for a bit?"

I sat down. She slid next to me. "Yeah, no one I really need to talk to anyway...."

"Your mom is really very sweet, you know?" She leaned in close. I grunted my agreement. The air was getting uncomfortably thick and making it hard to breathe. "In fact, I think you take after her quite a bit."

"Really?" It was more of a croak than a question.

"Oh yeah." She kissed me.

With all we'd been through, this wasn't on my list

of things to expect, especially after seeing my folks this afternoon, but I'm a good Boy Scout, always prepared. I kissed her back. And then some.

Wednesday

Wednesday Morning

I woke up with August in my arms and a blissful smile on my face.

I'd love to tell you we spent the entire evening wrapped up together, enjoying each other's bodies in a cornucopia of wild sexual delight. But I'll bet the fact we were both still completely dressed and on the couch, TV droning, would give some indication I was lying.

The truth of the matter was we kissed for a bit, did a serious amount of spit swapping, and then we both passed out. Hey, I'm not proud of it, but we were both exhausted. It had been a really long day.

"Besides," I thought. "There'll be plenty more time for that later, right?" At least I was hoping there'd be plenty more time, since there were people out to kill me.

It was that thought which brought me back to the sobering reality of where I was and what I was involved in. Then I thought about who I had to call.

Carefully, so as not to wake August, I extricated myself from her and slipped off the couch. I turned the TV sound down (but not off) and went looking for the phone. I found a cordless cradled on the counter near a clock. As I picked it up, I noticed two things: First, it was only 9:30 in the morning and second, I couldn't get another "C" word into that sentence if I tried.

I punched in my number first. I wasn't sure if Guantanamo would answer it, or if he was even home, but it was worth a shot. The phone rang four times and I figured I was shit out of luck and neither Guantanamo nor the machine were going to answer. I decided to let it ring a couple more times, just to make sure.

The phone gods were with me; on the seventh ring the machine picked up. It told me I wasn't home but I would be happy to return any call left by people trying to get hold of me, with the exception of creditors and women named "Butch," if only they'd leave a message with their name and number. Then I crossed my fingers and waited for the beep.

I lost a slight bit of circulation in the tips of the crossed fingers before it finally went off and let me leave my message, which consisted of me channeling my three exclamation point spouting dad and yelling "Guantanamo!!!" as loudly as I could. I had, if memory and my machine served me correctly, about 60 seconds to wake Bey and get him to pick up the phone and talk to me. Any longer and the machine would cut me off, and I figured the odds I had for getting it to pick up again were about the same as me ever getting on a Honda, and we all know how bad those odds are.

I was on my third round of "Pick up the phone you inconsiderate, wasted lump of human flesh" when I heard a click on the other end. Damn. Out of time.

"Wasted lump of human flesh? Is that the best you could come up with?"

Oh, thank God. "It's early, I'm tired and you know I don't mean it anyway."

"Yes, you do, but that's okay. I know where you live. In fact, I live where you live, and I know where you keep your beer. Now, why are you calling me at this ungodly hour of the morning? Where are you?"

"I'm around and I'm calling because I'm awake. Did anyone call for me?"

"Where are you? Are you in town? Never mind, don't answer that. I don't want to know. But are you going to get your mail from the post office? I'm expecting a package and--"

"Shut up. Did anyone call for me while I was gone?"

"A couple of people. Publisher Steve called late yesterday and some guy calling himself Detective Collins called in the morning. Why would you even joke about a thing like that? Detective Collins. Just thinking about it gives me the creeps. Although there was a guy in the service we called 'Officer.' Although, now that I think about it, that could have been because he actually was one."

"What did they want?"

"They both wanted to know where you were."

"And did you tell them?"

"I'm not stupid. I told them you were working on a story and in the field doing research. Said you'd get back to them as soon as you could."

"And did either of them buy it?"

"Nope. But Publisher Steve offered me your column."

"He can't do that. Deadline isn't until Wednesday."

"Yeah, that's today. He said if--"

"Today is Wednesday?"

"Yeah. That new giant squid movie opens Friday. You wanna go?"

"Don't think so. Did Collins leave a number?"

"He did, but I didn't write it down."

"What, exactly, do I pay you for?"

"Not my secretarial services, that's for damn sure. You gonna be home soon?"

"I hope so, why?"

"I just want to know if I should have people 'round."

"As long as you clean up when you're done."

"Deal."

I started to say something else, but I caught myself in time. See, for Guantanamo, when he ran out of things to say, the conversation was over, and he'd hung up as soon as he'd gotten what he wanted. Me, I was in trouble. I had a column to write and a police detective to contact, not to mention a beautiful woman asleep on a wanted friend's couch. So many choices, so little time.

But, as always, work before pleasure. I dialed the number to the office. The special number that went directly into Publisher Steve's office. It was one of the advantages to being me. There were so many downsides that a perk every now and again was nice. That's the official reason. I think the unofficial reason I got the direct line was that most of the secretaries were scared of me and if I wanted to talk to Publisher Steve, it was best to let me.

He answered on the first ring. "Revolution Magazine Group."

"Publisher Steve? Skids here."

There was a brief pause. "Who is this?"

"I told you, it's me, Skids Poppe."

"Listen, I don't know who you are or what kind of game you're playing, but imitating Skids is certainly not a way to get ahead in life."

"What? Imitating me is a great way to get some head in life. Why do you say it's not me?"

"What time is it?"

"About a quarter to ten."

"Exactly. The real Skids would never call me this early, especially on deadline day. If this was really you, you'd have waited until a few hours after you got up, say around five or so, and then immediately launched into an excuse as to why your stuff is going to be late. So you see, it's not you."

"But…" I tried to find fault with his logic, but it made sense. I gave in. "Fair enough. It's not really me. But if it was me, do you think I could convince you to run one of my 'run in case of death' stand-by columns?"

"If you had any left, maybe. But you don't and I need to fill the space."

"When do we go to press?"

"Tomorrow at 5."

"Can I get it to you tomorrow by 3?"

"10 p.m. tonight."

"Noon tomorrow."

"What's the topic?"

He was relenting. I had him and I knew it. Now, just to close in for the kill and - "Topic?"

"Yeah. What's it about?"

"You know I never know until I write it."

"Humor me."

I thought about it. What could I tell him that he would believe? I took a gamble. "The low budget film industry and a guy murdered in Venice."

There was a long sigh on the other end of the phone. "Fine. You don't want to tell me, don't. Just have it here in time."

He hung up. He and Guantanamo must have some very short conversations.

Next I dug the number for Detective Collins out of my notebook. After a short period of time on hold, when, I'm sure, they traced the call, Collins picked up the line.

"Skids, that you?"

"None other. Heard you called."

"You didn't leave town, did ya?"

"Never. I love this city."

"I've read your columns; I know exactly how you feel about this city. Wanna tell me what happened at your place a couple nights ago?"

"Not really. I think that's between me and a certain young lady."

"Speaking of...did the same people who got your place get hers, too?"

"I don't know what you're talking about."

There was a pause on his end, like when something's going on and you're distracted but you don't want to let the person you're talking with know. I figured they had finally tracked the call and discovered where I was. Collins, meanwhile, had decided to switch tactics.

"Where were you yesterday?"

"Right where I am now." It was a ploy. I wanted to see if they knew.

"So you don't answer the door when people come over?"

They knew. "Not my place. I have to respect the owner's privacy."

"And where is the owner?"

"How should I know? All I'm doing is watching his place until he gets back."

"So how long will you be there?"

"Weeks, months maybe. Really depends on the season. He's got cable and the bowling championships are on."

"Look, Skids." He was losing patience; I could hear it in his voice. "Here's how were going to play it: We want to question your friend. If we can't question him, we will question you, for at least 72 hours, and then book you on aiding and abetting, possibly harboring a fugitive from justice. If we're in a particularly nasty mood, accessory after the fact or even, and this is the one I most like, murder one.

"Now, we both know you didn't do it, but it would make me a local hero with the boys if I could bring you down and make your life miserable. I don't want to do that. I never thought being a local hero with the boys was all that much to aspire to. So, what do ya say? You talk to your friend and see which one of you comes in for questioning. Like I said, as long as I have someone, I still come out smelling like a rose."

I thought about it for a second. There was no way this piss-ant of a detective was going to threaten me, Skids Poppe, with any type of legal action. I'll show him, I thought.

"I'll see what I can do," though, is what came out of my mouth.

Collins grunted something which sounded vaguely affirmative then hung up without saying good-bye. Great. I'd be willing to bet money - Bernie's money, mind you, and duly noted on my expense report - that Collins was serious. He'd actually try to arrest me.

I wondered if he had a case. Could I account for where I was Thursday night? Probably. At least to a point. I'm sure I was drinking. Okay, so that wasn't a big stretch. I'm drinking most nights. Guantanamo could back me up on that. Mutt was with us as well, although I'm not sure that either of them were tipping the scales on the side of credibility. Jerry B., the bartender at the Zero Bar, could vouch for me up until 2 a.m. or so but I still didn't know what time Jā was killed so I didn't know if that helped at all. Besides, what kind of a motive did I have?

"Skids? You up?"

I looked up as my motive walked into the room. Regardless of the fact that I didn't officially meet her until Saturday night, she was certainly a plausible reason to kill a man who was treating her wrong. Especially if they just wanted to make life uncomfortable for me. Shit.

"Yeah, I'm up."

"You look depressed. Everything okay?"

"Fine. I just remembered I have a column due tomorrow which I haven't started yet."

"Well I'm sure you'll be able to knock it out in no time. You have breakfast yet?"

I smiled at her. She looked great in the morning. No make-up, hair a mess, and bits of sleep still crusting her eyes and she was gorgeous. "Nope, I was waiting for you."

"For me what? To cook?"

Sounded good to me.

"All right, but don't get used to it. I'll see what Bernie has in the fridge. Is there anything you don't like?"

I shook my head.

"Be ready soon." She turned and walked down the hallway and disappeared into the bathroom. Someone had their priorities straight. Me? I was still holding the phone figuring out who to call next. The clock was creeping past ten so it was now into the safe time to call anyone with a real job. I dug out the Goldman Galleries card and examined it.

My notebook was still open to Detective Collins' number; I flipped back to the fax number for Producer Dave. Yup, I was right. Sometimes it pays off to have a great head for remembering phone numbers. Producer Dave and Goldman Galleries were both getting faxes at the same place and unless it was a Kinko's in Beverly Hills, they were interconnected.

I toyed with the phone, running through a few conversation scenarios in my head before I dialed. Behind me, August flushed and came back into the kitchen. She kissed me on the lips and her breath smelled minty fresh. By her look, I could tell mine didn't. She was too polite to say anything. At least not that directly.

"Why don't you go freshen up and I'll have breakfast waiting when you get out. I found clean towels and extra toothbrushes and put one of each out for you."

I had a toothbrush in my bag, but if she went to all that trouble who was I to say no? I nodded and headed off to get clean. At least this solved my problem about whether or not to call right then. Now I would have the whole of the shower to help me figure out how to ask the right questions to let me know if these people killed Jā.

Clean, well fed and ninety minutes older, I picked up the phone and made the first of the rest of my calls. I didn't want to do it with August there, so I took the phone and dialed as I made my way to the roof-top sun deck. Bernie's was much more well apportioned than mine. Spring answered on the first ring.

"Did you find him?" She sounded anxious.

"Waldo? No. I did see Elvis once, though."

"Who is this?"

"It's me. Who's this?" Turnabout is fair play, I've

always said.

There was a pause, as if she couldn't believe what she was about to say. "Skids?"

"I'm flattered. You recognized my voice after only one meeting. How's Jack?"

"What do you want? Where are you?"

"That's really the question, isn't it? Can't tell you where I am. Who were you expecting?"

There was silence from the other end. She didn't know what to do. I figured if I let her think about it for too much longer, she'd hang up and I'd be stuck with one more dead end. I jumped into the conversation.

"Was it Ian? What's going on with you guys? Let me guess, you were pissed at Jā, so you had Ian knock him off?"

"No one was supposed to die."

"What? I was kidding."

"So was I." She wasn't. She knew something.

"Bullshit. What do you know? Is Ian involved? I don't care if he is, I just need to clear Bernie. You got to tell me, who killed Jā?"

I don't know how much of that she heard. I stopped talking when the recorded voice came on telling me if I'd like to make a call to please hang up and try again. Spring was going to make a move and I had to get to her first.

I was back down the stairs before I'd finished the thought. August met me at the landing. I think somewhere along the line I'd yelled her name.

"What is it?" she asked.

"Where does Spring live?"

"Mar Vista. Why?"

"Where? Address." I was frantic. August was following me as I ran down the stairs into the garage.

"I don't know. I just know how to get there."

"Fine. You're coming with." I tossed her a helmet and gunned the bike to life. She was still looking a bit dazed as I backed the bike out into the alley. She started the garage door closing and ran out under it. I waited until I felt her weight on the seat before I took off.

On the way, I filled August in a little about what we were doing. Not everything, because I didn't know everything yet, but enough. I'd say it took me, all told, from the time we left the house to the time we got to Spring's street in Mar Vista, about four minutes. Add in the two minutes it took to get out of the house and that gave us a six-minute lag time. Maybe eight if I miscalculated, but no more.

We turned onto Charnock and August pointed down the road, about halfway, to a house on the left. It was a nice little cottage, the kind built during the twenties as day-getaways for silent film stars. I would have found the place on my own by the big dog lounging in the fenced-in front yard.

I stopped the bike across the street.

"Her car still here?"

August looked around. "Don't see it, but that doesn't mean anything."

I walked over to the gate. Jack took notice as I approached. He got up to have a look. "Hey Jack, how's it going, boy?"

The dog looked up at me, searching its memory to see if I matched. I watched the tail, usually a good indicator.

It twitched. Then it started wagging in earnest. Then I noticed August standing next to me. Well, at least the dog recognized one of us.

"She'd never leave him," August said, rubbing a hand across Jack's grateful forehead. The dog didn't need much. As we walked up to the door, he followed for a few steps then found his spot in the yard to resume his morning nap.

I knocked on the door, then thought better of it. I ducked aside and put August right in front. A minute later, Spring opened up.

"August, what are you doing here?"

Before my girl could answer, I stood up, twisted around and found myself inside the house alongside a screaming Spring Tyme. I put my hand over her mouth and stayed with her as she backed into the living room. August followed and shut the door behind us.

It was a good thing August was there. She noticed the little things I kept missing. Like shutting the door. And the fact the phone was off the hook. She hung it up, after telling whoever it was on the other end Spring would have to call her back, her dog had just been hit by a car. Then August looked at me. I smiled and nodded and would have given her a thumbs-up if I'd had a hand free. As it was, I was walking with Spring, trying to guide her into a wall. Not easy, but I did it. Then it was my turn to talk.

"I don't want to hurt you, but you know something I

need to know. If you tell me, I'll let you go and then I'll go away. How's that for a plan?" I took my hand away as a measure of good faith.

"Fuck you."

"Look, I already know enough to cast at least a shadow of doubt on whatever alibi Ian might have. If you don't tell me what you know, I'll place an anonymous tip and your boyfriend gets questioned."

"Big deal. Questioned is nothing. They got nothing on him. Besides, he was with me the night Jā was killed."

"Implicating yourself?"

"Fuck off."

Spring sat down on the couch and wouldn't look at me. August stood across from her.

"Why are you with him, August? What kind of a hold does he have on you?"

"He just wants to help his friend. And ours. This isn't about getting anyone in trouble, it's about getting Bernie out of it."

For a long time, no one said anything. Jack barked at someone walking past (I know, I looked).

I walked out of the room, looking for the kitchen. "You got something to drink in this place?" I asked as I rummaged her cabinets.

As soon as I left, the two girls started talking amongst themselves. I made a big show of finding a glass and opening a beer. "Ew, domestic," I shouted out.

Pouring the beer into the glass was about the end of my stalling techniques. While I drank, I rested against the door jamb, out of site, and listened to the girls.

"Jā was doing something with the money," Spring was saying. "Ian was flipping out because all the accounts at the equipment houses were drained. Jā said he was paying them, but he wasn't. When he needed to calm Ian down, he came to me."

"Why you?" August asked.

"I knew Ian. I'd met him a few times and he liked me. Jā told me to go out with Ian, take his mind off his troubles, and then Jā would leave me alone."

"And you did?"

"What else could I do?"

"You could have said 'no'."

"I could have, but then he would have told you about us. He said if I did this, he wouldn't ask me for anything else. No money. No nothing. This was it and we were through. I thought it would be the easy way out."

"What happened?" August asked.

"What do you think happened? I went out with Ian and it actually went well. We ended up back at his place and I convinced him to calm down and trust that Jā would work things out."

"He believed you?"

"I had his dick in my mouth, of course he believed me."

From where I stood, I felt she made a valid point. If someone had my dick in their mouth, I'd take their word for whatever. Hell, I think that's how my subscription to Architectural Digest started.

"After that," Spring continued, "we saw each other off and on. We were together Thursday night."

I decided it was my turn to come back in.

"All night?"

She looked up. I think she'd forgotten I was there. "Yes. All night."

"Even after you went to sleep?"

"What do you mean?"

"Did you wake up together?"

She was getting pissed off. "No. He was up before me. Said he had an early call."

"You have no idea what time he left?"

"I would have noticed if he'd left the bed."

"You didn't notice when he got up for work."

"That's different."

"No, it's not. And from what I hear, Ian likes to work at night. Heard he doesn't sleep all that well. What time did you guys go to bed?"

She got up and walked over to the door. It was open and Jack was standing at the threshold wagging his tail, hoping to be allowed in. Spring counted to ten slowly then spoke.

"I think you'd better leave."

Like I care what she thinks. "Hell, you could have convinced him to kill Jā and that would help you both out."

By now, August was getting uncomfortable. She got up and grabbed my arm, trying to lead me to the door. I still hadn't finished my beer.

"Look," I went on. "I'm not saying you did. I just want to know what you know."

Spring was near tears. "That's all I know."

"Who were you expecting when I called?"

"Ian."

"Bullshit."

She took a breath. "No, I was. Him and a guy named Dave. One of the producers of the film, the guy that got Ian into it. After your call the other day, when you knew about Ian and me, I got scared. Ian thought you might be dangerous."

She hid her eyes. She was frightened and nervous and her best friend was sitting beside her. Either she was telling me what she knew now, or she would never tell me. I took the positive view and assumed she just didn't know much.

I drained my beer and set the glass down on the coffee table.

"Now aren't you glad your fears are unfounded?" I let August lead me out. "Thanks for the beer," I offered as we passed.

I was strapping my helmet on and about to check on the address for our next destination when August started in on me. I knew it was coming, but that still didn't make it any nicer.

"What the hell was that all about?"

You know, it seems a lot more pleasant when you see the words on paper than when you are being assaulted with them by the woman you lust after.

"I needed to know some stuff and she needed to tell me."

"In case you didn't notice, she happens to be one of

my best friends."

"Who was also sleeping with your boyfriend." Oops. There are times when that defense mechanism jumps in a little too quickly and very deftly inserts your foot into your mouth in such a way no amount of surgery will ever take it out again. This was one of those times. I really shouldn't have said that.

"You really shouldn't have said that."

I wasn't sure what to do. I could apologize, but it wouldn't sound sincere, or I could continue and not acknowledge the fact I had seriously hurt her feelings. Either way, I was fucked.

For her part, I think she was undecided as to whether to get on the bike or go back into the house. Before she could decide, I made my move.

"Look, I'm--"

"Don't say you're sorry because you're not. You knew what you were saying, and you meant it. And I can't fault you for it because it's true. I just don't like the truth being thrown in my face as a trump card for you to use whenever you need to talk yourself out of trouble."

We both looked at each other for a few seconds. I don't know what went through her head, but mine was filled with thoughts long-time friends would swear I had never had in my life. Mostly about how put-together this girl was to start calling my double-deals this early in the game. I put my hand in my pocket, just to have something to do with it, and found the Goldman Galleries card there.

"I have to go. Are you coming with me?"

She pursed her lips and looked away. Then she

reached for her helmet.

"When we talk about this... and we will talk about this... you will not bring up Spring or any of her…indiscretions. Is that clear?" I nodded.

She got on the bike first. I handed her the business card so she could check for addresses while we drove. Neither of us said another word the entire way to Beverly Hills.

Goldman Galleries took up an expensive bit of real estate on Cañon Drive near yet another Wolfgang Puck restaurant. And theoretically, it would start paying for that real estate - and then some - as soon as it opened.

Thankfully, Harley Davidson motorcycles were not an unknown sight in the Mecca of movie stars (thank you Jay Leno) so no one paid any attention as I backed into the curb in front of the gallery. Sure, we might have if any one of the tourists rushing about from store to store to get in all their shopping before the bus left had realized I wasn't a movie star, but instead a journalist wanted on a murder rap, but when you look like me and have someone who looks like August with you, people assume you're famous. The only giveaway was me ducking my head as a Beverly Hills Police squad car cruised past. They turned the corner and we rang the bell on the gallery door. The timing couldn't have worked out any better.

We were buzzed in and immediately greeted by a secretary or assistant letting us know the gallery wasn't open and how could she help us.

"Hi. I'm Skids Poppe," I put out my hand to be as

friendly as possible. "I'm looking for Dave. Is he in?"

The girl shook my hand. It's an automatic thing, really. You put your hand out and, unless they're prepared for it and really want to slight you, if they see it, they'll take it.

"Dave Black?"

"Is there another Dave working here?"

August was confused and so was our receptionist.

"Dave Black would be the only Dave, but he doesn't really work here. I mean, he works with Mr. Goldman, and he's been using our offices for a few weeks, but he's not employed by the gallery."

I nodded. That made sense. "Is he in?"

She shook her head. "No. He hasn't been in all week."

"That explains why he hasn't returned my calls. No problem. Is Leonard in?" Before she could repeat her earlier question, I volunteered a last name. "Leonard Goldman? It is his gallery, right?"

"Yes. He's in. Please wait here and I'll see if he's available." She turned to go. "What did you say your name was?"

"Skids Poppe. With three Ps." I nodded smugly as she walked away.

"Smooth," August said. I hoped she was talking about me and not the girl. "It's amazing how much you can get away with using pure bullshit."

I took it as a compliment. "It's not really bullshit; more like restrained arrogance. But the effect is generally the same."

"I see."

Poppe Culture

I looked over at her. This could go either way. She was looking at me and while she wasn't exactly smiling, she wasn't frowning either. It looked like we might be able to fix this.

"Do you think he'll see us?" she asked.

"No idea. I can only hope. Hell, I have a column to turn in tomorrow. If this doesn't get wrapped up soon, I'll have to find the time to write and catch the guy who killed Jā. But I have faith."

"What's the column on?"

"Can't tell you."

"You don't know, do you?"

"Never do, until I sit down to write it. Spontaneity works better when it's not planned out."

That got a smile. The journey to recovery had taken its first step.

"Mr. Goldman has a few minutes to spare." It was our receptionist, coming back. "If you'll follow me, you can wait in the office."

She led us into a utility office in the back of the gallery. This wasn't the office the clients would ever see. This wasn't where contracts for $50,000 drawings were signed. This was where the real work was done. Where the fax machine and the water cooler were. In short, it was a mess. Papers were everywhere, stacked on books opened to paint-spattered pages (they might have been art reproductions, but it was hard to tell). Our girl deposited us here, promising the imminent arrival of Mr. Goldman.

"Can I get either of you something to drink while you wait?" she asked.

I looked at August, wondering if she was going to order waters for both of us again. She didn't.

"We're fine," said August. I nodded my agreement.

The girl smiled and walked away without saying another word.

As soon as she left, I started rummaging through the papers on the desk. "Keep an eye out," I whispered to August. "Let me know when somebody's coming." She gave an exasperated sigh and got up to stand by the door.

Everything on the desk was art related. There were books and framing quotes and artists' contact numbers, but nothing about the film. I looked at August. She may not have been happy about it, but she was being a dutiful look-out. I decided to risk it and went for the filing cabinet.

The top drawer held nothing under the "B" file. On a whim, I tried the third drawer down.

Sure enough, there was a file labeled "Film Projects." I thumbed through it, leaving it in the drawer in case I needed to close it quickly. There were general notes on Jā, then some on a project called "Aces." There was nothing on "Body Mechanics." I was just about to close the whole thing when something caught my eye. It was a contract made out in the names of Haifisch, Alweighz and Acton. I tried to lift it out to read it, but I was interrupted.

"Someone's coming," August whispered. Then she sat down hard in her chair, trying to look bored.

I grabbed the contract, plus several pages behind it and crumpled them in a ball as I closed the drawer. I stuffed the wad in my pocket and started leafing through one of the open books on the desk. I'd just turned the first page when Leonard Goldman walked in.

He was short and round, not what you would have expected from Kim Goldman's father. My guess was she got her genes from Mom's side of the family.

"Hello, Mr. Poppe. Enjoying the Klimt?"

I was about to take offense when I realized he was talking about the book I was leafing through.

"Some of it's very…" I groped for the right word. "Colorful," I finally managed.

"I'm not a big Klimt fan myself. But he sells, and we are in the business here to make sales." It was then he noticed August. "Forgive me. I'm Leonard Goldman. Welcome to my gallery." He made it a grand gesture, as if the only reason the gallery existed was so he could show it to people like us.

"I'm August Everywhere."

"A pleasure." He took her hand and held it a second too long.

It was nice to know Kim got her brains and charm from Mom's side of the family, too.

Goldman walked around the desk to where I stood. He was shorter than me by about four inches, with graying hair holding tight to his head. In a way, he reminded me of Michael Tucker during his "LA Law" days. Only I suspected Goldman was a bastard once you got him in court. You don't spend as much time with the kind of guys I hang out with and not recognize a scrapper when you see one. And this guy was the worst kind.

Back in school, I used to always say given a choice

between fighting the geek and the football player, take the football player. It's more of an even fight and if the jock kicks your ass, at least it's over then and there. With the geek, you may pound him to a bloody stump, but he'll get even. When and where, you don't know, but it will happen.

Guys like Goldman were the reason I created that little axiom. I'd be willing to bet he'd destroyed more than his fair share of school-yard bullies. I could see no possible advantage to getting on his bad side. Of course, this meant a whole new approach, but that was okay. I could roll with the punches.

Goldman didn't wait for me to offer. He took the seat behind the desk, leaving me in the undesirable position of standing next to him. I could continue to stand, or I could walk back and take the seat next to August. Goldman waited for me to make up my mind.

I took the seat.

As soon as I had settled in, Goldman started talking. "So, Mr. Poppe, what can I do for you?"

"You can tell me about Jā Alweighz."

"He's dead."

"You're one up on your daughter. She doesn't know."

"She told me you came to see her. What did you want to know?"

"I wanted to know what Jā's connection with you was?"

"With me? None. He was involved with my daughter. I'd met him a few times, but I didn't know him."

"So, you're not producing his film?"

"Me? A film producer? No. I'm a lawyer and an art dealer. I do a couple other things here and there, but I'm afraid the film industry is just a bit too glamorous for me. If that's all you wanted to know, I'm sorry I couldn't help you more. But if you'll excuse me, I do have a lot of work to do." He got up, smiling.

"Who's Dave Black?"

That stopped him. He looked at me, the smile slowly fading from his face. He sat back down.

"I'm sorry, Mr. Poppe. I seem to have forgotten for just whom it is you are asking these questions."

The friendliness was on its way out. Replacing it was the shark-toothed lawyer I had sensed when he entered. Okay, it wasn't that much of a stretch, since I knew he allegedly worked for the mob, but looks can be deceiving. I'll bet it was the smile that got him off the indictment. Now though, the heavy guns were coming out and I was in the line of sight.

"I'm writing an article for 'Hollywood Insider' magazine. You know, 'We get the outsider in?' It's on financing independent movies."

"And what do I have to do with this article?"

"Well, we thought you were funding Jā's film. I mean, Kim did say he had gone to Vegas to see you about a business deal and one of the producers of the film, Dave Black, his fax number is for that fax machine." I pointed for dramatic effect.

"I believe this interview is over." Again, he got up to leave.

"But wait, we haven't even talked about the four

hundred grand." It was a risk, sure, but then I've never been one to play it safe, have I?

"Listen," Goldman said. He was leaning on the desk in the stereotypical pose of an angry bad guy. "I don't know who you are or what you want, but you are wading into water which can get very deep, very quick." He moved around and stood by the door, waiting for us to leave. August stood up and walked out the door. I started to follow her, but Goldman stopped me as I walked past.

"In a city of 17 million, people die all the time of unexplained causes," he whispered. "Do your best not to be one of them."

I could be in serious trouble here. August was already near the front door. I joined her. The receptionist was standing by the door as well, ready to let us out.

"Mr. Black just arrived, if you still wish to speak with him," she said. She motioned towards the back. A big guy was talking to Leonard Goldman. Goldman pointed towards us and Black turned to look. For a second, he and I locked eyes. I recognized him, although the last time I saw him, he'd been lying unconscious on the floor of my apartment.

"C'mon, we have to go." I hurried August out of the building and onto the bike. I didn't look back to see if we were being followed. Three blocks later, at the first red light, I finally stopped long enough to put on my helmet.

"Now do you want to tell me what happened back there?" August asked.

We were sitting at an upstairs table at Van Go's Ear.

Poppe Culture

What I was really in the mood for was Ships, but they had gone the way of Tiny Naylor's so now the Ear was it for comfort foods. Well, there and the Library Alehouse, but that was more of a dinner place.

We were finishing up lunch and I hadn't been doing a lot of talking. I had been thinking, but ever since I stopped moving my lips to read, I've been a bitch for mind readers.

"Near as I can figure, Goldman had Jā killed for stealing money."

"Why?"

"He threatened me as we were leaving and, whether you recognized or not, his friend, Dave Black, was one of the guys who tried to kill me at my place a few nights ago."

"I still don't see where you're getting your info."

To tell the truth, neither did I. But it made a certain kind of sense if you took gut feelings into the picture.

August moved our plates aside and took my hands. "What do we do now?"

"I'm not sure. Leaving town would be a good idea, except I have a deadline tomorrow."

August stared into my eyes. She took a moment to come up with the right words then asked the question I was hoping - since we left the gallery - that she wouldn't ask. "Are we in danger?"

I nodded. "I think so."

She sat back in her chair. "Shit."

I felt bad. I didn't know how to help her. I'd been in trouble before, more times than not, but it was always just me. Okay, me and Guantanamo, but he was there of his own volition (and nine out of ten times, had gotten us into the trouble to begin with). This was the first time in a while I had dragged someone else into the fire with me. "Sorry," I said.

August smiled weakly. "Not your fault. I was dating the wrong guy at the right time. These things happen." She paused. "Will you get me another Coke?"

I went downstairs to place the order. Reaching into my pocket for the money, I pulled out the papers I had snagged from Goldman's office. I looked through them while I waited for the drink.

My eyes went wide. "Holy Shit," I thought. "Goldman didn't kill Jā. But I think I know who did." I ran back upstairs to get August. I had some phone calls to make and one or two things to check out first, but I thought I could get everything taken care of by midnight.

"Hey, Skids, you forgot your coke...." was drowned out by the sound of my Sportster leaving the parking lot.

Wednesday Evening

I looked at the clock. 6:28 p.m. I'd been in Gina Acton's apartment for close to an hour and still hadn't found what I was looking for. Thankfully, it was still bright enough in the apartment to see everything without having to turn on the lights. I love Daylight Savings Time.

If August was with me, maybe she would have found it, but then, I really didn't want her here. Besides, she had work of her own to do.

I started my second go-round of the place. My first trip through Gina-land had turned up the usual, blatant stuff. You know, pictures of her with Bernie, some with other people. A bulletin board with a variety of papers tacked to it commemorating a hell of an active social life. Concert tickets for the Airheads of State gig I missed, a couple of used lift tickets, several postcards and a dollar bill folded into the shape of a swan. None of it did me any good. What I wanted wouldn't be out in the open.

I went for the underwear drawer. Nothing but net. Well, lace, actually, but still just panties and bras. More drawers contained more clothes, mostly shirts. A junk collection in the bottom of the armoire looked promising but it was nothing more than dead batteries and empty film canisters (plus a few Happy Meal toys, still in their wrappers; off-hand, I'd say the girl was a collector).

This is why I never became a second-story man. Sure, I could break in (this time, I had the key from Bernie's ring, but you get the idea) and rummage, but I could never find anything valuable. Now you understand why I admire Bernie Rhodenbarr, even if he was fictional. At least he could break into a house and immediately find the stuff worth the most money and get out clean in a fraction of the time it was taking me to discover Gina Acton had way too many burnt-out D cells for an actively dating woman.

I stopped for a minute. Maybe I was going about this entirely the wrong way. I knew what I needed to find would be in this apartment somewhere, so I just wasn't looking in the right place. That had to be the answer.

What would a real criminal do in this situation? He'd rip the place apart. Of course, this is what I was trying to avoid, but since it wasn't working there seemed no better time than the present to change tack.

I started with the bookshelf. It wasn't an impressive collection, mostly high-brow romance stuff like Nora Roberts and Danielle Steele. I'll give Gina points for having them in hardcover, but still. Nothing behind or in any of them anyway (this was a factual comment, not a quality-of-writing comment, although you can take it however you want).

Then I saw a section which I had dismissed earlier. The cookbooks. Face it, if I was a girl and I wanted to hide something from a guy, especially a guy like Bernie, I'd put it somewhere I was sure he'd never look. Outside of a Proust novel, a cookbook would be the place. And I saw no Proust anywhere.

I picked up the biggest one on the shelf, a red and white checkerboard baby from Betty Crocker, and opened it at random. The three-ring-binder approach proved incredibly helpful in searching for things which didn't belong. And there it was, near the end, in one of those clear plastic pouches. Pay dirt. I quickly sorted through the motel receipts, deposit records and bank statements to make sure they were what I needed. The Polaroids of Gina in compromising positions were an added bonus. Oh, baby, this was getting good. Amazing, really. When you know what you're looking for, you often find it.

Back at Bernie's place, I made two more phone calls. The first confirmed Guantanamo was home and the news crews weren't around. The second was to Vegas. I gave Bernie some explicit instructions, then I talked to Brandy.

"When is he gone?" were the first words out of her mouth.

"Why? What's the rush? I thought you liked him there."

"Sarcasm was never your strong suit. Answer the

question."

"Tomorrow, if everything goes well tonight."

"You're about to do something stupid, aren't you?" I couldn't decide if there was a hint of concern in her voice. I figured it was that or a bad piece of dinner stuck in her throat.

"What makes you say that?"

"Please. Look who I'm talking to."

It was definitely the food option.

"I need one last favor. You have to--"

"No."

"What do you mean 'no?' It'll help get him out of there."

"All right, one. What is it?"

"You're gonna be a pushover as a parent, you know that?"

"I'll change my mind...."

"Okay. Let Bernie make a couple of long-distance phone calls."

"He's got a cell phone, Skids. I've seen it. Why doesn't he use that?"

"That's easier to trace than a credit card," I said. I wasn't sure if it was true, but I was pretty sure I'd seen something about it on the Discovery Channel late one night. In any case, it wasn't worth the risk.

She thought about it for a second. "He's out tomorrow?"

"That or I'm dead. Either way, you don't have to deal with one of us anymore."

"Serious?"

"No. Even if I was dead, you'd still have to deal with me. Just let him make the calls. I gotta run."

She was saying something as I hung up. A small part of my large ego would like to think it was "good luck."

It was getting close to eight by the time August and I headed back to my place. I'd let her in on most of the plan, but she still didn't know everything I did. Why burden her with too much information at a time like this?

Guantanamo was waiting for us, the contents of his bag of tricks scattered across the living room floor. That's one of the great things about having Bey as a sidekick; makes no difference what you ask him to do, he's right there as a willing accomplice.

Of course, this was an easy one. It wasn't like I was asking him to do my tax returns or perform emergency first aid on one of my girlfriends (both of which he'd done in the past, albeit under protest). Nope, this time I was asking him to do something he really enjoyed doing. You could tell by the way he had lovingly assembled all his gear and how he was getting ready to pack it into travel bags that he loved this part of his job. I was glad. Every now and again it gave me a great deal of pleasure to make him happy.

The only thing I'd forgotten was that he and August hadn't yet met, and I'd made the mistake of telling him she was coming with me. When we walked in, he stopped what he was doing (well, actually, he froze completely in his tracks) and looked up cautiously, his hand tensing around an object hidden from view. I think the desired effect was to let us know if we were anyone but us, we'd be dead. It worked on August. She squeezed my hand tight until Guantanamo exhaled and released whatever it was he had his hand wrapped around inside his rucksack. Then he smiled and stood up.

"Skids," he nodded at me. "How you doin'? Everything going okay?"

"As can be expected."

Then he set his eyes on August. "You must be dead guy's girl," he said as he walked over, hand extended. "I'm Guantanamo. I'm sure Skids has told you a lot about me... and most of it is probably true."

August looked at me for approval. I shrugged my shoulders. There was no way I was taking responsibility here. She hesitantly shook his hand and when he didn't bite her, she introduced herself.

"Actually, my name is August."

"He told me." Then he went back to packing his bag.

August looked at me again, unsure of what to do. I understood. Like I said before, I've known Guantanamo for a long time. Long enough to know other people don't always get him. Hell, I don't always get him myself, but what the hell. He was still my best friend.

But August was, allegedly, my girlfriend. I had to get the two of them to meet in the middle. More accurately, I had to get Bey to take at least one step towards the middle and have August cover the extra ground. It wasn't exactly fair, but what was?

"Play nice or I get someone else to do the job," I told him.

His eyes went wide. I'm sure he was thinking there was no way I could be serious.

"There is no way you could be serious," he said. "You don't know anyone else who could do the job."

"There's always Happy Ellison."

"Oh, bullshit. You know Happy couldn't do the job nearly as good as me. Happy's color blind, for chrissake! He--" Guantanamo stopped. Probably he could see the twinkle in my eye. "You're bullshitting me, aren't you?"

I smiled positively and shook my head "No."

"Fair enough." He walked over to August. "Sorry, August. You being the dead guy's girl is no fault of yours. Sometimes people just make some stupid choices. There was this one time Skids and me, we were in Vegas, right, and he had long hair back then. Anyways--"

"Enough." I had to cut him off. It was way too soon for a new girl to hear about the haircut incident. "How're you coming along?" It really was alarmingly easy to get Bey sidetracked.

"Great. I even had everything I needed right here. Should be no problem at all."

"That's what I want to hear. How long do you think it'll take you to finish up?"

"Another two hours and I'm ready to roll."

"Perfect."

August was standing uncomfortably through all this. I'd wager she would have liked to hear about the haircut incident. If I wasn't careful, she'd corner Guantanamo and pry it out of him. Like it would be hard. I offered her a seat and a beer. She agreed to both and sat down.

In the kitchen, I realized Guantanamo had made a serious dent in the suds supply while I was gone. I'd have to put shopping on the agenda. I grabbed two and reached for an opener.

"Guantanamo? You want a beer?"

"Is the Pope named after the Beatles?"

I took that to mean yes and grabbed a third bottle.

"Hey Skids," Guantanamo called out. "Now that you're both here, what is the plan?"

I went back into the living room with the bottles and told him. To his credit, he never once asked "Why?"

I was nervous. Those of you who know me know it takes a lot for me to get scared. Well here it was, one of those few and far between times, so you'd better make the most of it.

According to my watch, late night hosts would be starting their monologues about now and the person I was supposed to meet was five minutes late. Well, people, really. Provided my phone calls proved successful, there should be several parties here by now.

"Here," in this case, was the top floor of Parking Structure Three on 2nd Street in Santa Monica. I was firmly ensconced against a wall, hidden by a shadow. My bike wasn't too far away if I needed it. Hopefully, I wouldn't. Hopefully, everything would go just as I'd planned it and the real killers would quietly turn themselves in and we could all get home in time for the late movie. I'm nothing if not overly optimistic.

I looked around to see if I'd missed anything. Nope.

There were still only five other cars up here, and none of them, as far as I could tell, belonged to any of my people. I thought about going over my notes again, but the moon wasn't nearly bright enough and there were no other lights. I could barely read my watch.

Eleven forty and still nothing. I didn't get it. What was the point in arranging a meeting if everyone was going to be late? This is not how professional people did business. At least I was pretty sure it wasn't.

Headlights. Thank God. Someone was coming. I shrank back as far as I could into the wall. A new Infiniti swung around the final turn and pulled into a parking spot just up from where I was hiding. Quickly following the Infiniti came a large pick-up and then a Mercedes. It looked like the whole gang was here. If I did this right, I would get out of here clean and Bernie would be a free man. If I didn't, well, Guantanamo knew where the spare set of keys to the bike were.

As car doors started opening, I decided it was time to go to work.

Marty Haifisch was the first one out of his car, the Infiniti. He looked pensive and uptight. He didn't see me. "Bernie," he called out, looking for his cousin. "Bernie, where are you?" Well, at least I knew Bernie had made the call.

"Bernie's not here, Marty," I said, stepping out from my hiding place.

Marty came closer. "He called, said to meet him here at a quarter to twelve."

Well that explained it. "It should have been eleven

thirty, but that's okay. And it was me you were going to meet, not him."

"Well that's great. I have nothing to say to you." He turned to leave when he saw the rest of the group I had invited. Leonard Goldman and Dave, his erstwhile associate, had left the doors to their Mercedes open while Ian, the D.P., had taken the time to lock and alarm his truck. What a world we live in, huh?

Goldman was the first to greet me by name. "Good evening, Skids. I assume you have a good reason for claiming you had my daughter hostage?"

"Actually, I just hoped it would get you here. Personally, I have no intention of holding your daughter hostage."

"I know. I called her. She said you were harmless. You'd make a lousy kidnapper."

I shrugged. What was I gonna do? He was right. Dave still didn't say anything.

When Marty saw Goldman, he held his ground, waiting for them to reach the same spot. I walked forward to meet them. Ian joined the group the same time I did.

For a minute, everyone just looked at everyone else. I tried to tell by their eyes who knew who or what and how much of each, but the same poor lighting which let me hide did wonders for facial subtlety. We just stood there, checking each other out.

Suddenly, I realized this was my chance to say one of those lines people wait their whole lives to say. I jumped at it.

"I assume you're wondering why I called you all

here."

Nailed it. Even the Romanian judges would have to give me high marks for that one.

"You bet your ass we want to know what the fuck we're doing out here." That was Dave. I could see how this guy became a producer.

I went for my opening gambit and hoped the other members of my team were in position and taking care of their end of things.

"We're here because a friend of mine has been accused of the murder of Jā Alweighz."

"And this has what to do with me?" Ian asked.

Since he had asked, I felt it was my responsibility to answer him. "You had the most to gain, at least right off, by killing Jā. You took over his film, not to mention you were sleeping with a girl he was sleeping with."

Goldman butted in. "You're sleeping with my daughter? You bastard! I thought we had a deal." He lunged at Ian and our little circle widened a bit.

"He's not fucking Kim!" I yelled and jumped in between them. Dave was holding Goldman back and Marty was just trying to stay out of the way. Leonard took a couple of deep breaths, enough to calm his breathing down.

"What…" he said, gasping for air. "What are you talking about?"

"He's not sleeping with Kim. He's sleeping with a girl named Spring. But that doesn't change the fact he took over the film. What kind of a deal did you guys have, anyway?"

"I promised I could bring the film in on time and on

budget," Ian said.

"Before or after Jā disappeared?"

Ian took a deep breath. He looked to Goldman for support.

"Hey, we're all friends here. If you can't trust us, who can you trust?"

Goldman wasn't giving anything away. If I ever got in trouble again with the law, I was going to do my best to hire him – provided he wasn't in jail himself.

"Before," Ian said. "There were some financial problems and I told Dave and Leonard I could do it right if they got rid of Jā. But I didn't kill him!"

He was scared. He was the one to go after. The others were all used to intimidation, but not him. He was way out of his league. Then again, so was I, but I wasn't about to let that stop me.

"Please. You're playing with some heavy hitters here. You telling me you didn't know what 'get rid of' meant? It was Jā's project. Getting rid of him any other way killed the project. This way you get your name above the line and a beautiful dedication in the credits to your friend Jasper. Seems to me it was all your idea."

Now was the moment of truth. If it was his idea, which I didn't think, but you never knew, he was going to bolt. If he didn't, well, I've been wrong before.

I watched him decide what to do. It didn't take long. "I swear to God I didn't kill him. He was an asshole, sure, but I didn't want to see him dead. I just thought Dave was going to scare him a bit and--"

"Shut your fucking mouth." Dave's fist came out so

fast no one had time to react. Ian was down before we knew it, holding a bleeding lip.

I reached down to offer Ian a hand up. He refused and stayed where he was, nursing his lip. I turned to Dave. "Well, what of it?"

"What of what? Listen you greaseball, I didn't kill no one."

"That's your story and you're sticking to it, right?"

"You betcher ass." Then his expression changed. "Wait a minute... you making fun of me?"

Dammit. I was getting rusty. Usually, I was long gone before this happened.

"Of course not. I know you didn't kill anyone. Although you really tried with me. Sorry about that conk on the head, by the way." I almost had him back. One or two more lines and I could fuck with him again, but now wasn't the time.

"'Sides," I continued, "You wouldn't have killed anyone without the orders of your boss Leonard here, and we all know he's as clean as they come, especially with someone like Marty doing the books. Right, Marty?"

Marty was surprised. I guess he thought we were going around the circle and it would be a little while before we got to him. Tough.

"What are you talking about?" he asked.

"Tell you what. I'll start talking and you let me know when it starts making sense. Anyone feel free to jump in at any time."

"I don't need to be here for this," said Marty. He turned to go.

"I believe you do. Somehow I don't think you're going anywhere." I held up a small remote control, the kind with three buttons you use to do various things with your car, like lock the doors or activate the alarm.

"What are you going to do with that?" asked Marty.

"Just ensuring you don't leave. Three buttons for three bombs in... one, two, three cars. I mean, hey, no use having a sidekick who can blow things up if you never use him, right?" I hoped to God Guantanamo had taken care of things like he was supposed to. All I had to do was press a button and "Boom!!!"

Thing was, no one knew whether or not I was kidding.

Marty stopped and stared at me. I held the detonator tightly, waiting for him to call my bluff. He didn't. He came back. I held onto the remote, just in case.

"I have nothing to hide."

"Of course you don't. At least not anymore. You've already hidden everything."

Marty jumped for me. I wasn't expecting it and besides, my reflexes were a little slowed by the beating I'd taken from Dave and his pal a few nights earlier. I moved, but not quickly enough. He connected with my side, knocking the wind out of me and the remote out of my hand. Suddenly, I found myself sitting on the ground.

I stood up as fast as I could, trying to stop Marty's foot from connecting with my head. It worked, to a certain degree, and he hit my knee instead. But at least I was standing. I was ready for his next punch and side-stepped it completely, letting my fist come down on his head. He crumpled to the ground. I'm sorry, but accountants just can't fight.

I stepped back, wiping the sweat from my forehead, and let Dave help Marty up. Ian had stood again to get out of the way and was now taking up his old position in the group. Goldman was the only one untouched.

After a moment of heavy breathing on my part, Goldman spoke. "You were saying?" he asked. He was very cool.

"I was," I gulped. I held up my finger to ask for a minute more while I tried to get my breathing under control. I looked at Goldman. "How much did you invest in Body Mechanics?"

"Body Mechanics? Oh right, the first film. Close to half a million. Jā was going to finish that and then he had a Vegas film, Aces, which I was also going to finance. That was the one I was really interested in."

"How did you get involved with Jā?"

Goldman looked at the accountant, who was rubbing the back of his head. "Marty introduced us. It seemed like a decent investment."

"I can imagine. I've seen the budget for the film, and I know another guy who put up a chunk of change to see it get made. How come bills weren't getting paid? What happened to the money?"

We all looked at Marty. He started to take a few steps but a subtle move from Goldman and Dave's hands tightened on Marty's arms. He wasn't going anywhere.

"Jā took it," Marty said defensively.

"And how would you know that?" I asked.

"It's the only explanation. He took the money and got killed for it."

I looked at Goldman. "Is that what you normally do to people who steal from you?"

Goldman was getting into the game.

"No, Skids. Usually we break their legs. But if someone steals from me and from someone else and the other person kills him, who am I to get involved?"

I stopped short. "You knew about Bernie?"

Goldman nodded. "If he wanted Jā dead, that was his choice. It certainly didn't hurt my investment. I was out some money, but Marty said we could make it back with Ian shooting the film."

"What about Aces?"

"I had the notes. I could always hire another writer. You can't spit in this town without hitting some poor bastard willing to sell his soul to write a screenplay."

For me, everything was almost in place. There was only one other question I needed to ask to put it all in order. "Did you know Gina Acton?"

Goldman looked at me as if I'd asked the dumbest question possible. "Jā's wife? Yeah, she came to dinner with us a few times while we were discussing Aces."

"While he was also seeing your daughter? That's rather ballsy."

Goldman shrugged. Business and pleasure stayed separate in his world.

"Gina was also dating Bernie," I continued.

"Really?"

"She got him to agree to finance Body Mechanics."

"I see. So Jā was playing both sides against the middle."

"See," Marty said. "Bernie had every reason in the world to kill Jā,"

Now was the time to play my trump card and hope everything worked out okay. I pulled a slip of paper from my back pocket, one of the fascinating collection I had taken from the back of the cookbook. I held it out to Goldman. "Yup," I said. "If the name on the Bahamas bank account was Bernie's. Shit, if that was the case, he'd have close to half a million reasons."

I looked down at the paper. "Unfortunately, the name here is Martin Haifisch." I looked over at Marty. "Christ, Haifisch, as an accountant, I would have thought you'd at least put a fake name on it."

Marty bolted. Remember what I said before about accountants not being able to fight? Forget it. They can when the have to. And Marty did. He elbowed Dave in the stomach and took off for his car. Dave was right behind him, but when your life is on the line, you can usually kick ass in a sprint.

Marty made it to the Infiniti with time to spare. I reached into my pocket for the detonator before I remembered it had gone sailing. While I was looking for it, Marty got the engine started and was heading straight for us.

Dave jumped out of the way, heading directly for Goldman's car. I found the remote and hit the button as fast as I could, hoping the shrapnel of the exploding car wouldn't hurt too bad.

There was a huge WHOOSH as air was suddenly

sucked up and flames from the Mercedes singed my eyebrows.

Shame Guantanamo got it wrong.

Marty's Infiniti fishtailed as he looked to see what the noise was. I had just enough time to jump out of the way as it came screeching past. He barely made the first turn going down, scraping the paint down the side of the car down to the steel.

I had to do something. I had counted on Goldman or Dave to take care of Marty. Now Dave was lying face down on the concrete in front of the burning wreckage of the Mercedes. Ian had rushed to his aid, but I couldn't wait around to see if he survived. I had to get Marty. Hopefully, August had taken care of her part a little better than Guantanamo and the police would be waiting downstairs, but I couldn't count on it.

I jumped on my bike and headed down after Haifisch. The great thing about a motorcycle is it can take those parking structure turns at a much higher rate of speed than a car. Which meant I was nearly even with the Infiniti when he pulled out of the structure and headed north on Second.

I got close enough to yell at him to stop, but he ignored me. Then I looked for the cops. They were nowhere to be seen. Doesn't it figure? The one time I actually want to see a squad car, they're all playing hide and seek with the meter maids.

Marty turned into me, swerving sideways. I gunned it to avoid being cut off and pulled out in front. This was fucked up. I was supposed to be chasing him.

He was right on my ass as we ran the light on Wilshire. I went straight through. I got lucky.

A block later and Marty was closing.

As we went through the intersection, he pulled up next to me, sticking a gun out the window. I have no idea what kind it was, I'm a knife guy, remember? But as far as I was concerned, it was the biggest fucking gun I'd ever seen. Maybe that was because it was pointed at my head.

I slammed on the brakes as the first shot went off. It missed, and the car shot past, but Marty wasn't stupid. The Infiniti's tires bit into the pavement, turning the car completely around to face me.

My only escape was to turn right and get out of his line of fire. If he had to control the car through turns, he wouldn't be able to aim. I took the path of most resistance and drove on the left side of the road, hoping to use oncoming traffic as a screen. Unfortunately, there was none.

I saw my salvation dead ahead, in the form of a topiary dinosaur. Again, I paid no attention to the light on Wilshire and headed straight into the Third Street Promenade. The barriers were up and I slid between them easily, cutting to the left around the leafy brontosaurus. I hoped Marty was paying more attention to me than the road.

Over the roar of my engine, I could hear metal crunch behind me. I swung the bike around and skidded to a stop behind the dinosaur. I looked back and saw the Infiniti sculpted around the metal poles designed to keep cars from entering the pedestrian mall.

I wasn't sure if I wanted to get close, but from head on, it didn't look good. There was an arm hanging from the driver's side window, limp and empty-handed. I inched my bike forward.

The airbag had gone off, which I guess was a good thing. Marty looked like he was breathing, but he wasn't going anywhere anytime soon. He turned his head to look at me, blood dripping down his face. In his eyes, I saw the reflection of red and blue flashing lights.

August had come through. She was just a little later than I would have liked. Now, she and I were sitting in the back of Detective Collins' car and I was explaining the entire thing to him. How Marty had basically killed everyone for the loot. It was more difficult than it sounds, because I couldn't use my hands. They were still handcuffed behind me. An hour earlier, Collins said they were just temporary, but they were still on. I think he was pissed over my leaving town. Well, that and blowing up a car on public property. Thankfully, nothing Guantanamo used could be traced back to either of us.

It must have been around four in the morning when Collins finally let us go. I was exhausted and wanted nothing more than to go home and go to sleep. Guantanamo made another suggestion.

"Norms for breakfast?"

I shrugged. Why not? Tomorrow would be a late day.

Guantanamo and I each had a steak and eggs meal which would make a farm boy's mother proud and talked about what had just happened. August slowly worked her way through a short stack of pancakes as she listened.

"Now what?" Guantanamo asked.

"We get Bernie back and it's business as usual," I said.

"As usual?" August asked.

I looked at her.

"Skids," she continued "I am not usual. I'm now dating a bona fide film producer and that makes me one of the elite."

I smiled. That's right. Now that Bernie was in the clear, the film could be finished and I would get my credit line. Me and Dave and Bernie. What a trio, huh?

Guantanamo had a pensive look. "Do you think Marty will make it to the premier?"

August and I looked at each other. Who would be the one to tell him? I cocked my head to let August have the honor.

"Guantanamo," she said gently. "Marty is going away for a long time."

"He should at least get an invitation."

"Done," August and I said at the same time.

I paid the check and put it on Bernie's tab. As we walked out of the restaurant, August stopped me.

"Let's call Bernie."

"Do you want to wake him up to tell him about Gina?"

"He could probably handle the part about her being Jā's wife," Guantanamo suggested. "But the dead part should wait 'til morning."

We agreed with him.

It felt good to be home. Stifling a yawn, I invited August to spend the night and headed into my room to get ready for bed.

"Why not?" she said. "You're going to need the company."

I was about to throw my shirt into the wash bin but stopped. "What are you talking about?"

"You still have a column to write."

"Shit."

I put my shirt back on and powered up the computer.

Then I told my readers exactly what I'd been up to the last five days.

Fade Out

About the Author

Jaq Greenspon is a dad, as well as a world traveling, dog loving, scuba diving, book collecting, writer, currently residing somewhere in Eastern Europe. His words have been spoken by Capt. Jean-Luc Picard and Robin Hood, been read by David Copperfield, and criticized by his 7th grade English teacher. He'd like to thank the members of the Academy, although he doesn't know why. In his spare time, he's a university professor and a kick-ass uncle.